THE
TURNING

EMILY WHITMAN

THE
TURNING

GREENWILLOW BOOKS

AN IMPRINT OF HARPERCOLLINSPUBLISHERS

The Turning
Text copyright © 2018 by Emily Whitman

The text of this book is set in Cochin Medium
Book design by Sylvie Le Floc'h

Library of Congress Cataloging-in-Publication Data is available.

ISBN 978-0-06-265795-4 (hardback)

18 19 20 21 22 CG/LSCH 10 9 8 7 6 5 4 3 2 1
First Edition
Greenwillow Books

In memory of my father

Another wave comes crashing down,
The world is sudden strange.
From pelt to skin and back again,
Our life is naught but change.

—Ancient Selkie Song

⸎ WHERE IT STARTED ⸎

I'd thought being left on Spindle Island was the worst thing that could happen. I was wrong.

People kept coming into the white room to stare at me, trying to get me to speak. But I hadn't spent all those months alone at sea to give in to humans now. That's where it started. When I dove from the cliff, searching for my clan, and the fishermen's nets snagged me and hauled me up on deck. I was cold—me, who'd never been cold before—and the motor pulsed through me, drowning out the rhythm of the waves. "It's him," they said. "The boy from Spindle Island. The one they were searching for. The one they never found."

Or maybe it started before that. When Nellie brought me the words to the song, and they fell in the whitecaps, soaking the pages with salt. When we faced the walrus. When I thought she could be my friend.

No. It started long before any of that. Before I'd ever seen a human. Back when I lived with Mam and the rest of the clan at sea, hauling out on rocks slick with spray, swimming in kelp forests, riding the waves. Before I knew the truth . . .

PART ONE

OCEAN

CHAPTER ONE

ᴇᴄᴄ LONGLIMBS ᴄᴄᴇ

We were heading home from hunting. I rode on Mam's back because we had so far to swim. The sun slipped down between sea and sky, the last long rays painting Mam's fur as pink as my skin.

"Let's dive," I said.

With a flip of her tail we slipped under the waves, swimming close to the surface where I could still see.

Mam was in sealform, sleek and strong. Her muscles flowed beneath her beautiful pelt. One day soon I'd have my own pelt, have the flippers and tail—the breath!—to travel the ocean roads all by myself. I'd greet the deep-water whales and swim for hours in spiraling coils. My eyes would be huge and black, able to see in dark water.

We rose so I could gulp in a lungful of air.

"Deeper!" I said.

Mam shook her head. "Not until you turn, Aran."

I sighed in frustration. Each day it grew harder to wait. For eleven years now I'd been stuck with legs instead of a tail. My skin was thinner than a translucent kelp leaf. My feet were as clumsy as chunks of driftwood, my toes as separate as pebbles on the shore.

The sky deepened to purple. A pale glow appeared on the horizon, and the Moon began to rise. She was waxing toward full. Now the waves were tipped with silver, and drops of light hung on the ends of Mam's whiskers.

The shape of the waves shifted and the island rose before us, black against the starlit sky. I slid off Mam's back to swim the rest of the way on my own. She slowed to stay by my side, her alert eyes scanning the sea.

I rode ashore on a wave, jumping to my feet in a crunch of pebbles. I ran over to the tide pools and started searching among the sea stars for something good to eat. There was a fat cluster of blue mussels and I twisted one free. The Moon was so bright, I could see my moonshadow, like another, darker me.

Mam stretched out long on the rocks above the reach

of the tide. If it were just her, she'd have her tail in the surf, but for my sake she always settled higher up.

"Aren't you coming to sleep?" she called.

"I'm getting a snack." I cracked the mussel shell on the rocks and slurped out the meat. "Want some?"

"Maybe a taste."

I brought her a handful. She crunched the shells with her teeth.

It was a good haulout Mam had found this time, with flat rocks for sleeping and basking, and plenty of tide pools, and a cove too shallow for sharks. She found all our haulouts when the rest of the clan was away on the long journey. They'd been gone for almost two moons now. I sat gazing out across the waves.

"Do you think they'll be back soon?" I asked.

Mam didn't answer. I looked over; she was already asleep.

When I was little, we'd watch the clan swim away, and Mam would wipe the tears from my eyes. "Once you have your pelt, we'll go," she'd say. "It will be soon enough." She called the time we spent alone our special time, and filled it with games and songs and stories, and I didn't mind that much. It was just the way life was.

Besides, Mam used to change all the time back then, when we were alone. I'd ride on her back to a new haulout, and as soon as we slid ashore she'd get that special, inward gaze, the look of the turning. Her pelt would grow loose around her and she'd slip it off, the flippers hanging lank, the black claws clattering on the stones. She'd give a long, luxurious stretch before carefully folding her pelt and stashing it in the rocks. Then she was in longlimbs, like me, except for the webbing between her fingers and toes. "You'll have that, too, when you turn," she'd say. She taught me the full-Moon dances, and we played chase, and legs seemed like a fine thing to have.

But the bigger I grew, the less often she changed. And when the rest of the clan was around, she hardly ever turned. Why would she, when she had a pelt? She'd been born in hers. Most selkies are.

I couldn't stop asking how my pelt would come. Would I wake one morning to find myself flicking a tail? Or would it be waiting for me on the shore? Would it be silver, like hers, or brown with golden spots, like my hair? Mam didn't know. "Trust in the Moon," she'd say. "It will come when the time is right."

But I could tell Mam was tired of waiting, too. And though she'd never admit it, she was worried. It was dangerous, having me in longlimbs. Humans don't believe there are selkies anymore; they think we're seals, and it's safest that way. One night I overheard Grandmam telling Mam, "You need to be more careful, Oona! What if they saw him, a boy living with seals? They'd take him away, that's what they'd do! They'd trap him on land"—her voice dropped, and I crept closer to hear the rest—"and he'd never get his pelt, and his selkie-soul would die."

The memory made me shiver.

Now I sat up tall and lifted my face to the Moon.

Please, I prayed. *Please*.

The rest of my prayer didn't have words. I closed my eyes and imagined the Moon—she who calls the waves—calling to me. I pictured myself with graceful flippers, my pelt sleek and shining.

I opened my eyes and spread my fingers wide, searching for webbing, a sign of the turning, the beginning.

They still looked the same.

Maybe the change was too small to see. I ran a finger down from the top of my thumb and along the arcs of skin.

Mam sighed. She was awake, her eyes following my finger as it traced every dip and rise. Her mouth set as she tried not to show me the ache she felt, the place in her heart as hollow as the gaps between my fingers. The place that only my pelt would fill.

CHAPTER TWO

THE KELP FOREST

The sun peeked over the rocks and nudged me awake. Mam wasn't there and my stomach growled; she must be getting breakfast. I ran down to the surf as she came scooting out of the waves, a little silver fish flapping in her jaws. She dropped it at my feet. I snatched it up and crunched off its head. The rest soon followed.

"I'm still hungry," I said. "Where did you catch it?"

She pushed at a scrap of fish skin with her flipper. "A lovely kelp forest, a short swim southwest."

I edged into the shallows. "I think I'll go catch another."

Her head jerked up. "Not on your own, you don't. What about orcas and sharks? What about—"

"There hasn't been a boat in weeks," I said. But she was already splashing in beside me.

I kept up a steady stroke as the sun rose higher and higher. A short swim for her was a long swim with legs. When the sun was past its midpoint, Mam said I should ride the rest of the way. I climbed on her back and we sped away, splashing through the crests. In no time at all, she was twirling to spin me off.

It was one of the prettiest kelp forests I'd ever seen. A wall of rock towered up to the surface. Sun seeped down thick, waving strands of bull kelp. Everything was dappled with light, from the specks of algae and miniature wiggling shrimp to the kelp's great, round air bubbles.

Mam swished up behind a young rockfish and gulped it down before it even had time to look surprised. Hunting was so easy with those teeth and curved black claws. All I had was fingernails, and those were worn to stubs from scrambling on rocks.

I swam along the rock face, searching among the sea stars and corals. I reached in a crevice and snatched out a baby octopus, then kicked up a warm current to the surface. I rode up and down on the waves as I ate.

I filled my lungs and dove again. I chased an anchovy through the waving fronds. There was a flicker of red on the seabed—a crab, a beauty! I swooped down and grabbed its shell by the sides, then swiveled around to show Mam. She was nowhere in sight.

My chest was growing tight. It was my stupid lungs, straining toward the surface like the bubbles in the kelp. I didn't have the air in my veins yet. In sealform, your blood carries enough air to stay underwater a long time. You close your nostrils and dive, and you don't have to worry about breathing for ages.

I flapped my arms to force myself farther down. The crab had to swish along, its eyes waving on their long stalks. Suddenly it twisted and snapped. A sharp pain sliced through the back of my hand.

"Ow!" The last of my breath escaped in a rush of bubbles.

The crab scuttled away as I kicked upward, my chest straining, my ears pounding. I burst through to the surface and gulped down a lungful of air.

A bright ribbon of blood trickled down my arm.

Mam swam up beside me, a green strand of kelp dangling from her mouth. "Here," she said, laying it across my arm. "Wrap this around it and then hop on for a ride."

I glared, embarrassed. "I can swim."

She shook her head. "You know perfectly well about blood and sharks."

"There aren't any sharks," I grumbled. But I climbed on her back, wrapped the seaweed tightly around my hand, and lay down flat for the ride back to shore.

Mam swam without speaking. It took forever. We swam and swam and still we were only halfway back.

That's when I felt the water change.

My muscles tensed. "Something's coming," I said.

Mam swam faster. She could feel it, too. We were in open water—no islands, no rocks, not even a chunk of driftwood to climb out on.

"Hold on," said Mam in the crisp voice that signaled danger. "Sharks look up, not down. When I nod, take your deepest breath and I'll dive."

My arms tightened around her neck. The end of the seaweed flapped loose in the waves.

The beast was approaching fast. Mam would never get away with me on her back. I started to let go—

"Don't even think about it," she snapped. "Don't—"

The beast zoomed beneath us, rocking us in its current. My heart was pounding hard enough to burst from my chest. Why hadn't it attacked from below? Was it playing with us?

I raised my fist. It was the only weapon I had.

CHAPTER THREE

ᨑᨑᨑ THE RETURN ᨑᨑᨑ

A black head broke through the waves a stone's throw away. Mam gasped — why wasn't she baring her teeth to fight? — and now it was surging toward us, water sheening its broad back —

It swerved to a stop a whisker away.

"Lyr!" cried Mam, her voice rich and warm.

That sleek black pelt, those whiskers — it was Lyr, our chief, the fastest, strongest selkie in the sea.

"You're back!" I cried.

Lyr drifted forward to nuzzle Mam's nose. Then, with a swish of his flippers, he was bobbing upright in the water, gazing at her with delight.

"Ah, it's good to see you, Oona." His voice rumbled dark and deep, like waves at night.

Mam was too busy smiling to answer.

If Lyr was back, then the rest of the clan was, too, home from the long journey. I sat up higher, scanning the waves for their shining heads.

Lyr followed my eyes. "They're not here yet," he said. "They were messing around an old shipwreck. I came ahead to find you."

My grin stretched as wide as an orca's.

He wore the special expression that was for me alone. "Look at you, Aran! You've grown a flipper's length since I last saw you." He grinned at Mam. "How can you still be carrying that pup? Why, he's as big as you are!"

He was joking, but the air sighed out of Mam, like an anemone closing back in on itself.

I shrugged it away. There'd be so much to do now that the others were back! We'd have chasing games, and lively discussions that Mam always said weren't really arguments, and more kinds of fish than you could count on all your claws put together. And stories. Grandmam's stories.

Lyr asked Mam if we'd found a good haulout, and she told him how to reach our cove. "Perfect," he said.

"I'll fetch the clan and see you there." He somersaulted backward and was gone.

I slipped off Mam's back and started swimming. When she flicked up beside me with a frown, I paused to show her the cut wasn't bleeding anymore, and then I took off again.

We were a small clan. It was just the seven of us, and I was the only pup. I could hardly wait to see them — bold Cormac, and Mist with her gentle wit and sweet smile. Even Maura, who meant well. But most of all I was thinking about Grandmam and the briny smell of her pelt, and the way she always tickled my ear with her whiskers.

After a while, I stopped to tread water and catch my breath. Mam asked if I wanted a ride; I shook my head. Then, staring across the waves so I wouldn't be looking at her, I asked, "What did Lyr mean?"

"About what?"

"About you still carrying me. Am I too old to be riding?"

Her smile went off-kilter. She was thinking hard how to answer. Finally she said, "Being born in longlimbs is special. It doesn't happen very often. Lyr's never known anyone else who had to wait for their pelt. He doesn't always see that we need to do things differently."

She'd only raised more questions.

"Does *anyone* know when I'll get my pelt?" I asked.

"The Moon knows," said Mam.

It was about time for the Moon to tell me. I splashed past Mam, swimming as fast as I could toward my clan.

CHAPTER FOUR

~ COME TO ME! ~
COME!

We swam around the point and there they were, scattered on the beach like sun-silvered driftwood.

"Hey!" I called, stopping to tread water so I could shout louder. "Over here! It's me!"

One of the logs arced up a shining head.

Beside me, Mam sang out, "Come to me! Come!" It was the ritual greeting after a long time apart. The notes hung sparkling in the air.

In a flash they were scooting toward the water, flippers slapping shale, bellies thumping. They splashed into the waves.

I struck out toward them. I'd only gone a few strokes

when Maura zipped up from below, rolling me over and over in a spiral. We broke apart at the surface, grinning at each other. Then Cormac grabbed my foot in his mouth and tugged me down to where the water grew dim. I kicked free and grabbed his flippers. We sped to the surface and burst through in a backflip as high as a rainbow. I splashed down, laughing so hard I had to tread water to catch my breath.

"Hi, Aran," said a soft voice next to my ear. Mist's warm eyes glowed in her pale gray pelt.

And then there was Grandmam, with her smile like midsummer sun, swimming up next to me and turning sideways for a hug.

"I've missed you," she whispered, tickling my ear with her whiskers, like always.

"Come on!" called Maura, heading back to the beach. "Do we have tales to tell you!"

We all turned to follow.

I glanced back once to make sure Mam was coming. She and Lyr were behind everyone else, swimming slowly, and so close together their flippers were almost touching.

As soon as we came ashore, Maura flopped up beside me. "We brought you a present," she said.

I looked around eagerly. Presents were usually something special to eat.

Maura turned to Grandmam. "Where did you put them?"

"I hid them away," said Grandmam. "Close your eyes, Aran."

I shut my eyes as she thumped toward the rocks.

"I helped with the carrying," said Mist.

Cormac chuckled. "Mist and your grandmam are the best at carrying things in their mouths. Lyr and I chomp down on everything."

"And I'm always swallowing things by accident," said Maura. "Or I would have helped, too. You'll love them, they—"

"Quiet, Maura," said Cormac and Mist together.

Grandmam thumped closer. Something clinked onto the pebbles.

"Open your eyes," she said.

At my feet were three golden suns, small and flat and round. I dropped to my knees and gathered them in my cupped hand.

"What are they?" I asked.

Cormac tossed his head proudly. "There was an old shipwreck off the mainland, where a river twists the currents around. We found a chest."

"Actually, it was your grandmam who found it," said Mist. "The rest of us helped break it open. It took a while. That's why Lyr swam ahead to find you." She smiled at Mam. "He couldn't wait."

The suns were heavy in my hand. Even in the gathering twilight, they glittered and glowed.

"They're called doubloons," said Maura. "Humans make them out of gold. Well? Do you like them?"

"I love them." I leaned over to give each member of the clan a hug. Grandmam I hugged the hardest and longest of all.

"Now," said Mam, settling beside Lyr on the flat rocks. "Tell us everything! How far north you went, and if you met anyone interesting, and where the currents are shifting, and where the fish are fattest, and—"

"Hold on," said Cormac, scooting next to Maura. Mist stretched out long beside me, and Grandmam gazed in contentment at Mam. We were together, every single one of us, the way it was meant to be.

I always told Mam that the times we spent alone were just as good, and she always agreed. But now she strained forward, like she was leaping into the water, eager to explore every shore, to ride every wave—to live the journey that she'd missed. A pang of guilt twinged in my chest.

"Start with where you went," said Mam.

"Up the coast," said Lyr. "Past the island with two pines, past the delta where the currents make a whirlpool."

"The water was low there," said Mist.

Cormac got a mischievous twinkle in his eye. "That's where Maura saw this handsome selkie in the water, and she stopped to brush her whiskers and smooth her pelt—"

"I did not!" said Maura.

"Yes, you did," said Cormac. "Maura never can resist a handsome face. But when she swam up to introduce herself, it splashed backward—it was nothing but a seal! You should have seen its expression. It practically flew out of there."

Everyone laughed good-heartedly, even Maura. Finally she said, "Well, it's not like we meet lots of other selkies. You have to hope!"

Lyr went back to describing their route. After the delta there were fewer boats and fewer houses along the shore, and the waters grew colder. They swam farther than ever before—so far north, floating boulders of ice sparkled in the water. And that, he said, was where they met three members of the white selkie clan.

Mam gasped. "The white selkies! I thought they were just a tale."

"Their pelts are as bright as snowdrifts," said Maura. "Do you think, when they're in longlimbs, their hair is white, too?"

Cormac shook his head. "Hair is always black in longlimbs."

"Not Aran's," said Maura. "He's got those light spots."

Grandmam gave me a warm smile. "Dappled like a pelt."

I'd never met any selkies beyond my own small clan. I scooted forward. "Do they talk like us?" I said. "Are there lots of them?"

But Grandmam had turned to Mam. "They said they're coming to Moon Day."

"Moon Day!" Mam sighed with longing. She hadn't been to the rites since I was born.

Moon Day only came every few years, when the Moon circled closest to Earth, huge and round, and her pull on the tides—and the folk—was the strongest. I'd begged Mam to take me last time, even though I knew full well I'd need tail and flippers for the journey. It was days of open-sea swimming to reach the Spire. Without a pelt, you can't sleep in open water, or close your nostrils to swim fast and far beneath the waves. And you have to swim there by yourself. No one can help you.

The funny thing is, once you get there, you slip your pelt right off again. It takes legs to climb the steep path, up and up until you're practically in the Moon's realm. That's where you whisper your prayers in her ear.

"All the clans are gathering," said Grandmam. "The Moon hasn't been this close in eighteen years."

Mist turned to Mam. "We came back to find you instead of heading right there, in case . . ." Her voice trailed off as she glanced at me; catching my eye, she tilted her head, as if to say she was sorry.

"Is it this full Moon?" I said.

Mist nodded.

"I wish I could go," I said.

This time everyone nodded.

"Then I could meet other selkies," I went on, half dreaming. "I bet there are lots and lots of them, aren't there? Are all the clans different? Do any of them come from the old shores? Maybe there'd be some pups my age, and I could play with them and—"

"Aran," said Grandmam gently. "There will be plenty more Moon Days when you *can* come."

My shoulders slumped. Mist nudged me with a flipper

and said, "We won't be gone for long. It's only a three-day swim if we sleep on the rocks off Black Cove."

Lyr shook his head. "Don't you remember? There are humans on that island now. They've built houses."

"Humans!" Cormac's voice dripped with scorn. "They should stay on the mainland, where they belong."

And then they were talking about which route to take, and old friends they hoped to see, and suddenly I didn't want to hear any more. I slipped away and walked down the beach, scuffing at stones, all the way to the tide pools.

The tide was out; the seaweed lay flat and shapeless. I poked at a hermit crab. It drew back into a shell covered with tiny barnacles and scraps of kelp. It was a good disguise. Unless you looked closely, you couldn't tell who was hiding inside. I was about to pick it up when Grandmam appeared at my side.

"Come on, I'll tell you a story," she said.

I jumped up, but then stopped. "I'm too old for stories," I said.

"You're never too old for stories. Come on, let's go where we won't disturb the others."

She scooted down the shore and I followed, relieved she hadn't left me time to protest.

CHAPTER FIVE

ᏉᏉ RIONA THE BRAVE ᏉᏉ

Grandmam's granite-gray pelt blended in with the rocks, so her three white spots floated ahead of me like little moons. She found a place to her liking and lay down long, the surf lapping her tail.

"I've brought back some wonderful new stories," she said. "Do you want to hear how Cormac outwitted the whale?"

I stretched out beside her. "Tell me Riona the Brave."

"But you've heard that a hundred times!"

"It's my favorite." I shifted so my head rested on her side. "And it's why we go on the long journey, right? Because of Riona?"

"It is indeed," she said, giving in.

She closed her eyes to summon the story. I could feel it gathering in the air. A gull poking around in the seaweed must have felt it, too, because it raised its head to stare, then strutted over. "Story?" it asked, plunking down beside me.

Seabirds and selkies don't speak each other's languages—there are so many, since each kind of seabird has its own—but we can communicate in a very simple pidgin called birdtalk.

"In selkie talk," I chirped, but the gull stayed anyway.

When Grandmam next spoke, it was in her deep, rich, story voice.

"Long ago, on the old shores, there lived a selkie pup named Riona. Her clan had always hauled out on the Skellig Islands, a long swim from the mainland. The waters teemed with fish, and the skies were aflutter with orange-beaked puffins and gray guillemots. Best of all, there were no humans anywhere near.

"Then one day a coracle crested the horizon. It landed on Big Skellig and men in brown robes clambered out. They trudged to the top of the peak and built round stone huts. They kept to themselves, singing strange songs of worship to their god, and they posed no danger.

"But other men, greedy men, came in their wake. Their

boats dragged huge tangles of rope called nets. Those gaping maws gulp down everything in their path. Turtle, dolphin, seal—edible or no, nets don't care. Death itself is woven into every strand. Riona's mam warned her time and time again, 'Don't you ever, ever go near a net! They'll swerve around, and snatch you up, and bind you till you drown.'

"Now, one evening Riona was chasing a dolphin and lost track of time. When she finally swam back, her mam cried out, 'You thoughtless pup! I was so worried, the chief himself went out looking for you. Won't he give you a piece of his mind when he returns!'

"Riona curled up small on the rocks, dreading her scolding. But the Moon rose, and the Moon set, and still the chief hadn't returned. A different kind of dread now filled Riona's heart. The clan gathered on shore, staring silently into the darkness. When dawn broke, cold and bitter, they swam out in all directions, searching.

"Riona swam to Big Skellig and along the coast. She rounded the point.

"There swam a great, black boat, a laden net sagging from its side. Two men grunted as they struggled to heave it up. Oh, it was a terrible sight—fish thrashing, gills gaping. But most terrible of all was the still, gray weight hanging at its center. The body of the chief, unmoving in death.

"The humans jerked the net higher, and one of them crowed, 'I'll have me a fine sealskin coat this winter!'

"The words stabbed Riona like a shark's teeth. The chief would never have neared the net had he not been looking for her. A shift in the current, a sudden swerve — it caught him and held him under till he drowned.

"Riona sank beneath the waves. Her heart was a stone dragging her down to the depths of the sea. Past the last hint of sun she sank, past the last fish, into total darkness. She wanted to die.

"And then a silver light blinded her and a voice spoke. It was the Moon. ''Twas the humans' net that killed your chief, not you,' she said. 'Will you let this evil bring your death, too? Or will you live to fight for your folk?'

"The blinding light shifted. Now Riona saw a band of selkies braving unknown seas in search of a new home. At their head swam a pup. Riona.

"*I can't*, she thought.

"'You must,' said the Moon. 'Your folk need you. Your journey awaits.'

"Then Riona was atop the waves again. Gathering all her courage, she swam back to her clan. She told them about the chief, and they mourned. Then she told them of her vision. Many doubted her. They clung to the past;

they feared the unknown. They said she was only a pup. But a small group heard the Moon's strength in her voice. 'We will go if you lead,' they said.

"Through the wild-storm winter they swam, riding strange currents, snatching moments of sleep in the waves. Finally they came to a cluster of islands scattered like bright stones in the sea, with many a cove and nary a boat. The waters were rich with salmon and herring, haddock and smelt. One island was as like to Big Skellig as could be, with a peak that pierced the clouds. They named it the Spire.

"That clan became many clans, spread up and down the coast of this new world. Now each year we undertake the long journey to remember Riona and the courage she found to swim off into the unknown, in search of a place where we can thrive. A place we can call home."

Grandmam's voice stilled, and she gazed across the waves. "Now the humans are here, too," she said, slowly shaking her head. And she whispered the old rhyme:

"Beware the ship, beware the net,
Beware the black gun in his hand.
He'll take you for your oil, your pelt.
He will, because he's man."

CHAPTER SIX
ᕫᕫ THE RED BEAK ᕫᕫ

We were basking in the morning sun when Lyr slid in on the waves. Everyone lifted heads and tails in interest. I rolled onto my belly and made my own crescent arc, legs as tight together as a curving tail.

"There are salmon to the west," said Lyr. "And so many, you've only to open your mouth and they swim right in. Who's coming?"

The beach came alive with bodies scooting to the water. I raced ahead, my feet pounding the pebbles, and dove in. An instant later Lyr popped up, blocking my way.

"We're going too far for you today," he said, in a voice that meant there'd be no discussion. Then he saw Mam back on shore. "Come, Oona," he called. "He can fend for himself until high sun. And the salmon are huge and sweet."

Mam was tossing back her head to reply when Grandmam slipped ashore. Her quick eyes darted between us, reading our faces. Then she gave an exaggerated groan. "These old bones of mine! I'm still sore from yesterday." Her head drooped. "I think I'll stay here after all."

Mam glanced from Grandmam, to me, to Lyr.

"Off with you, Oona," said Grandmam. "Leave Aran and me to our stories."

Mam and Lyr exchanged smiles, and then she was rushing into the waves. A moment later two heads rose in the center of the cove. Their bodies twined, and then they were gone.

I stomped ashore, kicking up angry sprays of water. Left behind again, and not even on my own. Didn't they trust me to do *anything*?

As soon as I reached Grandmam, she backed into the water. "I'm starving," she said, all groaning gone. "Wait here and I'll catch us something."

"I can catch my own," I said, but she'd already disappeared.

A moment later she popped up with a herring

struggling in her jaws. She took the fish in her claws and neatly bit off the head, then used her sharp teeth to peel back the skin, baring glistening flesh.

"Come on, then," she said.

I splashed over and she dropped a chunk in my hands. It wasn't nearly as good as salmon.

Up on shore, Grandmam stretched out long in the sun. She patted the rocks beside her.

"I don't want a story," I said, crossing my arms.

She grunted. "That's good, because I feel a nap coming on. These old flippers need their rest." Her voice was growing slow with sun and sleep. "Stay close and stay out of the water, or your mam will have my pelt. Go on, say it: *'Rough tides, riptides . . .'*"

I sighed, then chanted:

"Rough tides, riptides,
Orca's thrall,
Sharks and man —
Beware them all."

"That's right," she said, yawning. Her flippers hugged her belly, her head fell back, and a moment later a snore escaped from her flat black nose.

I sat there scanning the waves. After a while I found my doubloons and started experimenting, flashing bright shards of sunlight off their backs onto the water. I pounded them on rocks to see how hard they were.

"Stop making that noise!" grunted Grandmam.

I cupped the disks in my hand and waited until she was snoring again. Then I crept to my feet. I wasn't going to lie there waiting for the others to return, their faces fresh with adventure, their bellies stuffed. If I had to be stuck here, at least I'd go exploring. Grandmam would never even know I was gone.

I crossed the shore and scrambled up a rocky hill. At the top I turned back. Below me, Grandmam looked so small, she could have fit in the curve of my palm.

A gull flew in low from the north and swooped up to land at my feet. It was the gull from last night.

"Story?" it squawked, peering up at me. When I didn't answer right away, it pecked at my foot. "Story!"

I was the best in my clan at birdtalk, but all I said was, "Big swim. No gulls." I jingled the doubloons in my palm.

The gull's eyes sharpened. "What?" it said, staring at my hand. "Give!"

I bent down to show it the coins. It pecked at one suspiciously. "Not good," it said. It must have been expecting something to eat. Then it cocked its head, listening to something I couldn't hear, and flew off without saying good-bye.

I followed, jumping from rock to rock. A crag blocked my way, and I clambered to the top.

Below me, a cliff dropped down to a cove sheltered by curving arms of rock. Gaps in the rock opened to glimpses of whitecaps on the other side. A flat-topped boulder stood alone in the center of the beach, as grand as a great chief's throne. It would be a good place to make stone pictures.

I found a crevice just wide enough to brace myself, and I shimmied down. It squeezed to an end, and I grabbed handholds until I could jump to the ground.

In the rattling surf, I found the roundest, smoothest stones. Then I hauled myself up the chest-high boulder and sat on top, arranging them in a rising curve. It became a bold spiral—white stones, then black, then blood red. At the end the doubloons blazed like a comet's fiery tail.

But the center was empty. It needed something else.

I waded back into the surf and a shell tumbled across my feet—a moon snail, round and swirling like my picture. Perfect. As I carried it back, I scooped a finger inside, hoping for a snack. Instead, a flash of green fell into my palm. It was hard, like a stone, but it carried light like a wave. I held it to my eye and gasped. I could see right through!

Back atop the throne, I set the shell in the shining spiral. Then I sat gazing at the world through my new treasure. The shore, the sky, the cliff—everything was a hazy, underwater green. The stone turned land into ocean. Magic! If only I had someone to show it to.

The gull shrieked, "Look!"

It was peering out through a gap low in the rock wall. I didn't see anything but waves. Then came a strange kind of splashing, like no beast or bird I'd ever heard before. It neared the gap, growing louder, and louder.

A gigantic red beak swam into view.

Another splash and the creature surged forward. A curved belly filled the gap, blocking out the sea. It was as big as a full-grown orca.

But that wasn't whale skin. *It was wood*.

CHAPTER SEVEN
~ ALONE ~

A boat. And not just a speck in the distance like I'd seen before. I stared, spellbound.

A flat, wooden flipper dug into the water. Clutching the top was a hand. A human hand. It had to be. But the skin turned orange at the wrist. I leaned forward, straining to see through the gap. The boat splashed ahead, leaving only a swirl of foam—

And then the water exploded in front of me.

I leaped to my feet, my heart pounding, as a shape surged toward me in a blur of spray—Grandmam!

"Run!" she barked, her eyes blazing.

I startled to my senses. The boat was heading toward

the point. Soon the human would round the rocks. He'd see the cove. The boulder. *Me*.

I leaped off the boulder. The instant I hit the ground, I was racing for the cliff.

Another splash: louder, closer. I glanced back over my shoulder—and skidded to a stop. On top of the rock, the sun flared off the doubloons in a spiral of blinding gold.

I swerved back. Grandmam was at my heels, snarling and butting. The gull shrieked in alarm.

"He'll see it!" I hissed. "He'll know I'm here."

Grandmam followed my eyes. Her head reared up. "I'll do it. *Go*."

I sprinted to the cliff and scrambled up to the crevice, pressing back into the shadows.

A splash, a swirl, and into the cove swam the blood-red boat. A sharp beak. A broad belly. At the back, a straight line, like its tail was chopped off.

Was it a boat like this that killed Riona's chief?

It swam through the breakers. The man's back was toward me. On his arms and upper body, orange flesh hung loose and saggy, like an elephant seal's. It wrinkled as he dug in the flippers. Now he swiveled his head toward shore. His hair was hacked short. Dark-brown fur sprouted from his cheeks and chin.

My stomach churned. I'd thought humans looked like selkies in longlimbs. Not like . . . *this*.

The boat slid ashore. Rocks scraped its belly like teeth on bone.

A flash of movement caught my eye. Grandmam was hauling herself up the side of the boulder. It was so steep, she almost stood on her tail. With a grunt of effort, she crested the top and slapped down, her flipper shoving the swirl of gold and stones into a cleft.

The man climbed out of the boat. His feet were black and swollen. Or—or was something covering them, like part of a pelt? Was the saggy skin an extra layer, too? It fit so badly, it must weigh him down. Why would he wear it?

Maybe there was something wrong with his own skin.

He grabbed the boat's beak and jerked it higher ashore. He looped a cord around a log, tugging it tight. Then he turned and looked at Grandmam.

She glared back, swinging her head from side to side. He started walking toward her.

With a shove of her flippers, she slid off the rock, landing in a crash of pebbles. Now she'd attack to keep him from finding me. She'd drive him off, like the time she chased a walrus away. I leaned forward, eager for those slashing claws and bared teeth, that ferocious growl.

But Grandmam was scooting away from him. Away from me. She was rushing into the waves.

A swirl of foam and she disappeared.

I was alone.

CHAPTER EIGHT

~ EVERYONE KNEW ~

The air squeezed out of my lungs as if I were drowning. I was alone with a human, without fang or claw to defend myself.

I was shaking. I reached out a hand for support and a sharp rock shifted under my palm. If I could work it loose, I'd have a weapon. As quietly as I could, barely moving, I wiggled the rock from side to side.

Down below, the man leaped atop the boulder and stood gazing out to sea, a conqueror surveying his realm. Then he sat with his legs dangling over the side.

He reached into the baggy orange skin on his chest. He seemed to have a hollow in there, like the pouch of a pelican's beak. I watched in astonishment as he pulled out a monstrous, silver tooth. What beast had this come from, so long and thin and straight? The edge glittered like ice. I shivered, unable to look away.

He reached into his side again. Now he was unwrapping something that crackled like dried seaweed. He took out what looked like a hunk of flesh. The tooth glittered, slashed—the man lifted the thinnest of slivers to his mouth. He sliced and chewed, sliced and chewed.

Was it seal?

I shoved harder at the rock. With a snap, it broke off in my hand, sending a trail of dirt and stones rattling down. I froze.

The man turned and looked at the cliff as if seeing it for the first time. He jumped down and started walking over, stones crunching underfoot. His hands were empty. The silver tooth must be back in his chest pouch. It was so sharp, it could cut me to slivers, like the flesh he'd just eaten. Mam would never find the pieces.

I gripped the stone tighter.

At the base of the cliff, the man grabbed on to a nub of rock, raised his foot, and began to climb. He looked up for another handhold. His eyes were pale green, not at all like the dark eyes of selkies.

He climbed higher and higher. He wasn't looking at me, so he didn't hunt by smell, but soon he'd be eye-level with my hiding place. He'd hear my heart pounding. He was only a body length below me. I couldn't give him time to reach for the tooth. I'd have to shove past him and leap down. I stared out across the jumble of boulders at the foot of the cliff, trying to gauge the distance.

A head rose silently in the waves.

Mam!

Lyr rose beside her, and then the rest of the clan, their faces fierce and determined. Grandmam rose last of all, slower than the rest. How far and fast she must have gone to get them!

They slipped back under. A ripple showed their path toward the boat.

Mam crept ashore so carefully, it sounded like nothing more than pebbles rolling in the surf. She bared her teeth and bit through the rope, leaving it limp and twisted like a dead snake. She stole back into the waves.

The water swirled—and then the boat was scraping back across the stones.

The man's head whipped around. His eyes went wide. With my clan hidden underneath, it looked like the boat was swimming off by itself, backward against the tide.

"Stop!" he cried, as if the boat could hear him. But it sped up, rushing toward open ocean.

The man leaped down and ran, crying out in terror, as if the island were possessed.

The last of my fear lifted. He didn't look dangerous anymore, just ridiculous, his legs whirling faster than puffin wings. He swerved past the throne, grabbed the silver tooth—so it had been there all along—and dashed into the surf. He took off swimming, if you could call it that: with those awkward limbs, he was all splash and no speed. Gulls jeered and screeched overhead.

The boat stopped, defying the waves so the man could catch up. He grabbed the side. It tipped toward him, about to go belly-up. Then the water swirled and the boat hung there, waiting, while he hauled himself over. His feet were barely in when the boat sprang upright. It flew toward the point. He grabbed the sticks, flinging his body back and forth, and the boat disappeared around the rocks.

The splashing faded away.

Now head after shining head rose in the cove. The air exploded with snorts and grunts of glee and the loud smack of flippers hitting the water.

I leaned out from my hiding place and waved. Everyone grinned back at me. I scrambled down the cliff as fast as I could and ran across the sun-hot shale. My family, my folk! They'd all come back for me!

As they swam ashore, I ran from one to another, as light and free as if I were riding the crest of a foaming wave. I flung myself down to hug Grandmam, and we rolled on the warm pebbles. Lyr surfed up to land right at my feet, tossing his head as proudly as if he'd chased the man away all by himself.

I'd never loved my clan as much as I did at that moment. They gathered around me in a loose circle, wet pelts glistening in the sun, strong backs arching as if they were still guiding the boat from below.

"Did you see him?" cried Maura. "The look on his face!"

I jumped to my feet, searching for Mam. She was missing all the fun! There she was, still out in the cove, swimming in circles with her head underwater. I was about to shout when she dove and disappeared.

"If we hadn't held the boat, he'd still be trying to reach it," said Cormac. "Such skinny, useless arms!" He flapped his flippers around wildly to show what he meant. I was laughing so hard my stomach hurt.

But then his words echoed in my head. *Skinny. Useless.* I glanced down at my own arms.

Maura curved up into a crescent moon. "You think his arms were funny? What about those flailing legs?"

The laughter dimmed as I looked down at my knees. My ankles. At the only feet on the beach.

Lyr cleared his throat. "Now, Maura," he said in a serious tone. "We all have legs in longlimbs."

Everyone stilled, alert. Everyone, that is, except Maura.

"Oh, legs are lovely for dancing on land!" she went on blithely. "It's not the legs themselves I mind. But everyone knows you need flippers and tail in the sea."

She laughed, but no one laughed with her. Finally, realizing something had changed, she looked up to find everyone staring at her.

Then she did a terrible thing. She turned to stare at me.

Every head followed, swiveling as if they were pulled by the same string. Every eye was on me, and in those eyes, expressions I couldn't read. What was going on? The laughter was truly gone now. Silence grew into a thick, cold fog.

Finally Maura snorted. "Oh, for goodness sake, Aran, don't look so anxious. Of course I didn't mean *you*."

Everyone nodded. The tension started to lift.

"After all, you're *family*. You're one of us." Maura smiled warmly. And then she added, "Even if your father wasn't."

Grandmam gasped.

At first I didn't realize what Maura had said. But her words struck the clan like a stone thrown into still water. The ripples spread in a widening circle of stunned eyes and gaping mouths.

Even if your father wasn't.

I'd never thought to ask who my father was. Selkies don't care. Mates were a matter of a season, a journey, or a Moon Day gathering. But this must be different.

"What about my father?" I asked.

Everyone knew. I saw it on their faces.

"Well, now," said Maura. "You see—"

"That's for his mother to tell him," said Lyr.

Maura's mouth snapped shut.

"Mam's swimming," I said, my impatience growing like a bitter, tingling rash. "I want to know *now*."

Lyr and Grandmam exchanged a glance.

Maura was my only hope. I looked her right in the eye. "You can tell me, Maura. Who was he?"

"Isn't it obvious?" she said. "Your father was a man."

CHAPTER NINE

✐ THE KNIFE ✐

I ran inland so they wouldn't follow, my eyes stinging, the world a blur. On the far side of the island, I stumbled down to a lonely patch of shore. I threw myself onto the rocks and buried my head on my knees, clenched in a tight ball, as if I could suck my limbs into my body and make them disappear.

My father was a man.

They'd known, every one of them. They'd known for as long as I'd been alive.

How could I have been so stupid? Blindly believing Mam—"Any day now, Aran"—without once asking *why* I was different, *why* I was so late to turn.

My father was a man. What did that make *me*?

I heard someone splashing up from the waves. Drops of water fell on my back. I smelled Mam's pelt, and seaweed, and a scent I didn't recognize: a harsh, mineral tang. Then something clattered down on the pebbles beside me and I opened my eyes.

It was the silver tooth. The one the man had used.

A red drop fell on the blade. I looked up at Mam. Her mouth was bleeding at the sides where she'd carried it. The red lines ran down her fur, a brutal decoration.

"It's a knife," she said, smiling.

Knife. I reached out a finger and ran it along the surface.

Mam said, "Careful of the—"

Too late. With a gasp I held up my finger. The thinnest red line traced the tip.

Mam's voice was still happy. "It was hiding in a clump of seaweed. That's why it took me so long to find. When I was swimming back, I saw you heading off to explore. I had to circle the island twice to find you." She nudged the knife with a flipper. "It's made of steel."

Part of it wasn't shiny. It was black and rounded where the man had held it. I hesitated, as if the knife might bite me again, and then wrapped my fingers around the black.

"He dropped it when he climbed in his boat," she said. "Now it's for you."

For me. She'd brought it back for me. A man's tool. For a—

"I don't want it," I said, dropping the knife back down on the pebbles.

"Don't worry. Once you learn its ways, it won't cut you again."

I crossed my arms over my chest.

"I'll teach you how to use it," she went on. Her smile was gruesome with its red edges. I looked away.

"Don't you see, Aran? You can cut oysters from the rocks and pry their shells open. You can lash it to a stick and catch fish after fish."

"I already catch fish," I mumbled. But it wasn't fish I was picturing. It was the man's fingers holding the knife. I shoved my hands deeper into my armpits.

"You're a wonderful hunter," said Mam. "But now you can catch bigger prey and slice off their heads and peel back their . . ."

I couldn't hear her anymore. The anger was rising in my throat. She'd lied to me. She was still lying, pretending nothing was wrong.

Mam's voice came from far away. "Aran, what is it?"

And then my hands were fists and my head flew up. "I'm not like him!" I shouted.

Mam looked at me oddly. "That man? Of course not." She placed a soothing flipper on my knee.

I shoved her away. "No! My father. I'm not like *him*." She jerked back as if I'd hit her.

At the water's edge, a loon cried, sad and bitter. I already wished my words unsaid. What had I let loose in the world? I should have joked along with Maura. I should have pretended it didn't matter.

It was too late for that now. Very slowly, Mam nodded.

"It's time you knew," she said.

CHAPTER TEN

⌇⌇ LIKE ALL THE REST ⌇⌇

Mam stared out across the waves. I could feel the story starting to gather, like the sky darkening with a coming storm. When she spoke again, her voice was different and strange.

"There are those who say longlimbs is only for special rites. They say, in this day of boats and planes, we can't risk being discovered. But I always loved longlimbs. When I was younger I'd sneak away, slip off my pelt, and spend hours dancing. One night I fell asleep on shore in a tangle of seaweed. Then I sensed someone watching and my eyes flew open. It was a man. I'd never seen anyone so handsome."

"Did you run?" I asked. Because everyone knows

that's what you're supposed to do in that situation: grab your pelt and run, or swim away if you can.

She shook her head. "The night was silver with moonglow. I wasn't afraid."

"Was his face furry?"

"No, it was smooth. The hair on his head was as golden as the sun."

I hugged my knees into my chest. "Did he have . . . skinny arms?"

"Skinny? They were so strong, the sight of them made me catch my breath." Her flipper traced a circle on the stones. "He insisted on putting his coat around me and we talked until the Moon sank low. Once he left I pulled my pelt from its hiding place and swam home, thinking I'd never see him again. But the next night I went back and there he was. And the next night, and the next.

"Before long we were swimming together. I didn't even hide my pelt away. When I was with him, I only wanted to be in longlimbs. Each night I stayed longer. And then one morning I didn't leave.

"He built us what they call a house, like a cave made of wood. Each day he went off fishing in his boat, and each night he came home to me. He built a wooden chest and I set my pelt inside. Now and again he'd ask me to change and we'd swim together, selkie and man, but as time went on, my pelt just stayed in the chest."

"You didn't *swim*?" I asked.

"I swam in longlimbs near the house. I had no wish to go very far."

I shook my head in disbelief. Why would anyone swim with legs if they had a choice?

"Then I was pregnant. We sang to you as you grew in my belly, my songs of the sea and his songs of the land. He built a cradle shaped like a boat. We were happy.

"And yet, mornings, after his boat puttered away, the waves called to me stronger than ever before. I swam dawn to dusk, forsaking all else, and finally I realized why: a selkie pup needs the rhythms of the deep salt sea in his blood. To do right by you, I needed my pelt.

"I climbed to the house, opened the chest—" Her voice was trembling. She stopped and took a deep breath. "My dapple-gray pelt, my path to the sea: it was gone."

"No!" I said.

But Mam nodded.

"That night, when he came home, I ran up and told him about my pelt. He got a knowing look and said, 'You won't be needing that anymore now, will you?'

"My heart split in two. Oh, I'd heard the old songs

with their warnings, but I'd thought he was different. How foolish I'd been! He was like all the rest. He stole my pelt so I couldn't swim away. When you were born, would he steal your pelt, too? You'd be trapped on land forever. You'd never know your selkie soul."

Mam shuddered; her fear echoed down my spine, and I shuddered, too.

Her words came faster. "For your sake, I pretended to agree with him. But his arms felt different, like a net holding me down. That night I lay unsleeping by his side. Come morning, as soon as he sailed away, I ripped that house apart in a frenzy: dumping out drawers, prying up floorboards, climbing into the rafters. At day's end, I cleaned it all up and put my smiling mask back on. Day after day I searched. You kicked in my belly as if to say, 'Hurry!'

"Finally, I wrenched the doorstone aside. There, in a filthy, shallow hole, lay my pelt. I ran to the shore as fast as I could with my great round belly. I sat in the shallows and tried to tug the pelt on. How tight it had grown! I let out all my breath and squeezed—and then I was looking out from my sea eyes once again. I dove."

My heart was pounding. "You left so I'd be a selkie," I said, trying to sort it out.

"You *are* a selkie. One day your pelt will come and

you'll dive deep and strong and true."

"But . . ." I didn't want to say it. "Are there some . . . ?
Do some . . . ?"

Her voice grew hard and insistent. "It can happen.
Some children take after the human parent. They're left
on shore with human kin. But I knew you were a selkie
then. I feel it now. It's your nature, Aran. Your destiny."

She was so confident. And yet . . .

"One of my eyes is blue," I said.

"And the other is brown."

"My hair has light spots."

She stared at me fiercely. "You don't need to drink
fresh water, do you? Humans do. And you never get cold.
That's proof enough right there."

"They get *cold*?"

For the first time since telling me the truth, she smiled.
"Why else would they wear those ridiculous clothes?"

Clothes—so that was the baggy extra skin.

The surf splashed over my legs and I looked down.
They looked different. My whole body looked different.

I picked up a stone and hurled it into the waves.

Later, as night thickened around us, Mam laid her head
on the rocks. I stretched out higher up the shore. I was

grateful we were spending the night here, away from the rest of the clan. The tide turned and began to ebb away. . . .

I was swimming, but my body felt all wrong. Geysers of spray splashed up from my arms. Why were they so clumsy? A wrinkled orange hide covered my skin, sagging and shifting as I moved. Its weight was pulling me down like stone. I sank below the waves into darkness, deeper and deeper, until my chest was bursting. I had to get the hide off, now! I dug my fingers in and tugged, hard, and it peeled away— My skin came with it. I'd stripped myself like a fish. And blood brings sharks—

I startled awake in darkness, gasping for air. Then I felt the hard rocks under my back. I heard the waves and Mam's breath.

Mam kept saying my pelt would come soon, that all I had to do was wait. But how could I wait now that I knew what was lurking inside me? Any day it could start spreading like eelgrass, crowding out the rest of me, until nothing was left but a greedy, blackhearted, two-legged man.

A faint glow showed where the Moon was hiding behind a bank of clouds. Did she even know I was here? I wanted to reach up and rip the clouds away. Then maybe she'd finally see me. She'd remember she left me here, stuck in this skin.

CHAPTER ELEVEN

ᕽᕽᕽ HIM ᕽᕽᕽ

You can't swim very well with a knife in your hand. That's why I went overland the next morning while Mam swam ahead. At the top of the cliff, I looked down. The clan was gathered in a tight circle around Mam. Lyr glanced up and saw me; he said something to the others and they shuffled apart.

I climbed down and they greeted me too brightly, trying to pretend nothing had changed.

"Want a fish?" asked Maura. She dropped one at my feet, a little apology.

I shook my head and sat down with my back against a cedar log. Most of the rough bark had fallen off, leaving the tender inner bark exposed. I set the knife down on the pebbles in front of me and glared at the others, silently daring them to say something. They glanced at the knife uneasily and then looked away. So we weren't going to talk about that, either.

I started peeling off long strips of cedar like I was picking at a scab. A pile grew at my side. I wrapped a strand around and around my hand.

Cormac was the first to give up pretending. Turning to Lyr, he said, "Now that everyone is here, we should leave."

"But this is a beautiful haulout," said Mist.

Cormac tilted his head in my direction. "The man might have seen him."

Him. Like I didn't even have a name.

"He didn't see me." I pulled the strand so tight it gouged a line in my flesh. "And he didn't smell me, either."

"So we can stay." Mist smoothed the shale with a flipper.

"Stay?" said Cormac. "After what we did with the man's boat? He'll have already told other humans. Anything different gets their attention. They'll come."

Grandmam's eyes sharpened. "And if they see him, a boy living with seals . . ."

"No need to worry," said Lyr. "We'll be gone long before they get here."

I stared down at my hands, ripping off strands of cedar and twisting them together, binding them with knots. Anything not to look up. Lyr could say all the consoling words he wanted, but everyone knew the truth. The clan had to move because I was stuck in this stupid body.

Because the Moon had forgotten all about me.

"There's a cluster of rocks to the west," Lyr continued. "It's on our route. Oona and Aran can wait there until we're back from Moon Day."

The knotted cord was as long as my knife. I turned it and started another row. The others kept talking about the journey to Moon Day and the Moon's open ears. They were leaving me behind, like always.

But this wasn't like always. I jerked a knot tight. I couldn't keep waiting, now that I knew what was lurking inside me. Out of the whole clan, I was the only one who *needed* to climb the Spire. I had to stand where the Moon would finally see me, where she'd hear my prayers.

My shoulders straightened, my chin lifted. "I'm going to Moon Day, too," I said.

There was a sudden silence. Mam's forehead creased in dismay. I spoke louder. "You said it's the closest the

Moon's come in eighteen years. So close she'll hear every prayer. She needs to hear *mine*!"

"But Aran," said Maura. "You can't go without a pelt."

I shook my head, swallowing hard. "You just have to swim there."

"Exactly. And you can't possibly swim that far if all you've got is legs."

"If legs are all I've got," I said, twining two cords together, "then that's what I'll use."

Maura looked aghast. "Don't be ridiculous. You'd never make it. And besides, it isn't considerate. Think how you'd slow us down."

I jumped to my feet and glared down at her. "Then I'll go by myself!"

Suddenly everyone was talking about the dangers of boats and airplanes, of orcas and sharks; and how long it took to swim; and Grandmam said she didn't mind staying behind with me, and Cormac muttered about the risks to the clan if I were seen—

"Enough!" snapped Lyr. "We'll discuss this later. Be ready to leave tomorrow morning at high tide."

I didn't wait to hear any more. Grabbing a tangle of cedar, I ran to the cliff and scrambled up one-handed. I turned to look back at them, my chest heaving. Then

I hiked to the rocks at the island's peak. No one would follow me here.

I wasn't a fool. I knew how dangerous the journey would be, in longlimbs and alone. But I didn't have a choice. I had to get to Moon Day, come shark or come storm. I'd need the knife to protect myself, and a way to carry it that left my hands free for swimming.

I sat down cross-legged with the pile of cedar strands by my knee. Now that I knew what I was making, I worked fast, twisting and knotting the cords, row after row. Before long I had a sturdy, supple mesh as long as the blade and twice as wide. I folded it in half and wove a strand in and out to bind the edges. I measured a dangle of strips around my calf and braided a strap. The knife holder was ready.

I lashed it to my leg, slid the knife inside, and stood, feeling its weight. I reached down and pulled the knife out. Too slow. I'd never save myself from attack that way. I tried again, a little faster.

But I'd be using the knife in the ocean, not on land.

I headed down to practice on the far side of the island, away from the clan. I was passing a dark ridge when a voice came drifting up from the other side. Lyr. I stopped, trying to make out the words.

"You know you should come," he said.

I climbed the ridge and peered over. Far below, Mam and Lyr lay side by side in a small inlet, their shoulders touching. Waves lapped their tails.

"We'll never see such a gathering of the clans again," said Lyr. "And besides . . ." A new note filled his voice, firm and warm and sad. "You can fool the others, Oona, but you can't fool me. The Moon is calling you, pulling you as relentlessly as she pulls the tides. You can't hold her off forever. Even if Aran . . ."

A wave crashed, drowning out the next words, but I saw the devastated look on her face, and how he placed his flipper on hers. Something twisted in my chest. And then Lyr was saying, ". . . sleeping in open water. He'd never . . ."

The jagged rocks bit into my palms. I pulled back from the edge and jumped down. Then I ran all the way to a lonely patch of shore. I'd show them. I'd swim by myself to Moon Day and get my pelt, and then I'd be faster than anyone else. They wouldn't be able to keep up with *me*.

CHAPTER TWELVE
⸰⸰⸰ THE HARNESS ⸰⸰⸰

I was underwater out past the breakers, knife in hand, when Mam zoomed up and swam a spiral around me. Long cedar strands trailed from her mouth. She tilted her head toward the surface, and then darted up with a flick of her flippers. I stayed down another moment, setting my jaw as I put the knife in its holder. I wasn't going to let her talk me out of this journey.

But when I rose, she was already racing off through the gathering fog—*away* from the island. Away from the clan.

I glanced back toward shore in confusion. Had the others left early for a new haulout? Was she taking me there? I struck out after her, the knife an unfamiliar weight on my leg.

I didn't even see the rocks until Mam surged up from the water and landed on a stone shelf. I hauled up after her. She was dropping the cedar strands onto a pile so large, she must have made several trips.

"Where are the others?" I asked, looking around. "What are we doing here?"

Mam took a deep breath. "Aran, I decided you're right. You need to be at the Spire for the rites. I'm going to make sure you get there. We're going together."

"Together?" I said, hardly daring to hope. She nodded. *"Really?"*

"Really," she said. And then she beamed at me, a ray of light through the fog. A weight lifted from my heart, and I flung back my head, laughing in a whale spout of pure joy. I spread my arms wide and started spinning around, faster and faster, until I toppled over into the waves.

I hauled out, shaking the water from my hair. "Where's everyone else?" I asked, eager this time. "How did you get Maura to agree? Did you growl at her? I'll swim really fast, I'll hardly slow you down at all, and—"

"Well, you see . . ." Mam's smile faded just the tiniest bit. "It's going to take us longer, so you and I will swim on our own."

I shrugged off a twinge of disappointment. It didn't matter. I was going to Moon Day.

"We have some preparing to do." Mam nosed around in the pile and pulled out a thick cedar strand with her teeth. It was twisted and braided, like a fatter, stronger version of the cords I'd made. Mam must have been in longlimbs to make it, and that surprised me. She hardly ever changed anymore.

She draped the cord over my palm. "I'm not as clever with my hands as you are. It will be faster if you finish the braiding."

I looked at it, confused. "What is it?"

"A harness." There was the slightest edge to her voice.

"A harness?"

"You'll strap it around me and hold on so you won't fall off my back. I got the idea from watching you make your sheath." She nodded at the knife holder on my calf. "Don't worry, I'll tell you how long it needs to be and how the pieces go together. Work fast—we need to leave early tomorrow."

I still didn't understand. "But Mam, I won't be on your back. I'm swimming. I have to get to Moon Day on my own. That's the rule."

"Rule?" She poked at the pile of strands so she wasn't looking at me. "Different situation, different rules. It's not like you're a newborn, or too old or sick to climb to the top of the Spire. That's what the rule is about." She turned toward the north. "Besides, there isn't time for you to swim. The full Moon is only six nights from now. It's a three-day journey to get there, and that's in sealform. We'll need five with you on my back. And we'll be sleeping in open ocean. So you see, we need the harness."

Something about this didn't feel right. But Mam was so sure. And if this was the only way for me to get there in time . . .

I sat beside the pile of cedar and picked out two strands.

"Still," said Mam, "let's keep this between us, all right? The others don't need to know you didn't swim there on your own."

I swallowed hard, then grabbed another strand.

Mam nodded in approval. "Three of those braided together for strength," she said. "And twice as long as my body."

For a while the only sounds were the lapping waves and the rustle of my hands at work. Mam passed me strands as the cord grew longer. The fog thickened, wrapping us in white.

Mam started to hum. It was one of my favorite tunes from the story of creation. From the time I was small we'd told the story together, her calm voice letting me know all was right in the world.

Now I whispered, "In the beginning . . ."

Mam smiled and took up the tale. "In the beginning, there was the Moon. She circled a dry, barren planet called Earth."

"And she was lonely," I said.

Mam nodded. "Deep in her loneliness, the Moon sighed. Her sigh became music, a song so sweet with longing, it pulled tiny drops of moisture from the bone-dry air. They began to dance to her song."

"That was the mist," I said, reaching out a hand. Mam passed me another strand of cedar.

"Yes, the swirling mist. Now the Moon sang louder. The little drops became bigger drops, and those became rain, falling on the face of the Earth." Mam turned to me. "Sing it with me, Aran. Like you'll sing at the rites."

We sang together, *"Hail the rain, the blessed rain, sung by the Moon into being."*

"And what did the Moon do then?" Mam asked, as she'd always done.

"She sang louder still."

"Yes. And the louder she sang, the harder it rained, until the Earth was nothing but ocean."

I took a deep breath and we sang, *"Hail the ocean, great and gray, sung by the Moon into being."*

We began to sway gently from side to side, and the rhythm worked its way into the strands of bark.

"The Moon wandered the heavens," said Mam. "And the waters followed, straining to hear every precious note. They surged in her wake, curving in crests, crashing in hollows. And so the waves were born."

I sang, *"Hail the wave-foam, white as first mist, sung by the Moon into being."*

We stopped swaying because now came land.

"The waves pulled aside so the islands could raise their heads," said Mam. "Now the land was ready to welcome life. The Moon looked down at her work. There was one place she loved the best: the shore, with its ever-shifting dance, now water, now sand. What would be worthy of this place? Once more the Moon sang, and this time, as each note landed on that shimmering line, it turned into a selkie."

I sang the next words, my heart so full, it felt like the Moon was calling me then and there. *"Hail creation! Wave-riders, shore-striders, sung by the Moon into being!"*

The last notes drifted out to sea. With them, they carried the doubt that had been haunting me. I'd reach the Spire. I, too, would be sung by the Moon into being.

The fog wove into the growing darkness until I could barely make out the pile of cedar.

"That's enough for tonight," said Mam, all practical again. "Put that higher up so it's safe, and we'll finish in the morning. We need a good night's sleep." She scooted up past the reach of the tide and stretched out long, wiggling into a comfortable position.

But my head and my heart were too full to let go. I tried to make her keep talking.

"Did the Moon make humans, too?"

"The Moon created all life." Her voice was growing heavy with sleep.

"Why did she only give them longlimbs?"

"Well, she didn't want all that nice land to go to waste now, did she? Someone needed to live there."

She said it like joking, but it made sense. Some humans lived far inland; if they had pelts, they'd die of sadness for not being able to reach the sea. "Mam," I said, turning to tell her. But there wasn't any answer, just her breath matching the rise and fall of the waves.

I should join her. I should close my eyes. But how could I sleep? Tomorrow I was leaving on the journey that would change my life.

CHAPTER THIRTEEN
๑๏ THE JOURNEY ๑๏

A scraping sound woke me at dawn. Mam was using her teeth to spread out the harness. I jumped up and ran over to help. When we were done, it lay splayed on the shore like beached bones.

Mam rolled onto it, so she was right in the middle. I measured and fastened, tightened and trimmed. Then I stood back to check the fit.

I broke into a peal of laughter. Mam looked ridiculous, with her sleek, powerful body trussed up in that tangle of cords! But she glared at me so fiercely, I snapped my mouth shut and hurried to tighten a loose strap.

Blue sky peeked through the last scurrying wisps of fog.

Mam pushed off, strangely awkward, but once she was floating she looked right again. In thigh-high water I climbed on her back, fit my feet in the footholds, and hunched down low. "Away!" I cried.

"Away," said Mam, hard and determined.

I held my breath and she dove. The water closed over my head. Light danced and sparkled, and then grew dimmer as we swam down deep, faster than I'd ever gone before. An instant later, Mam turned with a flick of her tail and sped upward. We burst through the water's skin.

I gulped in air and then laughed, my joy spreading in ripples along with the waves and the water-strewn light.

"Again?" Mam asked. The hardness was gone from her voice. It was like swimming into a warm current.

"Again!" I said. "Deeper!"

This time she plunged, spinning in tightening coils like an eddy pulling down. A group of anchovies broke before us, making way, then turned to stare with amazement in their round eyes. Even in the dim light, I could see it all — fish with swirling fins; a shrimp, its legs scrambling; even a cloud of plankton — and we were twisting and twirling, part of the ocean's pulse. We reached the depth where we'd turned back before, and then dove deeper into darkness. A sudden swerve — a spiral — Mam was testing what she could do with my weight on her back. But playing, too, giving me a taste of the glories awaiting me. Her swaying ease was mine, the backward curve of her neck, then the forward curve of her tail—they were mine!

But my boy-lungs were mine as well—aching, insistent, pounding.

I defied the tightness in my chest. I *wouldn't* rise, I *wouldn't*! I tried to ignore the throbbing in my head, the dizziness. But the moment my hands began to loosen from the straps, Mam raced to the surface. She was panting as hard as I was.

"Tug on the straps when you need air," she said. "And not so deep the rest of the way. Now, enough playing. We have five days of swimming ahead of us. Let's go."

And then we were off. Northbound, away from the waters I knew. We'd speed along beneath the surface, and then ride a cresting wave where I'd gasp in a breath, my hair blown back by a lively wind, rich with the promise of change.

We didn't even stop for breakfast. When my stomach growled, Mam snatched a herring in her jaws, and with a flick of her head tossed it back to me. I'd never had breakfast on her back before. She slowed while I ate.

"Let's go faster," I said through a mouthful.

"No point in getting there early," she said, but I could feel her catching her breath.

All day we swam. Past the island with two pines, through the swirling currents where the river poured into the sea—I slipped off Mam's back there and she gulped down fish after fish—and then we were past the places I'd heard about.

We swam below in hushed blue light, cool water slipping over my skin. We rose and I called out a greeting to an auklet flying by—

"Quiet!" snapped Mam, glancing around for boats, even though the few we'd seen had been far in the distance. I closed my eyes so the sun blazed through my lids, brilliant and red. It was as if I could see the power— the strength and the grace—that would soon be mine.

The sun set in an explosion of orange and pink. We were out in open water with no land in sight. As dark descended, Mam told me to tuck my hands and feet under the straps and lie across her back to sleep.

"What about you?" I said. "How will you sleep with no one to keep watch?"

"Oh, you know me; I can sleep with one eye open."

I dreamed I was in my pelt. I dreamed I swam deep on my own. Each time I woke, Mam was still swimming, riding the swells where I could breathe.

The second day Mam swam slower. I wanted to swim alongside to give her a break, but her mouth got tight and stubborn and she said there wasn't time. She gave a sudden, strong push with her tail and we sped up for a while.

When I longed to slip off and swim, I pictured Moon Day instead. How would it happen, when the Moon called me into my true form? Maybe it would come during the ceremony, with the great chief chanting and all of us responding, and I'd feel a tingling along my arms and legs. I'd look down and see my skin growing sleek and dappled, and I'd hold my arms tight to my sides as the pelt grew up and over, and then my arms would slip into the flippers. Everyone would be staring at me, so happy. "The Moon has called him!" they'd cry.

Or maybe the Moon wanted me to don my pelt when all the others were donning theirs. After the ceremony, when everyone returned to the pelt cave to change back for the long swim home, the guardians would cry, "What's this? There's still one here, a perfect black pelt, the handsomest of all. Whose could it be?" I'd step forward, reaching out a hand. "It's mine," I'd say, and slip it on just like I'd seen the others do. Then I'd scoot into the waves, along with everyone else. I could almost feel the pebbles under the thick skin of my belly, the waves crashing over my head as I swam out and dove, deeper and deeper and deeper still. . . .

That night we stopped on an island for a quick sleep, and then we were off again.

On the fourth day—

"Look, Mam," I said, pointing.

We'd risen for air. Ahead of us, gulls eddied around a roiling patch of water, screaming as they dove for the remnants of someone's meal. The water rose in a dome.

Mam tensed, completely alert in the way that meant *predator*. And then we were speeding toward a rock in the distance. The water whipped past in a blur of foam. I freed my right hand and rested it alongside my leg, ready to grab my knife. Fish fled alongside us like shards of light. As we neared the rock, I slipped my feet free—

"Off!" cried Mam.

I leaped and Mam flung herself onto the rock, scooting as high as she could go. It was too small a refuge, little more than a granite fist thrusting up from the sea.

I turned to see huge dorsal fins swimming toward us, and then the black-and-white arc of a giant back.

Orcas!

I stood at the ready beside Mam, my knife pointed at the approaching fins. Five of them. They swam right up, paused, and then slowly began to circle the rock, as if they were examining it from every angle.

"Grab on to the rocks!" snapped Mam, wedging between two crags. "They'll splash their tails and make waves to flood us off. *Hurry!*"

I grabbed a knob of rock with one hand, but I didn't let go of the knife. My pulse was the pounding of wind-driven waves against stone. Power surged through me, hot and red and ready to fight.

Even the smallest dorsal fin was taller than Mam was long. They slowed, stopped. . . .

A monstrous head rose before me, and a huge dark eye stared right into mine. The rest of the world disappeared. There was only my hand brandishing the knife, and the cold intelligence of the orca's gaze, looking at me, at Mam.

And then, to my astonishment, the head sank back down until only the fin was showing. It turned away and the other four fins followed. We watched in silence as they dipped and rose, shrinking into the distance.

I slipped my knife back in its sheath.

"Thank the Moon they'd just eaten," gasped Mam. Her flippers were shaking. She saw me looking and rolled so they were tucked under her.

But my blood was still surging. I felt as if I could do

anything! I wanted to dive and kick some of my wild energy into the waves, but Mam insisted we stay on the rock for a while.

"So we can be sure they're gone," she said. But I saw her exhaustion, too.

We didn't take off again until high sun. Mam's body strained in effort, and there were sore spots where the harness rubbed her pelt. Again I said I'd swim. She only shook her head and kept on, now under the waves, now atop the crests. The sun dipped low and the light faded to gray, and still she swam.

When the stars came out, she said, "Sleep. You'll want to be at your best tomorrow."

I shook out my cramped legs before putting my feet back in the footholds. I lay against the curve of her back and closed my eyes, but I couldn't stop wondering about tomorrow, and the Spire, and meeting selkies from other clans, and if there'd be someone my own age. About the pelt cave, and the climb to the top, and the rites.

Hail creation! Wave-riders, shore-striders, sung by the Moon into being!

I didn't think I'd be able to fall asleep, but I opened my eyes to the shimmer of moonlight on the water, and then there was darkness again.

∾ ∾ ∾

I startled awake as Mam swerved to a stop and my toes touched sand. The sky was brightening. I splashed ashore.

"Are we there?" I cried, looking around for the other selkies. But the beach was empty.

"The Spire is that one." Mam pointed with her nose toward a bigger island, still a long swim away. While our resting spot was rounded and dark, the Spire was a silvery pinnacle piercing the sky. I caught my breath. No wonder you had to be in longlimbs to reach the top.

"I thought you'd want to swim the last bit yourself," said Mam, rolling onto her side.

I rushed to undo the straps. A few wiggles and the harness lay on the beach.

"Hide it up there," said Mam, nodding to rocks higher ashore.

I stared at the tumble of rope. "Why? I won't need it again."

"We don't want anyone else to find it." She looked at me intently, her eyes burning into mine. "Some things are best kept secret."

I found a hollow in the rocks well above the tideline and stashed the harness. Then I bent down, unstrapped the sheath, and hid my knife there, too. After tonight I'd have claws.

By the time I came back, Mam had caught a salmon. She chomped it in two and tossed me a glistening piece. But I was too excited to eat. She gulped it all down while I strode back and forth on the narrow beach.

And then we swam through the pink dawn toward the Spire. I was stiff from clutching the harness, but soon my arms were reaching out like wings, my hands slicing into the water with barely a splash.

The sky brightened to blue. All around us, the world was waking. Fish swarmed in the depths; jellyfish pulsed near the surface; pelicans plunged into the waves and rose with their catch thrashing in their beaks.

And then there were larger bodies surging through the water, sleek heads coming from all directions—selkies!— heading straight to the sunlit Spire.

Suddenly a selkie popped up next to me, staring wide-eyed. His pelt was white, without a single spot, and he was smaller than anyone in my clan. A pup, like me! I stopped and stared back. He smiled.

A flipper slapped the water ahead of us and a deep voice boomed, "Come along, Finn. Don't keep us waiting." The next instant the pup was gone, speeding underwater toward his clan.

Now my strokes felt impossibly slow, arm over arm

in a plodding pace. More and more selkies went zipping by, leaving us far behind. But Mam didn't look impatient. The merest flick of a tail kept her at my side as we swam to my very first Moon Day, and the great gathering of clans, and the Moon's open ears.

CHAPTER FOURTEEN
⟪ THE SPIRE ⟫

Everyone else was heading to the flat, pebbled beach, but Mam and I swam to a tumble of rocks on one side, where a crag blocked us from view.

"You and I will walk in together," she said. The fur grew loose around her.

From around the crag I could hear cries of greeting, flippers slapping and feet running, snatches of song. It was as raucous as a rookery at nesting time.

The pelt slid from Mam's shoulders. Her long, dark hair wrapped her body; her arms were pressed tight to her sides. In this pale face, her eyes were huge, and she had that mysterious, inward gaze, the look of changing.

I jumped on top of the rocks. "Hurry," I said, craning sideways, trying to see around the crag.

But Mam wasn't to be rushed, not now. When her pelt lay on the ground beside her, she stretched, feeling what it was to have arms again. She spread her fingers out one by one, the webbing between them thin and tender, almost translucent. She stretched her legs long, pointing her toes.

"Now?" I said, ready to jump down.

Mam took a deep breath. She picked up her pelt, folded it carefully, and tucked it under her arm.

"Now," she said.

Together we rounded the crag.

I stood in the shallows, staring, openmouthed. The beach was crowded with selkies. In sealform they surfed ashore, galumphed to greet loved ones, nuzzled noses. Pelts of every color lay in a glossy tumble: brown and black and silver, speckled and spotted and pearly white. And in longlimbs! In longlimbs they ran to one another with open arms, lounged on flat rocks, sat sifting sand with fresh-skin fingers. Still others were carrying their pelts up a path toward the black, gaping mouth of a cave.

I drew in a breath: the pelt cave! Three huge, muscular bull selkies protected the door. One was brown, one black, and the third granite gray. So those were the guardians, the ones who stay in sealform for the entire ceremony. A guardian needs the eyes of an eagle to watch out for intruders, the strength of a whale to fight them off, and a voice like thunder to summon the clans if need be. Selkies take no chances. If humans ever came upon Moon Day and stole all the pelts, they could wipe out the folk forever. Your soul dies without a pelt. That's what they say.

Maybe I'd be a guardian one day. I could see it now: my broad neck and muscular shoulders, the scars on my pelt proof of battles I'd fought and won.

Mam stroked her folded pelt. "Why don't you wait here," she said, turning toward the path.

I watched her walk uphill and take her place in line. She reached the cave and bowed respectfully, holding out her pelt with outstretched arms. The gray bull took it to store on the ledges within.

I was watching so closely, I didn't sense anyone near me. Then a voice at my shoulder made me jump.

"Why did you change early?"

I turned and stared. It was a pup, and in longlimbs! He was heavier than I was, with a broad chest and sturdy legs, as if all his ocean swimming had muscled him up. His dark hair flowed down to his shoulders. His skin was almost pure white; next to him I looked brown.

"Your pelt," he said, when I didn't answer. "Why didn't you wait and take it off here?" His eyes shone with an eager look — it was the white selkie who'd popped up beside me in the water. He gave me an open, welcoming smile. A smile of friendship.

I was overwhelmed by the surge of bodies, the splashing and calling, and the explanation was too complicated. "I just felt like it," I said.

"Lucky!" His laughter showered over me, a sunlit spray. "I'd swim in with legs, too, if I could do it like you. I never swim in longlimbs. Our chief won't let me. How'd you get so good?"

What an odd thing to admire! I shrugged. "Practice, I guess."

He leaned closer. "The ceremonies don't start for ages. Want to go climbing?"

Did I! I ran to tell Mam, and then I dashed off to play, for the first time ever, with another selkie pup.

CHAPTER FIFTEEN
~ FINN ~

We ran away from the crowd and up a stone staircase. As the island grew steep and pointed, we veered off onto a narrow path. One side hugged a wall of rock; the other was a sheer drop to the sea.

He stopped to peer over. "This is the highest I've ever gone. We don't have peaks like this where I come from."

"We could just explore around the beach if you want," I said. I didn't care what we did, as long as we did it together.

He must have thought I was scared, because he said, "I'll show you how. Watch your step. These skins are so thin, the stones cut right through."

I nodded as if I were learning something new. I let

him go first so he couldn't see how easily this came to me, how tough my soles and palms had become. His clan was probably like mine, only taking longlimbs for special rites.

"What's your name?" he said, heading up the path again.

"Aran."

"I'm Finn. Are you on your long journey, too? It's special when it coincides with the rites. We swam for more than a moon to get here. The elders told Brehan—that's our chief—that we had to come this year, even though it's so far from home."

"Did you come all the way from the old shores?" I asked.

He snorted. "Of course not! We come from the north, where the islands are made of ice. It's as far as you can go. Except some say there are ancient wise ones still farther north, at the very peak of the world. The wise ones are magic. They don't even need to come to Moon Day because they're always talking with the Moon."

We made our way toward a high ledge and lay down, our heads hanging over. Beyond a tumble of boulders, rock walls circled a clear blue pool. Late afternoon sun bounced off the water, reflecting red-gold ripples across the stone. And there, where wall met water, was a black arch.

"A sea cave," I said. "Let's go!"

We leaped to our feet and ran, searching for a place to jump into the pool. Now the trail was crowded with selkies heading upward. One group moved slowly, cheering on a tiny pup as she toddled on fat, wobbly legs. I looked over my shoulder as we passed them; she was only the second pup I'd seen.

Finn seemed to read my thoughts. "I'm glad you're here," he said. "I was afraid there wouldn't be anyone to play with."

"Where are all the pups?" I asked, speeding up again.

"There aren't many. Brehan says it's a disaster. It's because humans are poisoning the ocean, and netting all the fish, and making the water too warm. There need to be lots more pups for the folk to survive."

"But there must be hundreds of selkies here."

"This is nothing." Finn pointed out to the waves where a few stragglers were swimming ashore. "Brehan says these waters used to be so full of selkies, you could walk in longlimbs across their backs. That's one of the reasons we came so far to be here. Some of our clan"—he nudged me in the ribs—"are here to find mates."

The path curved. "There," I said. "If we climb to that rock, it's a straight dive down."

We scrambled over to the precipice. Then we were standing at the top of a great rim. The water glittered so far below, it was like looking down from the heavens.

"I feel like the Moon," I whispered.

A puffin whirred out from the cliff face below us.

"And there's your worshipper!" said Finn.

A feather floated off the puffin's back and we watched it drift down, down, down toward the water. Suddenly I wanted to grab it. I raised my arms overhead and dove. The air rushed past me and then I sliced into the water, the coolness closing over my skin. I rose with the feather in my hand.

Finn stared down in wonder. "How do you *do* that?" he called.

It wouldn't work to talk him through a dive. "Just jump!" I cried.

He flew out from the cliff, arms and legs waving like an octopus, and hit the water with a gigantic splash.

He rose to the sound of cheering from the hillside. "That's my clan," he said, giving them a wave. Then we swam to the dark arch of the cave and slipped through.

We paused, treading water. Near us, the low rays of the sun lit curving walls, but the cave stretched back into darkness.

"Wow!" said Finn.

Wavelets were lapping at something big in the center of

the cave. I swam over. At the edge of the light, a magnificent boulder rose from the water. The front was a long, smooth slope. I swam around to the back. Hollows were gouged into the rock, making steps. I scrambled up and sat at the top.

Just then, the sun dipped, shining a ray of light straight at me. I held the feather high, a chief brandishing a token of power. Finn gave a mock bow.

I started to slip—the rock was a perfect slide! I splashed off into deep water.

"My turn!" cried Finn, snatching the feather.

We slid down on our seats and our bellies, feetfirst and headfirst, the rock more slippery each time. Our howls of glee echoed around the cave until it sounded like there were hundreds of selkies crowded inside. I'd never had so much fun in my whole life.

I was on the rock, feather in hand, when Finn said, "I can hardly see you."

The sun had disappeared.

Then a blast of sound filled the cave, an unworldly voice singing a single booming note.

"The conch!" said Finn. "It's time for the rites!"

I slid down and swam off as fast as I could. I would not be late for this, the most important night of my life.

CHAPTER SIXTEEN
⟶ THE MOON'S EAR ⟵

I crested a final ridge and stopped, speechless. Before me, hundreds of selkies crowded into a vast hollow. The curving rock face echoed their shuffling and murmuring until it sounded like the surf far below. Above us, on a jutting ledge of rock just under the Spire, stood a broad-shouldered selkie. A white streak blazed in his hair like a bolt of lightning. That must be the Great Chief of all the clans. On a ledge below him stood the Caller, her black hair cascading to her feet.

Finn ran past me toward the group that had cheered his dive. They greeted him with hugs and exclamations over his scratched knees. I was following in his wake when a hand grabbed my shoulder.

"There you are," cried Mam, her eyes bright with excitement.

Lyr, Maura, Mist, Cormac, Grandmam: everyone was there, looking so different in longlimbs. They shifted to make room for me in the crush.

I was turning to point out Finn when a blast from the conch made me stop.

In the sudden hush, the Caller's clear voice filled the air:

"Sing, O Moon, the song of the sea!
Sing of the salt-spray, the tears, and the freedom
Erasing the border twixt wave-foam and shoreline.
Sweet comes the turning that sets the soul free."

The haunting tune swept me up like a current, and then its rhythms were surging inside me. My breath rose and fell to its pulse.

The notes drifted away, and a deep voice boomed like combers crashing ashore:

"IN THE BEGINNING!"

My eyes flew up to the ledge. The lightning-haired selkie stood with his arms straight out before him, palms turned upward. I caught my breath. This wasn't going to be anything like the warm, familiar tale I'd always known.

He raised his arms skyward, and we turned as one to face the sea. Before us was darkness. And then . . .

A single beam of light appeared at the edge of the world. It streaked across the waves toward the Spire like a brilliant, silver path. I gasped in awe.

A motion caught my eye. A tall, muscular selkie was resting his hand on Finn's shoulder. That must be Brehan, his chief. They gazed at the horizon together, the silver light reflecting in their eyes.

Slowly, gracefully, the Moon began to rise. Around her, the air shimmered blue and green: she had donned her halo to greet us. Now we would sing and chant her to the center of the sky.

"In the beginning," said the Great Chief, "there was the Moon. She circled a forsaken sphere of dirt and dust and rock. . . ."

The story was familiar and yet the words were new and strange. It felt like it was happening now, for the very first time: the barren Earth, the Moon's longing. He came to the part where the Moon began to sing, and softly, as softly as a breeze, a wordless tune caressed the air. It tugged at my heart like all the hunger and heartache and joy I'd ever felt. At first I thought the Moon herself was singing. But it was the Caller, her skin white as moonlight, her hair dark as night.

As the Great Chief's voice rolled on, I could almost feel the song tugging moisture from the air. It swirled into mist, and then rain; it fell upon the Earth. When the chief paused, I knew what to do. I'd been practicing my whole life. I chanted along with everyone else:

"Hail the rain, the blessed rain, sung by the Moon into being!"

I'd never heard it like this before. Each voice was swept up into something greater: the single voice of the selkie folk.

As the last word rang out, the Moon rose above the sea. She hovered, huge and round, waiting for us to sing her higher.

"Hail the ocean, great and gray, sung by the Moon into being!"

"The Moon wandered the vastness of space," said the chief, and the crowd began to sway. When Mam and I told the story, the swaying was gentle and playful. But now, hundreds of selkies swayed together from side to side, and the power felt primal, remorseless. We were the waves, surging in the Moon's wake, curving in crests and crashing in hollows, straining to hear every precious note of her song.

"Hail the wave-foam, white as first mist, sung by the Moon into being!"

We stilled, becoming as solid as rock. Now we were the islands rising from the waves. The Moon rose higher, her light filling me.

Finn looked toward me, his eyes full of the same wonder I was feeling. My hand rose in an instinctive greeting.

That's when Finn's chief glanced over. His brows lowered in a frown. I followed his gaze to my hand: I was still clutching the puffin feather, and it looked like I was waving it at Finn, playing during the holiest rites.

I dropped the feather in shame. The chief's cold eyes swept over my hair, my skin. He bent to whisper in Finn's ear.

I shivered, a leaf in a cold wind.

Then the Great Chief's voice swept me up again. "—the shoreline, where water meets rock, where dark sea meets bright sand, where borders are constantly changing. Once more the Moon sang."

The Caller sang one pure note, as round and shining as a pearl.

The Great Chief said softly, "As each note landed on that shimmering line, it became a selkie." He paused, and then his voice split the air like thunder:

"WE ARE THE FOLK BORN OF THE LINE WHERE WATER MEETS THE LAND!"

Another perfect note, and another, floated down to the shore and the shimmering line of foam. The Moon was gigantic now, filling the sky. The air felt electric.

Finn and I looked up at each other at the exact same moment, as if we were connected by our own strand of moonlight. *A friend*, I thought, with a longing deep and true.

The hairs on my arms stood on end, as though lightning was about to strike. I looked down. My skin was glowing with silvery light.

Suddenly everyone was chanting, *"Hail creation! Wave-riders, shore-striders, sung by the Moon into being!"*

The Moon was right above me! This was the moment!

I raised my face and prayed silently: *Please, Moon, let me live in my true form, the way I'm meant to be. Please.*

The air was thick with prayers swirling upward, and my skin was still tingling. This must be how it happened! First the tingling, and then the thickening of skin into fur. I stared at my arms. *Now*, I thought. *Now!*

CHAPTER SEVENTEEN
ꙮ STORM WAVES ꙮ

The conch blared and the Great Chief cried, "Let the dancing begin!"

I startled, looking around in confusion. Mam was there beside me, and then she was gone, swept away by Lyr. Selkies surged around me, grabbing partners, but I stood still, a rock in roiling waves, staring at my arms. The tingling was fading. I tried to hold on to it, but it was like grasping at air.

My skin was still skin.

But my pelt had to be coming now. I'd felt the Moon's magic!

My breath came short and shallow. I tried not to panic. At least I didn't stand out from everyone else. All around me, legs were dancing, kicking, leaping.

Of course—that was it! If the Moon changed me now, I'd be the only one not in longlimbs, still different from everyone else. I'd have had to take my pelt right off again. No, my pelt would be waiting for me in the cave, and the cave was sealed until daybreak.

Finn's hand clasped mine. "Grab on, it's the storm dance!" he cried, pulling me into a quickly moving line. The selkie at the head half ran, half danced, and the pattern passed from hand to hand so we were whipping along in his wake—a ribbon of dancers, cresting and falling like waves.

"I've been looking for you," Finn shouted over the music.

My feet stepped higher, lighter. Maybe waiting wouldn't be so bad after all.

Finn leaned closer. "You'll never believe what my chief said."

"What?"

"He said that your father—"

The line of dancers snapped back and forth, and I struggled to stay on my feet. Someone grabbed my other hand.

I raised my voice above the roar. "What about my father?"

"Brehan said he was human. I said that was madness!"

"No, it's true."

"It is?" He stared at me wide-eyed. "He *was*?"

How could I explain it to him here? I needed to take him somewhere quiet, just the two of us, so I could find the words. How my father wasn't a selkie, but it didn't matter, because I'd be in sealform before the rites were over. But the music grew faster and the dance's waves wilder, and I couldn't pull my hands away.

Finn shouted, "He said you're human, too."

"No, I'm going to turn!"

"Wind waves!" called the leader, as quick curves pulsed down the line. The rocks echoed back music and laughter and the drumbeat of pounding feet. We were nearing the Spire.

"That's what I told him," said Finn. "But he said to look at your hair with its funny bright spots. He said to look at your eyes."

"One is brown," I cried. The rocks echoed back in a mocking voice: *One is brown . . . brown . . . brown. . . .*

"Storm waves!" called the leader. The music thundered. A towering wave of a curve was surging toward me.

Finn looked right at me. "He said you're never going to turn, and I can't —"

The line flung me forward, and then *—snap!—* our hands pulled apart. Gasps and cries and sharp peals of laughter split the air as we went flying in all directions. I tripped and tumbled across the stony ground, crashing to a stop against the Spire. A jutting ledge above me blocked the moonlight.

From beyond the gloom came ripples of happy laughter. Someone called, "Find your partners!" The rocks warped the music into something dark and jarring. I didn't want to dance. I had to find Finn and explain.

I scooted out of my hollow and wiped the dirt from my arms. Around me, everyone was dancing in couples or small groups. At the sound of Finn's laugh, I looked up. There he was in a circle of six, hands clasped tight, feet moving in a complicated rhythmic step I'd never learned. His face was bright with joy. And holding one of his hands was his chief.

How could I wait until daybreak? I needed my pelt now. I needed to put it on right in front of Finn and his clan.

I could almost see it: their eyes growing wide with wonder and admiration, their voices begging forgiveness. *We should have known*, they'd say. *Of course the Moon provides for her own, on this night of all nights!* I'd smile humbly as

I accepted their apologies, and then Finn and I would belly-scoot into the waves, tumbling and tossing each other about, leaping in backflips. We'd spiral down to the depths, until our clan leaders slapped the surface hard with their flippers, calling us for our journeys home, and Finn would say he'd rather come with me.

It was all I could do not to run to the cave. I forced myself to sit there, rocks gouging my back, waiting for Finn to see me and come over.

One couple was dancing with such spirit, a circle of admirers had gathered to cheer them on. I saw an arm flung high, a wave of black hair flying. Then the circle shifted, revealing the pair, their faces glowing, step matching passionate step, the pull between them as strong as the tides —

It was Mam and Lyr.

I rocked, buffeted by a changing wind. I'd always been the center of Mam's life. It didn't need saying; it was just how it was, obvious each time the others left or an orca's fin broke the waves. But the way she was looking at Lyr now . . .

I clenched my fists. Mam could do whatever she wanted. Come daybreak, I'd have my pelt. I'd have air in my blood to swim deep, and flippers to speed me along with the rest of the clan. She didn't need to stay back for me.

The dance ended amid a burst of cheers. Then Mam was scanning the crowd, searching for me. I couldn't stand the thought of her rushing over, the joy in her eyes replaced by the same questions pounding through my veins: *How? When?* So I stood and waved to show her I was fine, and then I disappeared into the crowd.

Cormac was talking with Finn's chief, their heads bent close together. That meant Finn was free. I went looking for him.

The banquet was spread out on low, flat rocks. Finn was by himself, gulping down prawns.

I ran up. "There you are!"

He glanced around anxiously, grabbed my arm, and pulled me back behind a boulder.

"Listen," he said in a hushed voice. "I'm not supposed to talk with you anymore."

My heart plummeted.

"They say"—he paused and took a deep breath, the feelings battling across his face—"they say you're a danger to us."

"Why would I want to hurt you?" I said. "You're my friend."

"It's not that you'd want to. You couldn't help it. You'd

draw attention and make humans notice us. They'd see we aren't seals. They'd catch us and put us in zoos."

"In what?"

"Zoos. That's where humans trap you in a metal cage so they can stare at you. One of the elders lived on land for a while and he told us about zoos, and circuses, where they make you do stupid tricks to entertain them. We'd see humans coming and be trying to swim away and you couldn't keep up."

I tried to answer, but all I could do was shake my head, harder and harder.

"Maybe I'd stay behind to help you," Finn went on. "That's what you do for a friend, and then I'd get caught. It's too risky. And it's not just humans. What about orcas, and great whites? Sometimes you only have a whisker's advantage when they're on your tail. You'd be so slow with your splashing—"

"I don't splash!" My voice was too sharp. "And besides, it doesn't matter, because I'm turning. That's why I'm here!"

"They say . . ." He stopped all of a sudden. Pity washed across his face like a swirl of white foam.

I wanted to leave then, run away across the crags, as far as I could go. But I couldn't help myself. "What"—the words came out all twisted — "what do they say?"

He answered so softly, I strained to hear him. "Not everyone turns, you know."

Something snapped in me. My arm shot out and I shoved him back a step. "I'm getting my pelt!"

"Not if the human half is stronger. Some of your kind never turn. They're stuck forever in that—"

This time I shoved him so hard he fell to the ground, and then I was on top of him, my fist raised to strike. He rolled us over, gripping my arms, trying to pin me down. I jerked free and slammed him backward across the boulders, sending prawns and squid flying, and then we were on our feet, careening into the rocks, fists flailing—

A hand reached between us and grabbed Finn.

"What did I tell you?" It was Brehan, his face dark with anger. "That one's nothing but trouble."

I stumbled to my feet, my chest heaving. "But we didn't mean to—"

"And on Moon Day, too," he went on, ignoring me.

That broad hand clamped down on Finn's shoulder, leading him away.

CHAPTER EIGHTEEN
⁓ THE PELT CAVE ⁓

I waited, and I waited, and I waited. The sky faded to gray. The last star fled. From the hollow there rose a tune aching with loss and farewell: the Caller was singing the Moon down into the sea.

A streak of red slashed the eastern sky, and a conch blared. I leaped to my feet. The pelt cave was opening!

All around me, selkies began to move reluctantly, as if they didn't want the night to end. I shoved past them toward the stairs, and then I flew, leaping down two steps at a time. I reached the cave just as the guardians finished rolling back the boulder. I was the first in line. No one else was even in sight.

I stood at the door and held up my hands to receive my pelt.

"Name?" barked the great gray bull guarding the door.

"Aran," I said as loudly and clearly as I could.

He disappeared for a moment. My heart was pounding like it would explode.

The guardian came back, but he wasn't carrying anything. I peered past him into the darkness. Was someone else bringing my pelt?

"Didn't find it right off," said the guardian. "It might have slipped under another. It happens sometimes. Check back in a bit."

I stood there in disbelief until a tap on my shoulder made me turn. A line had formed behind me. Reluctantly I moved a half step, but as body after body nudged past me, I went to sit on the hillside. Young and old, male and female, short and tall: one selkie after another approached the door and left carrying a pelt.

They walked down to the surf; they slipped their pelts over their shoulders and pulled the fur tight. And then came that instant of turning, where it stops being a pelt draped across a body and becomes sealform and grace and strength. The shore was filling with a growing herd, gray pelts and brown pelts, dappled and pearl white. . . .

White was Finn's clan.

The guardians must have uncovered my pelt by now. I ran to the back of the line and took my place again. I craned my neck to the side so I could see how long I'd have to wait. There, at the door to the cave, was Finn, his arms outstretched. When he pulled them back to his chest, they held a gleaming white pelt.

As he passed by on his way to the shoreline, I leaned out and said, "Finn, wait for me!"

So I can show you it's true, I wanted to add. *So we can play under the waves.*

But his chief was beside him. He motioned for Finn to keep walking.

Still, Finn tilted his head toward me and whispered, "Bye, Aran." And then, "Good luck."

I shuffled impatiently, desperate to get my pelt in time for Finn to see me put it on. Maura ran past me with hers tucked under her arm. She splashed into the waves like she couldn't wait an instant longer. The line crept forward.

This time when I reached the cave, the guardian recognized me. "I'm sure I can find it now," he said. "Aran, right?"

"Right."

A long moment passed. Again, he came back without a

pelt. "Are you sure you left it under that name?" he asked.

Left it? I couldn't explain, not with the line behind me, and the eyes of that burly guardian burning into mine. So, "That's my name," I said. "It *has* to be there."

"Give us a little longer, then," said the guardian. "We've never lost one yet." And he nodded me aside.

The sky was already pale blue as I took my place yet again at the end of the line. Mam walked toward me, her dapple-gray pelt tucked under an arm. "Sorry I took so long," she said.

I saw Lyr at the front of the line, reaching for his sleek black pelt.

"I'll wait with you." Mam smiled, but something was wrong with the corners of her mouth. My stomach clenched. Of everyone, Mam should be the surest. She'd prayed as hard as I had; I'd seen her face. But doubt was reaching out from her with icy fingers. Suddenly I couldn't stand being next to her.

"Go away," I said sharply.

Her eyes widened in surprise.

"I want to wait by myself."

"Well . . . all right, then." She walked slowly toward the shore, looking back at me over her shoulder.

No one else appeared behind me. I was the last in line.

The sun's rays were streaking out over the waves when I reached the cave for the third time. The gray guardian saw me and nodded.

"I'll look once more," he said.

I heard the *slup, slup* of his belly heading into the dark. He was gone a long time.

When he came back, the other two guardians were with him.

"This is unprecedented," said the gray guardian. "We've looked everywhere. What color did you say your pelt is?"

I paused. Then, "I don't know," I whispered.

"What's that? I didn't hear you. Speak up! What did you say? Did you say brown?"

"*I don't know!*" This time it came out so loud, their heads reared back.

"Don't know?" the gray guardian barked. "What do you mean, you don't know?"

But then the black one was leaning over and murmuring something, and the gray guardian's face changed. His eyes—the eyes of this great bull selkie, chosen for his strength and valor—were filling with tears.

The ground grew unsteady beneath my feet. "I'm

getting it today," I insisted. "I prayed for it. It has to be in there. Look again, please!"

He shook his head. "I'm sorry."

The three of them scooted out. Behind them, the cave gaped, dark and empty.

"We have to close up here," said the black guardian. "Maybe next year."

They put their shoulders to the rock and rolled it across the door.

CHAPTER NINETEEN
⮿ WHAT REALLY ⮾ MATTERS

I dragged my feet toward the shore. The cove was almost deserted. A last few selkies slipped into the surf, and then only my clan remained, all back in sealform except for Mam.

Cormac was leaning aggressively toward the others. His words rose over the rumble of the waves. "And I say, you're not thinking about the dangers. Luck only lasts so long. I was talking with the white selkies and—"

Grandmam's head swung around. "Aran!" she cried, scooting toward me. Then she stopped, a question in her eyes. The question they all had in their eyes.

I shook my head. Their faces fell; it struck me like an accusation.

A pause, then, "All things in time," said Lyr.

Mam took a step closer, her eyes huge and aching—

I swiveled away in a spray of pebbles and ran. An instant later Mam's feet came pounding after me. I put on a burst of speed, and then there was hard rock underfoot, and the slick of seaweed. I hauled myself up the crag at the end of the cove and half jumped, half fell to the other side.

"Oona!" cried Grandmam. "Let him go. He needs time."

Mam's steps trudged, slow and heavy, back to the others.

Now that they couldn't see me, my legs buckled. I fell to my knees and my chest caved in. My fists were stone, cold and hard against my face.

"Are you staying longlimbs to go find him?" Lyr wasn't even lowering his voice. They must think I'd gone too far to hear.

Mam didn't answer, but a rock scraped aside—that would be her fetching her pelt—and then came a flap as she spread it out, and the gathering sound of it binding around her. Finally she sighed with such pain and sorrow, the world blurred into gray.

"What will you do?" asked Grandmam.

A pause, then, "I'll swim back with him," said Mam. "He's bound to come find me before nightfall."

"When he's done moping?" asked Maura.

The silence sharpened. I could almost see her looking around, wondering what she'd done wrong. Then she said, "I just meant, if he isn't going to turn, he'll have to get used to it. That's all."

A rough scrape across pebbles, the growl of Mam baring her teeth —

"Enough!" said Lyr. "We'll sort this out later."

I sank deeper into the rocks.

"No, Lyr," said Cormac. "We need to talk now. We all hope Aran will turn, but there's more at stake. It's a matter of our survival. Up north, the waters are cleaner, and you can go moons without seeing a human. The white selkies want us to come, but Aran can't —"

"Enough!" Lyr said, louder.

Cormac defied him. "The white selkies see him as a danger. And frankly, even if he could swim that far —"

Lyr's roar shook me to my bones.

In the shocked silence, he barked out commands. "Cormac, you're leaving. *Now*. Maura. Mist. Go with him. Go to the island with two pines. The rest of us will find you there."

A splash, and they were gone.

For a long time there was only the sound of the surf. Then Grandmam said gently, "Oona, my dear girl, you have to face it. It's possible he may never turn."

I waited for Mam to growl, defending my honor once again. But only a harsh keening reached my ears.

"There now, hush," said Grandmam.

The terrible sound was Mam crying.

Dark clouds rolled in toward the Spire, swallowing the sky.

No bird, no seal, no leaping fish—there was no one to watch me slip into the surf, under the waves, and away.

I swam underwater except to breathe. The sun was high by the time I reached the island. I pulled out the harness, threw it on the ground, and untangled my knife from the pile. I strapped it on my calf.

I was walking back into the surf when something knocked me off my feet.

"Don't you ever do that again!" Mam was yelling and crying at the same time, her face shoved up next to mine. "You stupid, stupid pup! You could have died! I searched every inch of the Spire. I thought you'd—"

"I heard what Cormac said," I shouted back, struggling

to my feet. "You're all going to die if you stay with me!"

"Don't be ridiculous." Her jaw clamped shut.

"It's true, isn't it? *Isn't it?* Humans will trap you. Or I'll slow you down and orcas will get you. They almost did on the way here."

"We were fine."

"I saw you shaking!" That stopped her. I stood taller, drawing strength up from the waves. "I won't live with the clan until I've got my pelt."

"Then I'll stay with you," said Mam. "I've done it for eleven years. I'll stay as long as it takes."

"Stay? I'm not staying. I'm going north, far north, past where the white selkies live."

She shook her head. "You'd never make it."

Her certainty cut me to the bone. But in that sudden slash of pain, I saw the truth.

"You don't think I can do anything. You didn't think I'd make it to Moon Day. But the harness was cheating. *That's* why I didn't get my pelt. I have to swim north by myself. I'll find the wise ones who speak with the Moon."

"Aran! No one even knows if they really exist."

"Finn says they do."

Mam froze. Then, interested, "He said that?"

The words spilled out of me, raging with anger and

hope. "They live at the top of the world, and they're magic. They'll know how I can get my pelt. You can't stop me. I'm going."

Mam's eyes got a quick, calculating look. She took a deep breath. "Aran"—her voice was so calm, it was as if I'd imagined the rest—"what really matters here? It isn't whether you make the journey; it's getting your pelt. Right?"

I found myself nodding, even though my heart was shouting at me not to listen to her.

"The wise ones, if they exist, may indeed be our best hope," she went on. "But I'm the one who should go. I'll get there faster. I'll convince them. You stay here with the clan—"

That startled me out of her spell. "No! Humans will find them and stick them in zoos."

Mam's eyes widened slightly; there was another quick readjustment. "Then stay behind while the clan comes with me."

I gasped in amazement. "Stay? Without you?" Mam had never even let me spend a night by myself. Did she really trust me to live on my own?

Her voice kept rolling over me. "I'll choose a place for you to stay. You must wait for me there, so I can find you again when I return. It's the only way I can undertake this journey for you. Will you promise?"

This wasn't giving in. The Moon would look down from the heavens and see me surviving on my own, living off my wits and my strength and my skill. Maybe it would make up for cheating with the harness. My resistance swirled away in the surf.

I'd have to catch all my own food, ride out storms, and outwit predators. There'd be no one to help if I got hurt. Was I ready?

"Yes," I said. "I promise."

If I'd known where she was taking me, I'd never have agreed.

PART TWO
LAND

CHAPTER TWENTY
❧ PROMISES ❧

I stayed with the clan while Mam swam off to find a place for me. Everyone spoke to me with soothing voices as if I were sick. They brought me fish, and when I told them to stop, they herded fish in my direction and then pretended it was an accident.

Why had I said I'd wait with them? By day I scanned the horizon for boats. At night I startled awake at the slightest sound. One week stretched into two. Even Grandmam was getting edgy. Why didn't Mam let me stay here? There were clams and mussels to eat if fish were scarce, and high rocks to wait out storms. But she'd said she had something special in mind.

Finally, after seventeen nights, Mam slid ashore. I ran up as the others circled around. Their questions piled on top of each other so fast, I couldn't even tell who was speaking.

Mam ignored them and turned to me. "We need to leave right away to catch this current. Go get your doubloons."

On our way back from Moon Day, we'd stopped at the old haulout to collect them. I didn't know why she thought they were important, but I wasn't going to argue now.

I ran to fetch them. When I reached into the crevice, my magic green rock tumbled out along with the gold. I slipped it all into the sheath with my knife.

When I got back, Grandmam and Mam were whispering with their heads close together. They saw me and startled apart. Worry lines creased Grandmam's forehead. At the sight, my stomach churned.

Mam tugged the harness onto the beach.

The others had never seen it before. They stared at the thick brown cords in confusion. Mam rolled on top of the straps and I started to fasten them around her body. Cormac reared back, his eyes narrowing.

"What on earth is that?" said Maura.

"A harness," said Mam, scooting into the shallows.

"Please tell me you didn't use that for *Moon Day*," gasped Maura. "Oona, you wouldn't . . . he didn't . . . "

"They need to go," said Grandmam. "Come here, Aran, and say good-bye. We'll see you soon as anything."

I crouched down to hug them. I buried my face in Grandmam's pelt, breathing in her warm, briny scent. Then I waded into the waves and climbed on Mam's back.

As she shifted to get comfortable, I glanced back at the shore. The clan lay in a row, watching. Suddenly Lyr arced up and opened his mouth to speak —

Mam dove. We were off.

"It's only for two moons," said Mam as the sun was setting. "A flick of a tail, that's all."

I stared at every rock and islet and haze of land, wondering what sort of place she'd found for me. Her tight mouth told me she was uneasy about leaving me behind, but she was as bound by her promise as I was by mine.

"How long will it take you to reach the wise ones?" I asked.

"Just shy of a moon, from what Brehan told Cormac."

"How do they talk to the Moon?" I went on. "Do you think they swim up to the horizon when she's resting there? Or maybe she sends down a beam of light and it turns solid like ice, and they shimmy up to her side."

"Maybe. I don't know." She sounded impatient, so I talked faster.

"How will you carry my pelt? Not in your mouth; you need to eat. Maybe they'll teach you a song to make me turn, or—"

Mam dove to say we were done talking.

The sky darkened and we swam through the night. Come daybreak, we found a rocky islet and took turns sleeping while the other kept watch. On the third day I was surprised to see several boats in the distance. On the fourth, we passed an island larger than any haulout I'd ever known. We'd always avoided big islands; they attracted humans.

I bent to Mam's ear. "Where are you taking me?"

"Wait and see," was her only reply.

Near dawn, as the Moon was setting behind swollen clouds, we swam into a current of fresh water. Mam headed toward its source. The water grew so sweet I started to gag. The sky lightened from black to granite, and a humpbacked island rose before us. Fir trees stabbed the sky.

High atop a bluff sat a huge, bulky shape. At first it looked like a boulder. But its top rose to a point, and its sides were too straight, as if a landslide had sheered them away.

I looked at it warily. "What's that?"

Mam's shoulders tensed. "A house."

House. I'd heard the word somewhere before. *He built us what they call a house.*

I jerked the harness. "Stop!"

Mam kept swimming toward shore.

"*Stop!*" I slipped off her back.

She swerved to look at me. Her eyes weren't cautious, like they should have been, but determined.

This was all wrong! I was supposed to be going to live on my own, proving myself by my skill and my wits. Instead she was taking me to a house, and in the house . . .

I reared back with a splash. "No!" I said. "You can't leave me with him!"

"Him?"

"My father. If I get my pelt he'll steal it and—"

"Aran, what are you thinking?" Mam shook her head as if I were the one who'd gone mad. "Your father lived far away from here. And I'd never leave you with him. Never. Why would I do that when I'm going to the ends of the earth to find your pelt?"

I treaded water, confused. "Then why are we here?"

"To get you clothes."

"Clothes? *Human* clothes?" Now I saw her terrible plan. "You said I'd be on my own!"

"No, I didn't," Mam said firmly. "I told you I'd find you a safe place to wait for me, and that's what I've done. Why do you think I was gone so long? I swam to island after island, searching for a woman who lives alone, and then I watched to make sure she can be trusted—"

"You can't trust any of them," I said.

"And then I had to convince her to keep you, without her suspecting you're a selkie. We'll grab clothes here and then swim to her island. You'll be safe there until I return."

"Safe? With one of *them*? I'll be safer alone. I have my knife."

"One little knife!" Mam gave a dismissive snort. "It can't make fish swim toward you, or keep the skies from storming, or hide you from men. On your own, you'd be at risk from all humans. I'm leaving you with one, a good woman." The tide kept pushing us closer to shore. "I'm not doing this for me, Aran. It's for you, to get you what you need. What you deserve." She paused. "And you promised."

I was trapped. Even if Mam had misled me, I wasn't the kind of selkie who'd break a promise. Gritting my teeth, I turned and swam to shore.

CHAPTER TWENTY-ONE
❧ THE SPIDERWEB ❧

Mam slipped out of her pelt and stashed it in a hollow, covering it with a layer of stones. Her black hair whipped in the rising wind. Behind a bank of clouds, the sun was threatening to rise.

She headed up a steep slope. I forced myself to follow. In my head I heard Grandmam chanting: *Beware the ship, beware the net. Beware the black gun in his hand.*

I was in the enemy's realm now.

We crept forward through the trees. A crow cawed, and then there was the house, monstrous and gray in the half-light. I could barely breathe. We tiptoed past a wall of wooden planks and around a corner.

Behind the house, a fat cord stretched from tree to tree like a strand in a giant spiderweb. And the spider had been at work: arms and legs hung in the web's clutches, the empty shells of people sucked dry.

"Clothes," I whispered.

"Shh!" Mam snuck up to the web, grabbed a pair of legs, and tugged. They tumbled down limp in her hands.

A light shone out from the house. Mam's head flew up, and she pushed me back toward the trees. We crouched down low.

"She's up early," whispered Mam, as taut as the web.

Something was banging and crashing around in the house. My hand hovered by my knife. I leaned closer to Mam. "Let's go. I don't need clothes."

Ghost clothes, shivering in the wind.

Before Mam could answer, the door flew open. A short, wide woman sidled out carrying a load on her hip. She set it down, pulled out a wet clump of cloth, and shook it roughly. Before my eyes it turned into a wrinkled pair of legs. She stuck them on the web and they hung there, kicking.

As she worked, a mangy animal came creeping around the side of the house. Its ribs poked through matted fur. I raised my eyebrows at Mam.

"A dog," she whispered.

It gave a hopeful whimper. The woman's scowl deepened. She picked up a stone and hurled it, striking the dog's side. It yelped and ran away.

I jerked back as if the rock had hit me, too.

I leaned closer to Mam. "How can you leave me with one of *them*?"

"They're not all the same. You can tell a lot by their faces. And their hands."

The woman's hands snapped more clumps into clothes.

A shrill ringing burst from the house. She hurried back in. Then another door slammed, a motor roared to life, and a battered hull chugged away from the front of the house.

I gasped. "A land-boat!"

"That's a truck," said Mam. "Thank the Moon she's gone! Now let's dress you for your visit, and me for my part."

She hurried back to the web. She grabbed a faded skin, so shapeless, it didn't even look like a body. "This will do for me," she said. Then she started pulling down arms and legs, holding them up against me one after the other until she found what she wanted.

I had to lie down to slide the legs on. They were dingy

blue. I stood and tripped over the ends; Mam rolled them up. When we were done, I was blue on the bottom and gray on top, like a crag jutting up from the sea.

"It itches," I said.

"You get used to it. It's just another skin."

But she was wrong. It was a disgusting joke of a pelt.

Mam put her hands on my shoulders and turned me around so she could see me from all sides. "It needs something else," she said. Her eyes landed on my hair. She led me to a tree stump. "Sit," she said. "Give me your knife."

She pulled a hank of hair away from my head and slashed if off, high and short. As she worked, she snapped instructions. "The woman you're staying with is called Maggie. Her house is isolated, but there are other people on the island, so make sure no one else sees you. That means no roaming around the island or out to sea."

"I can't even *swim*?"

"Only close to shore, and after you've made certain there's nobody about." She moved around to the back of my head. "Now listen, Aran, this is important. Maggie has to think you're human, so act human in every way. Watch what she does and copy her. She must never suspect what you really are."

A slash, and a hank of hair fell down.

"I told her your father's a cruel man who beats us. I'm getting a divorce—that means leaving him—and that makes him so angry, he might try to kill us both. That's why you need to stay hidden while I find us a place to live. I'll be back for you by the second full Moon."

"Divorce," I said, trying to memorize a word I couldn't understand. The story reeked of shame and deception. The worst part was how well it matched my own feelings.

Mam stepped back to judge her work. "Good," she said, looking at my face. "Try to have just that expression when we come to her door."

I reached a hand to my shoulder, then higher. My hair was a short, jagged fringe. I looked down. No arms, no legs: I'd disappeared. My body was buried in clothes.

Back at the inlet, Mam rolled all the clothes into a bundle for the swim. Then she reached into the hollow where she'd hidden her pelt. She carried it to the shoreline, spread it out, and pulled it up around her . . .

It didn't tighten.

Her eyes widened. She gripped the fur closer, but it hung on her shoulders, loose and lank and wrinkled, like it wasn't even hers. Like she was trying to force herself into a strange, borrowed skin.

I sucked in my breath. When I was little and Mam took longlimbs, Grandmam would warn her to be careful. "Don't take the Moon's gift lightly," she'd say. "Take off your pelt too often, and one day it won't go back on."

Now I smelled the sharp, bitter tang of Mam's fear. "Please," she whispered.

The wind grew stronger. It was starting to rain. The drops trickled down Mam's loose pelt like tears.

"Oh, Moon," she begged softly. *"Please."*

A dark hope swooped into my chest, a bat looking to roost. If Mam couldn't turn, she'd have to stay with me forever and ever and ever. She couldn't force me to wear clothes. She couldn't leave me with a human. The dark hope stretched out its wings to land.

No! I reached down deep, and with every drop of my strength, I pushed the darkness away. I thought of Moon Day, how we all stood under the Spire, our voices singing as one. Now that song rose inside me. I opened my mouth and the notes rang out, bright and clear, as if I were the Caller:

"Sing, O Moon, the song of the sea!"

The notes hung sparkling in the air. Mam gasped, then joined in:

"Sing of the salt-spray, the tears, and the freedom
Erasing the border twixt wave-foam and shoreline.
Sweet comes the turning that sets the soul free."

There was a sound like a quick intake of breath, a gathering together—and the wrinkles in Mam's pelt smoothed out.

She looked at me, her seal eyes deep and shining with tears.

We didn't talk for a long time. We lay there in the tiny inlet, surrounded by lapping waves, her flipper on my ankle. All around us came the sound of falling rain.

CHAPTER TWENTY-TWO
❧ SPINDLE ISLAND ❧

We waited until nightfall. The rain drizzled to a stop, but the air weighed heavy on my skin. The birds had fled. A storm was coming.

I tucked the bundle of clothes under my arm and climbed on Mam's back. We swam out from the sheltered inlet into a deafening roar. Waves crashed high around us, wind bellowed, and clouds pressed low. I stared ahead into darkness as we swam and swam, Mam's body straining forward, my hands aching from clenching the straps.

Finally, darker against the darkness, a brooding shape loomed before us. Land.

We rounded a rocky point. It blocked the wind, and

there was a sudden stillness. Mam paused to catch her breath. In an inlet that was little more than a gulp of water, a dozen boats rocked, roped and tamed. A cluster of houses huddled on shore.

"That's the only town on Spindle Island," said Mam. "The harbor is too shallow for fancy yachts or a ferry, and the undertow keeps tourists away. Hardly anyone lives here. Those who do keep to themselves." She nodded in satisfaction. "It's perfect."

I swallowed hard. "Which house is it?"

"Not here. I wouldn't choose a place with so many eyes to see you." She started swimming again.

Once we passed the harbor, the wind and waves rose with fresh fury. For a long time there weren't any more houses, only the jagged outlines of trees and rocks. Then we swam around an outcropping. There, on a curve of cliff, a lone house faced into the wind, as bold as an osprey. I stared—it was so different from all the rest!— and suddenly a light blazed out from its heart.

Mam dove. I pressed myself flat against her back as the ocean closed overhead.

We rose far past the house. Mam swam close to shore now, searching the cliff, until she found what she was looking for: a tumble of boulders and what was left of a steep path.

Sections had fallen away, leaving strips of sheer rock.

We landed on a flat boulder at the cliff's base. I helped Mam take off the harness. The wind blew her whiskers back.

"I need to catch my breath," she said. "You go peek over the top, then come back and tell me what you see."

"No," I said, my heart pounding louder than the surf. "I'll wait for you."

She shook her head. "Just make sure it's the right place."

Her voice was ragged. She was struggling to make her face a smooth mask, pretending everything was all right. So I pretended, too, for her sake.

I climbed up the cliff. Near the top I slowed, carefully lifting my head over the rim.

Past a stretch of lichen-covered rock, past tall grasses hissing in the wind, a small house hunkered down against the coming storm. It tilted sideways, like a shore tree bent by constant winds, struggling with all its might to hang on.

I scrambled back down to Mam. She'd opened the ball of clothing with her teeth and was separating my clothes from hers. I told her what I'd seen.

"Good," she said. "That's Maggie's house. I'll keep watch while you get dressed."

I struggled to pull on the sopping clothes, forcing my arms and legs through the clammy fabric. When I finally got them on, it felt like I was coated in mud. I rolled up the cloth legs higher than before, baring my knife. Just in case.

"Take out the doubloons," said Mam.

"Why?"

"To give to Maggie. People will do anything for gold, and I promised her some. Tell her it's to help with the costs."

I pulled my knife from the sheath and scrounged out the doubloons. The knife felt reassuring in my hand. I forced myself to put it back.

"Cover it," said Mam.

Reluctantly, I rolled the blue legs down. Then I grabbed the soggy clump of Mam's clothes and held it out to her.

"Your turn," I said.

But Mam was shaking her head. "I'm sorry, Aran."

A gust of wind grabbed my name, whipping it away. A few hard pellets of rain struck my skin.

"I was going to come up to the door with you, but . . ." Her voice grew harder. "What if my pelt doesn't close again? I can't risk it. This is as far as I can go if I'm to swim to the wise ones."

I shoved the clothes forward again. "You have to come!"

Mam's mouth tightened. She swept out a flipper, pushing the clothes—and the harness—off the rocks. They disappeared under the roiling foam.

"I found you a safe place," she snapped. "You'll stay here, and you'll be here when I come back." She pushed me toward the path, but now her voice turned pleading. "Don't you see? If I know you're safe, I can go, and I have to go to help you."

The pleading was worse than the hardness.

I stared up the cliff face, then back at her, my fear pulsing in my throat.

"Swear it," said Mam, fierce again, as she held back her tears. "Swear you'll stay in that house until I return. Even if the Moon brings your pelt first, wait here, or I may never find you again. Swear you won't let anyone see you besides Maggie. Swear it all by the Moon!"

A blast of wind sent me stumbling to the edge of the rocks. The storm broke with a roar of fury. The waves towered higher, wild with white foam, and then the rain struck—slashing down sideways, ricocheting off rocks, hurling in every direction. In an instant the whole world was water.

"Swear!" shouted Mam over the wind.

"I swear."

"By the Moon!"

Struggling to stay on my feet, I put my hand to my heart to make the vow. "By the Moon!"

CHAPTER TWENTY-THREE
❧ MAGGIE ❧

I climbed the cliff, rehearsing the lies that made up my new life. *Divorce . . . father . . . two moons.*

I pulled myself over the top and looked back. The rocks were deserted.

I turned to face the house, gray behind shuddering gusts of rain. I had to go now or I'd never go. I forced myself to take one step through the howling wind. Then another, across stone, and grass, the rain slapping my face, until I stood in front of a peeling wooden door.

I tried to think how a human boy would stand. I raised my hand, clenched a fist like Mam told me, and knocked. The sound echoed in the hollow behind the door. I was grateful for the dark and the wind snatching at the shreds of my hair and the rain pounding down so the woman couldn't see me too closely at first.

A harsh light blinded me from above and the door swung open. All I could see was an outline, a shadow without a body. Shorter than Mam in longlimbs, and thinner, and stooped. A voice spoke urgently but my heart was pounding and the gale blowing and I couldn't hear the words. She took a step closer—

A bony hand clamped down on my shoulder and pulled me inside.

The door banged shut. My breath rasped against the silence. The air smelled stale and sick.

"What happened?" Her voice was taut. A voice for emergencies.

She wasn't as old as Grandmam, but her hair was dull and faded, and lines etched deep gullies down the sides of her face. It was as if the life had been sucked out of her, leaving an empty shell behind.

I couldn't find my tongue.

"Was there an accident?" she said.

The room swirled around me in a confusion of colors and shapes. The walls were crawling with patterns, and the floor scratched my feet, and the heat pressed on my lungs.

"Can you answer me, son? Who's with you? Is anyone hurt?"

Her questions, her anxious voice—didn't she know who I was?

I took a step back. What if this was the wrong place? My body was screaming at me to run, but I couldn't; I'd sworn that I'd stay here in this house, stay with . . .

"Maggie," I said out loud.

She peered at me. "Do I know you?"

I gulped. "I'm Aran." She didn't move. "You told my mam I could stay."

"Told your what?"

"My mam, my mother, she came to you because of the . . . the divorce, and my . . . my father, he beats me and . . ."

A horrified realization came into her eyes.

"And you said you'd hide me from him," I sputtered on. "Because he . . . he might try to hurt us, or . . ."

"Oh my Lord!" She was shaking her head in dismay. "Is she still out there?" She ripped the door open and shouted into the dark, "Come back!"

The storm howled in reply.

"Come back!" she called, louder. Under the light, the rain slashed down like knife blades. Then she threw back her head, shouting so loud it was almost a scream, *"He can't stay here!"*

It was too much for her. She started coughing and her chest caved in. She coughed and coughed and it didn't stop, like she was going to cough her guts out. Like she was going to die.

I stared. I didn't know what to do. I wanted to run and dive off the cliff and find Mam. I wanted to tell her the human hated me and wouldn't let me stay. But I forced my feet to stay put. I'd made a Moon vow.

Maggie stumbled in and shut the door. The cough quieted, crawling back inside her like a beast settling into its lair. Finally she looked at me and croaked, "Come on."

She led me deeper into the hot, stale room. We wove past puffy, cloth-covered lumps with legs and wooden planks with legs. The floor wore patches of mangy brown fur, as if it needed clothes, too. Every surface was cluttered with clusters of objects, small and strange, neither wood nor shell nor stone.

"You must be frozen," she said. "Come sit by the fire."

I only knew fire from lightning, and the charred smell of logs left behind by humans on beaches. Now I sat where she nodded, beside a black box perched on four legs. It was the source of the terrible heat. She opened a door in its side, threw in a log, and nodded as it burst into flame.

I jerked back, biting down a cry. *Humans get cold*, I told myself. *Humans like fire.*

"Here, take this blanket."

She covered me with it, trapping the wet in my clothes. I started to steam.

She fell back into the perch across from me, her face drained and gray. I didn't know whether to look at her or the fire or the floor. The silence lasted a lifetime.

Finally she spoke. "Did your mom leave you here on purpose?"

"You . . . you knew," I said. "You told her I could stay."

"I thought it was a dream." Maggie shook her head. "A knock on my door in the middle of the night. There she stood, too beautiful to be real. Like a fairy-tale princess. She asked me to watch her son, and all I could do was nod, like I was under some kind of spell. I blinked and she was gone."

"You said you'd keep me."

"That's how I knew it was a dream. I woke up, and the idea was so wild, I had to laugh. I'd never say yes to a boy staying here. How could I, with Jack?"

Mam hadn't said anything about a Jack. The word bristled.

"You can stay here tonight," she said. "No one can get

here in this storm. But in the morning, you call your mom and tell her to come back and fetch you."

"I can't," I said. "She's gone."

Her mouth narrowed. "Then I'll call Social Services. They'll come to the island and take you to foster care. They're the ones can keep you safe from your dad, not me."

Take me . . . Was that the cages, the zoo? She was going to send me away and Mam would never find me again. I *had* to stay here! The room was spinning and the heat was smothering me and I clenched my fists—

Hard metal dug into my palm.

The doubloons!

I leaped up and thrust my hand toward Maggie. The discs glowed softly on my palm.

Her brow wrinkled in confusion.

"It's gold!" I said. "For you, to help with the costs."

She picked one up with a pitying look. "Gold. Did your mom tell you that?"

I nodded, clinking the rest of them into her hand so she could feel their weight.

She sighed. "Toys, that's what these are. Stuff they sell in little plastic chests at the tourist stores. Fake pirate gold."

"It's not fake! It's real!"

"And I'm the queen of England."

I didn't understand, but I didn't dare ask.

Maggie dropped the doubloons on a plank beside her and leaned closer, her hands on her knees. "Listen, son. I'm not going to sugarcoat this. A mom who dumps you with a stranger and doesn't even come to see you're all right—well, you'll be better off with the state."

"But I have to stay here," I said. "Mam's gone to get my—get help for us. She trusts you."

Maggie pressed herself to her feet. "Let's get you into a bath and then find you some dry clothes."

"The gold will pay for me," I said, following her across the room toward another door. "And I can help you. I'm strong. I can catch you fish. And it's only until the second full Moon."

Behind the door was a smaller room. This one wasn't cluttered; it was hard and white and shiny. She bent to a handhold and water gushed into a long hollow.

"I'm sure you'd be helpful," she said, swishing her hand in the water. "But my health's not good. You can't count on me. And you sure can't count on Jack."

"What's Jack?"

"Not what. Who. My husband."

"Is that like a mate?"

Her eyes told me I'd said something wrong, but she only said, "That's right."

"Mam said no one else lives here."

"Well, she got that wrong. He's up in Alaska, working on a fishing boat. You can't be here when he gets home. Jack . . ." Her lips narrowed and she shook her head, hard and quick. "You never know what Jack's going to do. Go on, take off those wet clothes and hop in the bath."

Steam was rising from the pool. I stared at it in horror. Did people really boil themselves in hot water? I took a step back, and a movement across the room caught my eye.

A human boy was looking at me through a gap in the wall. He was slim and wiry, with a thicket of hair like grass growing in all directions. His clothes were wet, too, and clung to his arms and chest like seaweed once the tide has gone out. I gasped, and his mouth fell open. I took a step back and he stepped back, his eyes blazing.

One brown eye, one blue.

"Are you going to take off those wet things or not?" asked Maggie.

But I couldn't take my eyes off the boy in the gap. I stepped closer, and closer; I reached out and he did, too. We touched fingers on a shiny surface.

The human boy was me.

CHAPTER TWENTY-FOUR
❧ ACTING HUMAN ❧

Maggie turned off the running water. The room grew still and steamy. The other me was starting to fade behind a cloud.

"No bath?" said Maggie.

"No bath."

She sighed. "All right, then. But we're getting you into dry clothes, and no back talk. You're so skinny, Tommy's things might work. Come on."

I followed her back through the cluttered room and down a dim passage. She stopped in the shadows and took a deep breath, as if to prepare herself, then opened a door. I couldn't see through the darkness.

"Who's Tommy?" I asked.

"He was my son," she said, and the darkness was in her voice, too.

The air smelled old and musty. Maggie coughed again, her shoulders shaking. I held my breath until she stopped. She touched the wall and a light shone down.

A broad ledge filled most of the room. It wore a cloth with a picture of a big blue whale. The walls had smaller blue whales swimming all over them.

"They'll be in the closet," said Maggie, opening another door to the smallest room of all. Why did humans need so many doors? They built walls to shut out the wind and waves, and then more walls inside, to keep everything separate and alone.

Maggie backed out of the closet. "Here you go. Dry shorts and a T-shirt. You hungry?" I nodded. "Okay. Get dressed and I'll get you something to eat."

She closed the door behind her. My heart started pounding again. I was trapped, like a fish you stash in a rock pool to keep fresh for later. She'd said she was going to call the child-taking people. Was she doing that now? I strained my ears, trying to hear if she was going outside to shout for them. I pulled on the handhold for the door — the wood rattled in its shell, but it didn't open. I stared at my hand, breathing short and fast. Then I remembered how Maggie's wrist had turned. I twisted and pulled again, hard. The door flew open.

"Everything all right in there?" called Maggie.

"Yes," I called back. "Everything is fine."

I peeled off the wet things and picked up the dry ones. At least the shorts left my calves bare, so I could grab my knife if I needed it. I pulled the T-shirt over my head. For a moment I was suffocating, and then I was through. I wiggled my arms into the holes.

I followed a sizzling sound and found Maggie leaning over a big, white box, poking at something with a stick.

"Hi," I said.

She turned and gasped. The stick clattered to the floor. When she bent to pick it up, her eyes lingered on my knife, but all she said was, "Funny, seeing you in his clothes. You with your two-color eyes. Sit down and I'll get your eggs."

I almost sat on the floor. Then I remembered the seats in the other room, and sat on a plank with four wooden legs. Humans put legs on everything. Maybe it made them feel better about being stuck with their own.

I was expecting eggs like I'd stolen from birds' nests, fresh and runny. But when Maggie set food before me, my stomach turned. Steam rose from a pale yellow mound. There were three black strips that might have been meat, but the life was all charred away, like a stump burned by lightning.

"Guess you need a fork," said Maggie, setting a silvery twig on the table.

What was it for?

"Want hot sauce?" There was a pause. "You know, this would be easier if you talked. How about some ketchup?" Red glop oozed onto the eggs, thick and dark, like a puddle of blood.

Fork, I said to myself, feeling sick. *Ketchup*.

Maggie sighed. "Well, if you don't like bacon and eggs, why didn't you say so? What *do* you eat?" She opened a shiny door and cold air wafted out. "Come see what you want."

Inside was a jumble that didn't look anything like food. There was a platter covered with translucent leaves. Maybe it was a new kind of sea lettuce. At least it didn't smell as bad as the meat. I pulled some off and opened my mouth—

She snatched it from my fingers. "Are you crazy? That's plastic wrap!"

It turned out there was something I could eat. It was called cornflakes. I picked it up by the handful. It crunched like little bones, and it was almost as sweet as salmon.

Outside the rain kept pounding. The sky lightened to a paler gray.

Finally, "Nine o'clock," said Maggie. "Time to call Social Services."

"No!" I followed her from the room. "I'm easy to keep, really I am. And my mam will be back soon, maybe even before the second full Moon!"

I waited for her to open the door and yell, though I didn't think that was so smart with all her coughing. But she only picked up a black bar and held it to her ear, then shook it in frustration.

"Phone's out," she said, setting it back down. She stared at the window, masked with mist. Rain pounded on the roof and streamed off its edges.

"Does . . . does that mean you can't call?" I asked. "Does it mean I can stay?"

"You can stay until the phone works, or until the storm lifts and we can get to the harbor," she said. "Whichever comes first."

All day long, the storm called to me to come outside; all day long I sat in a chair, because apparently that's what people did. Maggie kept shoving logs into the fire. She kept holding the phone to her ear with a frown. She kept staring out the window like that would make the storm pass.

By midday I was starving. I longed for fish, still pulsing with life, but I settled for more cornflakes.

"Here's a spoon," said Maggie.

In the closed house, the air hung heavy with the smell of charred flesh. I didn't know what to call things. I didn't know what they were for. I watched how Maggie touched each object, her expression as she held it in her hand, the use she set it to. I strained my ears to make out every word. *Cup. Sink. Stove.* The worst was *bathroom.*

As daylight slipped away, Maggie set the phone down one last time.

"I guess you're here for the night," she said. "And the way this storm is going, maybe tomorrow, too. Let's clean that room and make up your bed. Here, take the broom."

I stared in confusion. She showed me how to push dirt around and then put it in a place called *the trash*, where humans hoard their waste behind its own small door.

When we were done, mounds of covers buried the bed. *Pillow.* I had to put on new clothes for sleeping, thinner and closer to my skin.

Maggie stared at the knife. "You're not going to sleep with that thing on your leg, are you?" She reached out a hand,

and a low growl escaped from my throat. "All right," she said, raising her eyebrows. "It looks like you're sleeping with it."

She told me to lie on the bed. I had to. That's what people do.

"When will Jack be here?" I asked.

"When the season's over." She pulled the covers up until only my head stuck out. "About three months or so."

"But that's after Mam is coming to get me. I'll be gone before he's back."

Maggie crossed her arms tightly, blocking off her heart. "Jack drinks. If he gets himself kicked off the boat, he'll be back early. It's happened before."

I was starting to sweat under the covers.

"Don't you worry. You'll be safe in foster care." Maggie gave me a crooked smile. "Look at you, all wired up, and no wonder. I know what'll help."

She rummaged in the closet and came out holding a furry blue creature with four stubby legs. She thrust it toward me. "I bet you think you're too old for a teddy bear, but go on, take it. It was Tommy's."

I reached out reluctantly. It smelled like sadness. The grizzled fur was half worn away, and there were dead black circles where the eyes should be.

"It used to have button eyes," said Maggie, running

a finger around one of the circles. "Then one got lost, so I cut these out of felt. Stitched them on so tight, they'll never fall off."

It wasn't me she was seeing but another boy, a human boy. She leaned over like she was going to kiss me, then caught herself and stood up straight. "Sleep well, Aran."

The room went dark, and she closed the door.

CHAPTER TWENTY-FIVE

❧ THE CLIFF ❧

The covers clutched at me like an anemone's tentacles, pulling me down. I squeezed my eyes shut, forcing myself to stay in the bed, because that's what humans do. But the walls were creeping closer, and I couldn't stop thinking about cages and zoos, and people pointing, and my heart was pounding louder and louder, and my eyes flew open—

Black eyes were staring right into mine.

A predator! My hand shot out instinctively and grabbed it around the throat. I hurled it across the room and leaped out of bed, my teeth bared for battle, my knife already in my hand.

It didn't move. I crept closer, straining to see in the

dark. It lay on its back, belly bared in surrender, four stubby legs jutting out.

I sighed at myself in disgust. It was the dead boy's teddy bear.

I picked it up gingerly by one paw and tossed it on the bed. I buried it under a pile of covers. Now it couldn't stare at me with those hollow eyes.

I slumped down against the wall. I was an idiot. How could I have thought that bit of mangy fur was alive? In this house, in this world, I didn't even know what was real. I could feel myself slipping away.

My hand tightened around the handle of the knife. The one Mam brought me so I'd have my own sharp claw. It was all I had left to remember who I was. This, and my magic green stone.

I dug the stone out of the sheath and rolled it in my other palm.

Outside, wind wailed across the sea. Trees thrashed; a branch cracked and tumbled down. A gust slammed into the house like a fist.

The storm was calling to me.

I stood and eased the door open, listening. I snuck down the hall, through the room with the smoldering fire, to the other door. I turned the handhold. A blast of wind struck my face, and then I was running through pelting rain, gulping down lungfuls of crisp, raw air.

The gale shoved me across gravel and grass and rocks, the waves thundering louder and louder, until I stood at the very edge of the cliff. Combers crashed against it so hard, their spray flew all the way up to my face—salt and rain, rain and salt. I took a breath and raised my arms, ready to dive and swim through the whitecaps and find my clan.

Find them?

My arms dropped. I'd never find them. Without me to slow her down, Mam would be back with the others by now. Maybe they were already swimming to the far north. Wherever that was.

No. If I ever wanted to see them again, I had to stay on Spindle Island until Mam returned. Two moons of *fork* and *cornflakes* and *trash*.

I lay on the rocks and the rain lashed my face until I was too numb to feel.

Maggie stood over me, making clucking noises in the gray morning light. She wrapped me in a blanket and steered me inside. She wanted to put me in hot water again, but she settled for giving me a dry set of clothes, saying,

"Change in the bathroom while I straighten up."

I tugged on a T-shirt and slipped on the shorts. Then I reached to the sheath, pulled out my knife, and rummaged for my green stone. Before I joined Maggie, I needed to make the world look like the ocean, where I belonged. But the sheath was empty.

I ran back into the dead boy's room. The bed was neat again, the teddy bear perched firmly on top. The floor was too clean. *Where was it?*

I ran outside and searched along the top of the cliff.

Maggie stood at the door. "What's the matter?" she called.

"I lost it!" I ran past her back inside and started ripping the covers off the bed.

"Lost what?"

"My stone! My magic green stone!"

"Magic?"

"You can look right through it. It turns everything underwater green—"

"Oh, the beach glass." She headed toward the kitchen. "Come on, I put it with the rest."

What did she mean, the rest?

She picked up a container and tipped it over the table. A torrent of stones tumbled out, blue and green and gold.

Each worn smooth by endless waves. Each so clear, the light shone through.

I sucked in my breath. I'd thought mine was the only one.

I picked up a green stone. But no, the color was too dark. I threw it down and grabbed another. The shape was wrong. The stones made cool, tinkling noises, laughing at me.

A pale green stone peeked out from under the pile. It was the right color, and there were the curves that fit perfectly in my palm. But now I saw the scars pitting its surface, and the ground-in flecks of dirt. Against all the others, it looked dull and common.

I left it there and walked away.

That day Maggie only checked the phone six times. The rain slowed to a drizzle.

"I could start up Jack's precious truck," she said. "But I hate driving that thing. The phone will be working soon. You might as well stay another night."

And another. And another.

Each night I'd lie in the bed until the house was dark and quiet. Then I'd slip outside by the sea, my heart aching with longing for my clan, until the waves finally sang me to sleep. I woke before dawn to scavenge barnacles and seaweed, sneaking back inside before Maggie woke.

I copied how she made the bed. I used the broom. I brought in wood and stacked it next to the firebox in neat piles. If I was polite and helpful and human enough, maybe she'd stop talking about sending me away.

One day she picked up the phone and it buzzed like a swarm of flies. She reached a finger to its face, then paused, looking thoughtful.

"Another few days won't hurt," she said, setting the phone back down.

The sky was dawning a thin, pale blue. I crouched at the base of the cliff, swallowing another barnacle. I was tired of barnacles. I wanted fish, fresh and salty sweet. Maggie wouldn't be awake for ages. I had plenty of time.

I slipped from the rocks into the water. I wouldn't go very far, not so far I'd be breaking my vow. Just far enough to catch some real food.

I dove down and right away I found a fat crab. I surfaced to break off its legs and suck out the meat. I smashed its shell on a boulder and picked it clean.

I ducked and swam along the rock face, right into a cluster of little silver fish. I gulped one down, relishing the crunch of small bones against smooth flesh.

I kicked to the surface and turned a somersault. Here, in the water, I knew who I was. I dove down and rocketed back up, I spun and spiraled, floated and stroked, as graceful as you can be in a body without a tail.

But as I played, the sun was rising. Finally I had to admit it was time to go back to the house.

I belly flopped up on a flat rock, then scrambled up the cliff. I was hefting myself over the edge when I froze.

There was Maggie, staring at me.

"Where'd you learn to swim like that?" she asked, her voice full of wonder.

I knew better than to answer. I pulled myself to my feet.

She gazed out over the cliff to the sea, then back at my arms, my legs. "You look like you belong out there."

My breath caught. This was the last thing I expected, to feel understood. It confused me.

"I've lived by the sea my whole life, Aran, and I've never seen anyone swim like that. Like you're part of the waves. I knew you were different, but . . ."

"Oh no," I said. "I'm just a regular human boy."

She raised her eyebrows. "But a boy who needs to swim."

I gave a quick, hard nod.

She chewed her lip, weighing something. "So you need to be by the ocean. You're not going to like a foster home in the city."

I shook my head, pretending to know what she meant.

"When did you say your mom's coming back?"

I gulped, hardly daring to hope. "By the second full Moon. I know she will."

Maggie looked deep into my eyes, really seeing me for the first time. A struggle passed over her face, and then she nodded. "All right, I'll try to keep you here until then. But not any longer. My health isn't good. I could . . . I could have to go to the hospital at any time. And you have to promise me, if Jack calls to say he's coming home, you'll go to foster care. No back talk. Have we got a deal?"

The only part that mattered was about getting to stay. Mam would be back in time and the rest would never come to pass.

"Is a deal like swearing?" I asked.

The corner of her mouth twitched up. "I guess it is."

"Then we have got a deal," I said, holding my hand to my heart in the way of vow making.

She wrapped an arm around my shoulders. To my surprise, I didn't mind.

CHAPTER TWENTY-SIX

❧ THE PUFFIN ❧

I sensed the tides; I watched the Moon. Maggie had a different way of keeping track of time. It was called a calendar. Each day she took it out of a drawer in the kitchen and drew a line through one of its boxes. Then she put it back without saying a word.

I started swimming every morning before the sun cracked the horizon. Maggie warned me to be careful. "Someone sees you swimming like that, and next thing you know, your picture's on the six o'clock news. Your dad could hear about it." She thought for a moment. "Anyone finds you, say you're my nephew. Then tell me right away and we'll figure out what to do."

So I stayed close to shore. I dove deep and swam low, and I rose for breath cautiously, making barely a ripple.

I did that for two whole days.

But now that I'd had a taste of really swimming again, the ocean was calling to every drop of my blood. Holding back was torture.

On the third day, I was sitting, fuming, at the base of the cliff when a gull cried out overhead. I jumped to my feet. Of course! The seabirds! I started with gulls since they're the most talkative. I gave them food, setting out crabmeat in cracked shells and sharing my catch. Soon we had an agreement.

Word got around to the other seabirds. Gulls and guillemots, ospreys and oystercatchers: they all started warning me when boats were heading my way. Now I could swim farther from shore. As long as no other humans saw me, I wasn't breaking my promise.

Each trip made me bolder. My routes became longer. Out to the little islands in the strait. To the skellies that were too small to call islands. To the reefs that lurked near the surface, because boats avoided shallows. The best days dawned shrouded in fog. Fog meant freedom. In the white haze, I was just another splash of wave. On those days I swam far and long and hard.

My limbs had always been lean and strong. Now

they were growing more muscular. I could swim farther without needing to stop and tread water. If I swam hard enough, I didn't have room to think about Moon Day, or the dangers my clan was facing, or how long was left until the second full Moon.

I'd come back to Maggie's panting and dripping, exhausted enough to go inside and sit quietly, just like a human boy.

One day I was standing on top of the cliff when a puffin flew up and plopped at my feet. She looked exhausted. I was surprised to see her traveling alone.

"Where does the wind carry you?" I asked in birdtalk.

She cocked her head to look up at me. It was a long way for her to look; puffins have such short necks.

I held out my arm. "Come," I said.

She fluttered up, then sidestepped to my shoulder, her orange beak close to my ear. She was breathing hard. She preened and I stared out to sea politely to give her a moment to gather herself.

Then, "Help?" she grunted, in a low, rough voice.

I nodded to show I'd try.

She stretched out a wing. "Hurt. Lost flock. See flock?"

For the first time in ages I smiled. I *could* help! "Two

suns gone," I said pointing to a rock out in the strait. "Big flock. Sleep there. Fly west."

"What west?"

I pointed to show the exact direction and she chortled, relieved to know where to find them. She rubbed the side of my face in thanks.

"Me lose flock, too," I said.

She made a low, sympathetic rumble.

"Selkie flock," I said.

She bobbed her head up and down, then grunted, "Me fly. Me look."

I lifted my arm again and she waddled out to spread her wings.

"Good winds!" I called as she flew off.

A sudden crash split the air behind me.

I spun around. Maggie was standing, openmouthed, by the house. A fallen box lay at her feet and glints of metal were scattered all around.

"Mother of God!" she exclaimed, staring at me. "Were you talking with it?"

Her eyes, her voice—everything shouted danger.

Since I'd been here, I hadn't heard her speak with a single auklet or sandpiper or gull. She threw out crusts without saying a word. Not once had a bird flown to her feet for conversation or settled beside her.

So even though we'd come to some kind of understanding, I looked right at her and answered, "No, of course not. Who talks with birds?"

CHAPTER TWENTY-SEVEN
❧ THE NET ❧

I woke before dawn to find the world muffled in fog. I couldn't have asked for better. Today I'd test myself by swimming all the way around Spindle Island.

I dove in and struck out toward the point. I found my way by feeling the current's shape against the shore, by the sound of the wind soughing through the trees. I didn't have to worry about hiding, and after so many days of swimming underwater, it was a treat to ride the swell and dip of the waves. I fell into an easy, steady rhythm. Soon I wasn't thinking at all, just moving like part of the sea.

I rounded some rocks. The wind eased and the waves quieted. It was the same, sudden stillness from the night

Mam brought me. The harbor must be right in front of me, its buildings huddled together in a ragged flock.

Now I heard waves slapping against the curved bellies of boats. I tensed, ready to hide.

But then I took a deep breath. I was already hidden by the fog. And I felt strong from my swim in the dark. A wild idea came to me. The boats would be empty now, lashed to their moorings. What would it be like to set my hand on one? Not to let myself be afraid?

My senses heightened—the plash of the smallest wave, the smell of salt and smoke.

I turned and swam toward the dock.

I rose beside a small boat. It was open at the top. I reached for the rim, wary at first, as if it would bite. But then I grabbed on firmly and tilted the boat toward me. Its belly was braced with strips of wood, like a whale's curved ribs. Two planks stretched crossways—seats. Otherwise the boat was as empty as a crab shell picked clean by gulls.

One boat. That should have been enough. Mam would have been snapping at me to leave. But Mam wasn't here, and there was another boat only three strokes away.

This one was all hard lines. Instead of wood, its skin was white and cold. The box hanging off its back reeked of

smoke. That must be what throbbed the water. *Motorboats*,
Mam called them.

And I still wasn't ready to go. The fog was so thick,
only the slightest hint of dawn snuck through. No one
would see me if I explored a little more.

I climbed up onto the dock. No sound came from
shore. I crept along, peering down at the boats from
above. A rusty metal boat was full of buckets and ropes.
A sleek boat had a skinny pole jutting up from the center,
like a bone stripped of its flesh.

I neared the end of the dock and the lapping sound
deepened. Something big was lurking there. I lifted my
chin, took another step—

A metal wall rose before me. It was the side of a huge,
muscular boat. Ropes thicker than my wrist lashed it to
the dock. My breath caught, but I stayed there, staring.
And then, before I knew what I was doing, I'd grabbed
one of the ropes and was pulling myself up hand over
hand, my feet walking up the boat's cold skin.

I landed on deck in a crouch, listening. Nothing but
waves, and the whisper of wind on metal cords.

I stood slowly, my heart pounding. A small house
squatted before me. Silver pipes and black tubes snaked
up its side, their mouths clamped on like lampreys. I

grabbed one and climbed to a flat roof. A pole as wide as my waist thrust up into the fog, so tall it disappeared from sight.

I wouldn't waste time climbing it. It was the boat's guts I wanted to explore.

I jumped back down to deck. Wide metal cords stretched toward the boat's tail. I wrapped a hand around one and followed it back, the twisted strands rough under my palm. It ended at a shrouded shape, twice my height and curved on top. The thick cover crinkled when I touched it. I lifted an edge to peek underneath.

The cover started to slip. I tried to hold it up, but it kept falling, crinkling and crackling loudly the whole way. I tensed to dive.

No sound came from shore.

The cover lay in a crumpled pile at my feet. I stared up at the strange object before me. Two metal rounds hung suspended above the deck. Something was wound around them, like cloth, but coarse and uneven. I stepped closer. It was rope, layer after layer, squished tight. Some dingy white, some green. A string of white floats dangled down.

Why would one boat need so much rope?

A length stretched out at the bottom. Spread wide, it made a diamond pattern. A tight, gripping mesh. I traced a strand with a finger—and gasped. *A net*, that's what it was!

Beware the ship, beware the net. . . .

I had to see it better.

I reached for a diamond of rope and pulled. The circle cranked around, spilling net out at my feet. That's how they'd spread it in the sea.

A fire rose in my chest.

Soon, maybe tomorrow, this net would be gulping down swarms of fish. Killing turtles, porpoises, sea lions—not even to eat them, just to dump their bodies back into the waves. And selkies. It would snag them, like the net that snagged Riona's chief and held him under until he drowned.

NO! My grip tightened on the cords. *Not this net!*

There was a roaring in my ears like thirty-foot waves crashing down. Their strength was mine. I grabbed my knife and raised my arm—

The blade slashed through the net as smoothly as if it were flesh. The cut ends shriveled back, a mouth gaping in surprise.

Something cut through me, too, freeing the anger I'd kept buried too deep to feel. Anger at humans, and having to hide, and my own wrong skin—now it surged through my veins and the world turned red. I lifted my arm again and again. I was the downward thrust, the slashing blade! I was the ocean storm!

I jerked out length after length of net. With every slash, cords shriveled back in fear, their strength bleeding away. This net would never catch another porpoise—*slash*—or seal—*slash*—or selkie! The dock disappeared in a red haze until there was only the net and my knife flashing down—

A gull screamed from the top of a post.

I froze, my knife raised high. The sky was a dull, granite gray. Buildings peeked through ribbons of fog. Wooden slats. A light behind a curtain.

The creak of a door opening.

My breath rasped the air like it belonged to someone else. Shreds of net lay scattered at my feet. Severed strands drooped from the spool like moss dangling from a ghostly tree.

A shudder ran through me. The red haze was gone, leaving me panting and sick to my stomach.

I kicked and shoved a tangle of net back under the crinkled coat so the humans wouldn't see what I'd done. So they wouldn't see *me*. With a last glance at shore, I climbed onto the railing and dove.

CHAPTER TWENTY-EIGHT

❧ OUT OF THE FOG ❧

I swam back exhausted, stunned by the fury that had slashed out with the blade of my knife. For the first time, swimming to Maggie's felt like seeking refuge.

I was still catching my breath, so I swam on the surface, keeping to the wisps of fog. The shore wove in and out of view: trees with bold red bark, a doe foraging in the bushes, fresh water trickling down rocks to the waves . . .

A girl, my size, at the edge of a bluff, gazing out to sea.

She stood as alert and graceful as a deer. Her arms and legs were slim and wiry like mine, but her skin was a rich, shining brown. A tangled shock of black hair flew behind her. She held her head high, welcoming the wind like she was part of the earth and the grass and the trees. I should have ducked, but I was so tumbled and raw inside, all I could do was stare.

And then, to my surprise, I was lifting my hand high above the waves. A salute to this spirit of the land.

She turned. Slowly she raised a slender arm. And then she startled and bounded off across the bluff, her feet barely touching the ground.

The spell broke. I dove under, swimming unevenly, shocked at what I'd done. Why did I wave? And today of all days, with those nets hanging in shreds?

But the more I swam, the more I was filled by the beauty and strangeness of what I'd seen. That nimble spirit was nothing like Maggie with her dull hair and tired shoulders, or the coarse man who had flailed after his boat. I couldn't imagine her in a stuffy house. No, the land must have sprites like the sea had selkies. So even though I'd promised to tell Maggie if anyone saw me, this didn't count.

When I got back to Maggie's, I tried to pretend it was just another day. Eating a bowl of cornflakes. Helping around the house. It was midmorning when I brought in a last armload of logs. I was stacking them by the wood stove when someone banged on the door.

Maggie and I both startled, our heads swiveling.

"Maggie?" It was a rough male voice. He pounded again, rattling the door in its frame.

Maggie pointed to the bedroom. I set down the log silently, rose to my feet—

"You in there?" boomed the voice. "I need to talk to you."

The doorknob started to turn.

I flung myself to the floor and squeezed under the couch. The springs sagged into my back. Dust swirled around my face.

The door opened and a pair of heavy black boots strode into view.

"Maggie!"

"Hey, Harry. You always barge in like that?" There was a sharp edge to her voice. She didn't like this man.

"You didn't answer. Didn't think you heard me."

The boots tromped closer. One step. Two. I scooted back deeper. Dust flew up my nose, igniting a sneeze. I struggled to hold it in, but it grew, and grew—I stifled the sound, but my body shook the couch. An instant later, Maggie gave a loud, fake cough.

"I need some coffee," she said, walking toward the kitchen. "Join me?"

She never had coffee this time of day.

"Nope. I can't stay."

Water gushed into the kettle. "Then what brings you?" The kettle slammed down on the stove. "Come here where I can hear you."

To my relief, the boots walked away. My body shook with another silent sneeze.

"You seen anyone strange around here?" the man asked.

I froze.

"Strange?" said Maggie. "What do you mean?"

"We're all out searching. You know Stan Wylie? He had his boat tied up last night. Came out this morning and found the nets all pulled off the reels, hacked to shreds."

Maggie banged a mug down on the counter. "Bet it was kids. Teenagers, sneaking onto the island for a prank."

"Not in that fog. And you should have seen those nets. Slashed up like in a horror movie. We think there's a psycho on the loose."

"A psycho?" Maggie gave a harsh laugh. "Don't get carried away. I bet Stan did it himself. You know, for the insurance money. Why don't you go ask him? Now"—she walked to the door—"I have work to do."

His boots tromped after. "Keep your eyes open. Call me or Stan if you see anything unusual. I'm keeping my gun loaded. Stan's got a call in to the sheriff's office on the mainland." The door swung open and the boots stepped outside. "And hey, you know I told Jack I'd keep an eye on his things? That road of yours is all rutted up after the storm. I had to park before the turnoff. Glad to give you a price for fixing it."

"No thanks, Harry."

The door closed. The steps faded; in the distance, a motor started up and ebbed away.

"Come on out," said Maggie.

I crawled out and a cloud of dust went flying. I wiped off my arms, my legs. My knife.

Maggie's eyes narrowed. "Don't wear that knife anymore."

"But—"

"No ifs, ands, or buts. It doesn't matter what you did. Guys like Harry and Stan don't ask questions first. If they see that knife, your dad will be the least of your worries."

I didn't answer.

"You're not leaving the house if that thing's on your leg."

My hands clenched at my sides.

"We have an agreement, son. You planning on keeping it?"

I went into the bedroom and closed the door. I wanted to keep the knife close by, but hidden, in case Maggie decided to take it.

I couldn't hide it in the bed. Sometimes Maggie came in to crisp the covers and pat the bear, pretending to straighten up. The dresser was her territory, too. She'd filled it with more shorts, T-shirts, and a long-sleeved top. Sometimes I'd find her standing in front of an open drawer, folding and refolding the clothes like she needed an excuse to hold them.

That left the closet. I turned the knob, holding my breath, as if the dead boy's ghost would drift out along with the dust.

The closet was packed. Big boxes crowded a high shelf, clothes dangled across the middle, and the floor was hidden under stacks of smaller boxes. Stray shoes lay scattered around like a boneyard of old body parts.

I knelt and pulled out a stack of boxes. One was full

of wooden animals. Another had tiny trucks and colored sticks. But I didn't want my knife sharing space with the dead boy's things. I shoved the boxes and shoes aside and reached into the dark.

At the back wall, my fingers slid into a gap in the floor. I traced the edges. It was just long enough.

I had to force myself to unstrap the sheath from my leg. My knife, the only thing I still had from Mam and my life with the clan . . . I balanced it on my palm, feeling its familiar weight. Then I gritted my teeth and thrust it down into the gap.

As I let go, my hand brushed against something hard and cool. I wrapped my fingers around it—smooth, the length of my palm—and backed out of the closet. It felt like I was being given a trade for my knife. Slowly, I unfurled my fingers.

There, on my palm, lay a beautiful seal carved from dark green stone. Flippers, claws, the swish of the tail— all perfect. All true. Her head and tail lifted in a crescent, and she looked at me with a hint of a smile. A familiar smile. And those intelligent eyes . . .

This was no seal. It was a selkie.

I leaned against the wall, rocked by the strangeness of it. A closet, in a room, in a house—what was a stone selkie doing here, in this human place?

I brought the selkie up to the level of my face. She looked right into my eyes. Her head tilted a little to one side, like Grandmam when she had something important to tell me. Was it a message? Not from Mam; she hadn't been inside the house. From . . . the Moon?

She sees me, I thought. *The Moon sees me!* My chest filled, my heart too big to hold, like laughing and crying all jumbled together. She saw me stuck in longlimbs. She saw the clan swimming north through dangerous seas. I wasn't alone.

I pressed the selkie to my cheek as if I could soak in the courage I saw in her eyes. I took a deep breath. I'd be brave and strong here on Spindle Island. I'd be worthy of this gift, and I'd be worthy of the pelt Mam would bring by the second full Moon.

CHAPTER TWENTY-NINE
❧ THE SONG ❧

Maggie wouldn't let me go swimming for days after Harry came. I stayed close to the house, listening for motors and the heavy thud of boots. And thinking about the sprite. I pictured her on top of the bluff, firm footed and graceful. I saw the confident set of her shoulders, her chin lifting as she looked out to sea, her hand raising toward mine.

Harry had talked about the boat, and a gun, and people out searching. But he hadn't said one word about a boy seen swimming away from the harbor. That meant I was right about the sprite. She wasn't human. She hadn't told.

Maggie took out the calendar. "Full moon," she said,

drawing a line through a box with a circle in it. She turned a page and pointed to another circle. "One month till your mom's due back. And *that*"—another page, and her pen stabbed down—"is when Jack's coming home."

All those boxes! If I stayed in the house that long I'd lose my mind. I thought of the stone selkie in my shorts pocket. I'd vowed to be brave. Why was I cowering inside?

The next morning I woke with the first crack of daylight. I scanned the horizon. There wasn't a boat in sight.

Halfway down the cliff, a fist-sized hole in the rock made a perfect cave for the stone selkie. I settled her there facing out to sea, as if she'd be watching for my return. Then I jumped down to the flat rocks and slipped into the water.

The coolness rushed across my skin. For the first time in days I felt alive. I somersaulted and dove to the seabed. A striped greenling stared at me, flicking its fins. I grinned and gave chase. All along the rock face, crabs skittered and anemones waved. A wolf eel pulled its head back into a crevice.

I rose, treading water. I'd come all the way to the rocky point. On the other side was the bluff where I'd seen the sprite.

I was about to turn back when a song came rippling across the waves.

The singer's voice was clear and sweet. And the tune! In a few notes it curved from light to dark like the inside of a cresting wave. It called to me, to my blood, like I'd known it forever. It felt like home.

I swam around the point with my head above water so I wouldn't lose a single note.

It was the sprite. Of course it was. She sat cross-legged at the top of the bluff, her eyes closed, as if she were drawing magic from deep in the earth. The sweet, sad tune drew me closer. The waves hushed and now I could hear the words:

"Awake, awake, my bonnie maid,
For oh, how soundly thou dost sleep.
I'll tell thee where thy babe's father is,
He's . . . He's . . ."

She paused, then started again. *"I'll tell thee where thy babe's father is, he's . . ."*

The tune skittered to a stop, and in a cross voice she said, "Oh, rats!"

The song's magic fled. That didn't sound like what a

forest sprite would say. And the way her mouth pulled tight in frustration was more like a . . . a *human* expression. And those shorts and T-shirt she had on —

She *was* human! I startled backward with a splash.

The girl's eyes flew open and she leaped to her feet, staring right at me.

She was human and she'd seen me twice! She'd been lying in wait for me, luring me closer with her song. Now she'd tell everyone. They'd catch me and take me away, and I'd never see Mam or my clan again.

The current was carrying me toward the point. The girl started running along the bluff to keep up. I snapped to my senses and dove, kicking down to where the water turned dark. If she couldn't see me, she couldn't follow. I swam around the point and rose cautiously.

A gasp came from overhead. She was looking down from the top of the rocks.

"Don't go!" she cried, raising her arms to dive. "Wait for me!"

I kicked down deep and sped off. A moment later the water shook as she pierced the surface. The force of it rushed over me, circle after circle spreading out with the girl at the center. I swam faster. The water carried the beat of her strokes coming straight at me, as if the song had bound us together with an invisible cord.

I couldn't let her follow me to Maggie's! I swerved and headed out toward open water, where the waves were too big, the current too strong, for that feeble stroke of hers.

Behind me, her course shifted, too.

I swam underwater until my lungs were about to explode. When I was so far from land she couldn't possibly have followed, I rose in the trough of a wave and listened. The splashing had stopped.

I gulped in relief. She must have turned back.

But then why didn't I hear her swimming back to shore?

CHAPTER THIRTY
❧ THE ROCK ❧

The wind was rising, the waves breaking higher around me. I rode up a towering crest and looked toward shore. Halfway back, something thrashed to the surface.

A fish leaping, I tried to tell myself.

But two gulls flew over and circled, shrieking their danger cry.

The next thing I knew, I was swimming back toward the girl as fast as I could, riding the crests to keep her in sight. The splashing stopped as she sank underwater, then started again, wilder and shorter, and the waves were crashing, and the gulls were screaming, and I didn't know if I'd make it in time.

She was under the waves when I reached her. My hand closed around her wrist and I pulled. The moment her head burst through, her arms flailed out, raining frantic blows on my face and arms as she tried to grab on and climb above water. She was coughing and gulping, and kicking so hard I had to push her away.

"Calm down," I shouted, trying to get close again. But she was blind with panic—her nails raked my arm, and her fist struck my face. I backed off and dove. This time I came up behind her. I grabbed her shoulder, rolled her onto her back, and started swimming.

Finally she realized I had her. Her body let go into stillness. Now I could settle her weight and swim on my side. Her black hair floated around her face like seaweed at high tide.

It was too far to carry her to shore. Farther out in the strait, a crag jutted up from the water. It was our only chance. I lugged the girl through the rough chop, struggling to keep her head above water. Before long, I was short of breath and my arms were aching. The current sped up, rushing toward the crag. If it carried us past, I didn't know if I'd have the strength to turn and fight my way back through. We were hurtling closer to the slap and crash of wave on stone. I grabbed the girl tighter — I couldn't drop her now! — and, gathering all my strength, gave a powerful kick —

My feet touched rock.

The girl grabbed on to the solid stone, white-knuckled, coughing.

There was barely enough room on the crag for the two of us. I sat with my feet in the water and stared back at the curve of Spindle Island, struggling to catch my breath.

I could have left her then. I'd brought her this far, hadn't I? Saved her when she was certain to drown. Wasn't that enough?

But her breathing eased, and I was still there.

She sat up beside me, hugging her knees tight to her chest. She was shivering so hard, her whole body shook. But she was smiling. And her eyes, clear and bright and gray, were smiling, too.

"You saved me," she said. "Thank you."

To my amazement, I smiled back.

I looked at her closely. There was the same alertness I'd seen on the bluff. Her chin was determined, her limbs strong and thin, her feet almost as calloused as mine.

She nodded toward my upper arm. There were three long, red scratches.

"Did I do that?"

I shrugged. "It's all right. You couldn't help it. People don't swim very well."

"Except for you. That first time I saw you, I thought you were a seal. And then you waved." She rubbed her hands roughly up and down her arms. "You look so free in the water!"

"But that's how *you* are on land," I said. "Like you belong."

The rest of the world, with all its dangers and rules, had disappeared. The wind sang across the water, and the waves struck the rock, now high and light, now deep and dark, like voices blending in a tune.

"What was that song you were singing?" I said.

"Back on shore? It's one of Grandpa's old ballads. It's called 'Sule Skerry.'"

"Will you sing it now?"

She shook her head. "I only sing when I'm alone."

I looked at the vast stretch of white-tipped water separating us from shore. "This is pretty alone."

A smile played at the corners of her mouth. "Okay, but don't laugh."

She started singing in a clear, true voice,

"In Norway land there lived a maid,
'Baloo, my babe,' this maid began.
'I know not where thy father is,
Far less the land that he dwells in.'

"It happened on a certain day
When this fair maid lay fast asleep
That in there came a gray selkie —"

I missed the next line, because when she sang the word *selkie*, my heart stopped. No wonder the song had been calling to me! It was about my folk! But this was a human song. How could they have the rhythm of the waves, the joy and the longing, so right?

Now the girl was singing,

"'Awake, awake, my bonnie maid,
For oh, how soundly thou dost sleep.
I'll tell thee where thy babe's father is,
He's . . . He's . . ."

Her eyes widened. "Oh, now I remember! —

"'He's sitting close at thy bed's feet.'"

She stopped.

"Just a little more," I begged.

"Well, I know one more verse." She sat up straighter.

"'I am a man upon the land,
I am a selkie in the sea,
And when I'm far from every strand,
My dwelling 'tis on Sule Skerry.'"

As the last notes drifted away, the sun broke out from behind a cloud. In the sudden warmth, the girl stretched her legs long and gazed at me, bright-eyed. "Do you think there really are any?"

I gulped. "Any what?"

"Any selkies."

What would happen if I told her? If I let the whole story pour out, the truth I'd kept locked and silent for more than a moon? But before I could speak, a boat's motor throbbed the air.

It was heading in our direction. The world came flooding back in.

I leaped to my feet. "As soon as you see it, shout,"

I said. "Shout and wave as big as you can!"

"See what?"

The throb became a distant growl. The girl jumped up as she heard it, too.

I stared into her eyes. "Swear you won't tell anyone you saw me."

"I won't tell."

That wasn't enough. Not for how much I was risking.

"Swear to the Moon!"

Her face was solemn. "I swear to the moon."

The boat crested the horizon and I raised my arms to dive.

"Wait!" she said. "What's your name?"

"Aran," I said, and I dove.

CHAPTER THIRTY-ONE

❧ WHAT MAGGIE HEARD ❧

The house was empty when I got home. Maggie's shopping bag was gone. She must have walked to the store by the harbor. No matter how many fish I brought her, she kept going, even though she came back more exhausted each time.

The shadows had shifted by the time I heard her trudging up to the door. That's when I remembered the scratches on my arm. I ran to put on the top with long sleeves.

I came into the kitchen as she was setting her bag down on the table.

"You'll never guess what I saw at the dock," she said. Her body sagged, but her voice was lively. "It was the strangest thing." She started pulling cans out of the bag. "I was in Jane's store when Darlene Mitchell came running in. She grabbed the phone and called up old Bob Donahoe. 'Come down and get your granddaughter!' she cried. 'Harry's brought her in from the middle of the ocean!'"

I couldn't breathe.

Maggie picked up a can and carried it to the cupboard. She came back for another. Then, "Where's the coffee?" she said, rummaging in the bag. She pulled out a packet.

"Then what?" I said.

"Why, then we all went outside to see. And there she was, stepping out of the boat, wearing an orange life vest twice as big as she is. She's a skinny little thing, half black, if you can believe it." She poured the coffee into its canister. "Came to live with Bob, oh, it must have been three months ago. It surprised everyone. Bob's a loner, like me. Comes into the store to pick up his packages, but otherwise he keeps to himself."

It was the most words I'd ever heard from Maggie in a row. I hoped she wouldn't start coughing.

She pulled out a mug. "The girl just stood there with her mouth clamped shut while Harry ran on and on. Said he was motoring along when he saw someone out on those rocks in the strait. Thought he'd find a kayaker who got into trouble. But it was that wisp of a girl, all alone.

"Then Bob came running up, shouting and red in the face, and grabbed her tight. 'How in God's name did you get out there?' he said. And she said—"

The kettle whistled and Maggie turned to the stove.

My heart was pounding in my chest. But Maggie was measuring coffee, reaching for the kettle—

"What?" I said. "What did she say?"

"That she couldn't remember! Said she fell asleep up on the bluff, and the next thing she knows she's lying on this rock surrounded by waves and can't remember a thing in between."

I stifled a sigh of relief. The bittersweet smell of coffee filled the room.

"Bob was having a fit," said Maggie. "Going on and on about how they'd both promised her parents she wouldn't go swimming without him. It's not like the man knows how to care for a child in the first place. Alone up there with his books and his paints. Lets her run wild all over the island."

I looked out the window so I wouldn't be looking at Maggie. "What's her name?"

"Nellie. Well, that's what he calls her, anyway. She's got some long, complicated name, but he calls her Nellie." Maggie sat down opposite me, cradling her steaming mug. "There's more. Harry thought maybe he saw someone else in the water. But it was a long way off, and he wasn't sure." She took a sip, looking at me over the rim of her mug. "You wouldn't know anything about that, would you?"

I gave her my best innocent look. "It must have been a seal."

That song was haunting me. I hummed the tune as I stacked firewood. I whispered the words. *I am a man upon the land, I am a selkie in the sea* — without the rest of its verses, it was only half a creature, a ghost searching for its flesh and bones.

What happened between the selkie and the human woman? And their baby — the song didn't say *pup*, so it must be in longlimbs — what happened?

Mam would be back in less than a moon. Before then, before I left the human world, I wanted to hear the tune again. And every one of its words. And . . . and I wanted to see the girl.

I shouldn't. She was human and that meant danger. Maggie was different. She'd been chosen by Mam; she proved herself when Harry came. But the girl?

Then I thought of her clear, gray eyes, and her bravery

after she'd almost drowned, and her smile. When I sat beside her on the rock, it was so easy, as if the rest of the world didn't exist. And she kept her promise. She didn't tell.

I walked to the window and stared out at the darkening sky. Tomorrow morning I'd go back to the bluff. I hoped the girl would be there.

CHAPTER THIRTY-TWO
❧ THE BOOK ❧

A gust of wind woke me from my sleep. Dawn was cracking the sky. I settled the stone selkie in her cave and swam near the base of the cliff, catching breakfast. The sun crept up as slow as a snail. Finally I couldn't wait any longer. I took off swimming toward the bluff. A powerful current kept trying to push me back to shore.

I rose for air in the slap and splash of whitecaps. Maybe I should turn around and go back. After yesterday, the girl's grandfather would probably keep her inside for days. For a half-moon. Longer, until Mam came back and I'd left Spindle Island.

Above me, an osprey rode a wild swoop of wind. I kept swimming.

I rose at the tip of the point. There she was, sitting cross-legged, staring down at something in her lap.

I opened my mouth, but nothing came out. My voice was hiding somewhere down around my ankles. Finally I gulped and managed to call, "Hi!"

She leaped to her feet. "I knew you'd come!" She hoisted something flat and dark blue. "I brought it! The book with the song! I can sing you the whole thing now."

I swam a little closer.

"Come on up," she said, pointing to a split in the steep rock face.

It was a good place for climbing, with plenty of handholds and ledges. But I stayed where I was. The shoreline is the safest place to be: whichever direction danger comes, be it shark or human, you can slip out of reach in a flash.

"Sing it from there," I said.

"You aren't coming up?" She sounded disappointed.

I shook my head.

"Okay." She sat, settling the book in her lap. White pages flapped in the wind. She held them down and started to sing.

I strained to hear her over the blustery wind. I caught a strand of tune, but her head was bent to the book, and it swallowed the words back up again like a secret it wanted to keep.

"Sing louder," I called.

"It messes up the tune." She stood and studied the split in the rocks. "I guess I can sit on that ledge."

Clutching the book to her side, she started working her way down. She moved quickly, sure-footed and nimble. I backed away so the waves surrounded me. I was only here for the song, I told myself. That was all.

Now she'd reached the steepest part. She took a step—a stone teetered under her weight and slid, scraping and grating, and she reached out a hand to catch her balance—

The book flew from her grip and out over the waves, flapping wildly. Then its wings slapped shut and it dove into the roiling foam. Whitecaps crashed, pushing it deeper with every blow.

No! I dove under the chop, groping blindly, clutching at bubbles. Then my hand hit a hard, straight edge. I grabbed it and raced to the surface.

Nellie was standing on the ledge near the water. I swam back holding the book high above my head, victorious. I'd saved its life, and now I'd have the song as my reward. I climbed up beside her, grinning.

But she was staring at the book in horror, her breath coming in short gasps.

My smile dropped.

She held out both hands and I laid the book across them. The blue wing lay askew. Beneath it the pages were sodden and crumpled. Nellie reached out a trembling hand and lifted a torn strip of paper; it draped over her fingers like seaweed.

"Grandpa's going to kill me," she whispered. "I'm not supposed to take the books out of the house. For the special ones in the glass case, I'm supposed to ask before I even touch them. And I didn't ask."

She was going to be punished. But it was because of me she'd taken the book, because of me she'd tried to carry it down the steep path.

"Maybe . . . maybe we can fix it," I said.

"Fix it?" She bit her lip. "How?"

I wasn't about to tell her I'd never seen a book before, let alone healed one. I ran a finger along the cover. It was as blue as the ocean depths, and the paper inside was thick and rich. Even wet, it held its force like a living thing.

I lifted the crooked wing and gently tried to straighten it. There was a small ripping sound. I jerked my hand back.

"We'll need to see how they're made," I said. "Are there any more books like this?"

"This old? Yes, a few."

"Bring one here."

She shuddered. "I can't take another one out of the house. I don't dare."

A wild thought came into my head. I was going to push it away. But then I thought of the stone selkie waiting in her cave, and I wanted to be brave.

I swallowed hard. "Where's your house?"

She pointed toward the trees. *Inland*. Away from the safety of shore and the heartbeat of the waves.

I stood up straighter and took a deep breath. "I'll come there."

"You can't!" she said. "You need to stay secret."

"I can come if no one else sees me." I turned to climb.

"Wait," said Nellie. "It's too late to go today. Grandpa goes out painting early, but he might be back soon. Meet me here tomorrow at seven."

"Seven? When's that?"

She paused—had I shown myself as different yet again? Then she pointed to a spot low on the horizon. "When the sun's still down there, and the robins start to sing."

CHAPTER THIRTY-THREE
❧ THE AERIE ❧

The next morning I was swimming toward the bluff when my hand brushed against my side—and against the stone selkie in my pocket. I'd forgotten to put her in the little cave. I was about to turn back but then stopped. It felt good having her with me as I went inland. I pushed her down deeper in my pocket and swam on.

Nellie was pacing back and forth across the bluff. She waited silently while I swam to the rocks and climbed up beside her. Wildflowers tickled my ankles, and the rocks were speckled with green and gold lichen.

"Ready?" said Nellie.

I nodded.

She took off into a tangle of trees. Dark branches closed overhead, and bushes snagged at my legs. It was all I could do to keep up. Nellie ran like a deer, her bark-brown legs leaping along paths I couldn't even see. I'd always thought of myself as a fast runner, but now I lumbered along cracking every twig. At one point she stopped, waiting for me to catch up, and I felt my face flush.

The trees thinned; sun sparked off water. We crouched behind bushes and peered out.

A house perched atop a cliff, its back sheltered by trees, its face gazing out to sea. It wasn't much bigger than Maggie's. But her house was as tilted and ramshackle as an afterthought, and this one! I didn't know human houses could look like this, so solid and graceful, its beams rising as strong as fir trees. It looked like it belonged.

Nellie pointed to a room at the top, all windows. "That's where the glass bookcases are."

My heart beat faster.

"Wait here while I make sure he didn't come back early." She walked to the house and opened the door. "Grandpa?" I heard her walking around inside. Then she was at the door again, waving me in.

Maggie's house was built to keep the sea out. This

house, with its wall of windows, asked the sea in. There was warm polished wood and stone the colors of the rocks where I was raised. Everything was as spare and clean as the wave-washed shore. A picture on the wall made me catch my breath. It was just swirling shapes, red and black, but somehow they came together to make a breaching whale.

"Come upstairs," called Nellie.

I followed her up a dark, narrow chute. A door swung open, and I blinked in bright sunlight.

The room was nothing but windows on three sides. I could see everything from here: whitecaps breaking against rocks in the strait, a speck of a fishing boat far from land, a wisp of cloud on the horizon. A heron flew past, and I felt like I could swoop out and fly alongside. It was like looking out from an eagle's aerie.

Nellie's voice broke through my thoughts. "Which one do you want to see?"

I turned. She was standing in front of a wall made entirely of books. They rose from floor to ceiling, packed tighter than a guillemot colony at nesting time.

I took a step closer, my mouth open in wonder. There were so many! They seemed to shimmer with a kind of magic. Did each one have a different song? Would they sing to me, too? I wanted to open them all. But I had a task to do.

"It needs to be like the hurt one," I said.

"Then I guess . . ."

One group of books had their own little house of dark wood. They gazed out from behind its glass windows. Nellie opened the door and pulled one out.

"This has the same kind of cover," she said.

The book fell open. Black markings danced across thick, ivory-colored pages. Nellie placed it in my hands.

I felt like an imposter. How could she have such faith in me? I didn't know how to heal books. I barely knew how to hold one.

But I had to find a way. Like when I knotted the cedar strands: I'd never seen a sheath before, but I made one all the same. Or when the Moon-calling song rose in my throat to help Mam bind her pelt back on. Those were finding a way for the first time, too.

"Go get the hurt one," I said.

She ran downstairs and returned with the damaged book. It was still damp. That was probably good; some things got brittle when they dried, like seaweed.

I set the books side by side on the wood floor. I bent

over the healthy book and sniffed; I licked the page. Nellie's eyebrows shot up.

"No salt," I explained. "We'd better start by rinsing the other in clear water."

"Rinsing it?" Her voice rose. "I can't make it wet again! Look at the cover: it's already fading."

She was right. There were white streaks on the blue skin.

"If things aren't made for the ocean, it kills them," I said. "I think this one's more like a freshwater fish. It can't take the salt." I picked up the book.

Her eyes were huge. "What are you doing?"

"Taking it outside to wash it."

"*Outside?*"

"Look," I said impatiently, "do you want to fix it, or not?"

"But what if Grandpa comes back early?" said Nellie. "What if he sees —"

"Sees what?" boomed a gruff voice behind us.

CHAPTER THIRTY-FOUR
❧ THE WALRUS ❧

My head whipped around. There, at the top of the stairs, stood a great gray walrus of a man. His face bristled with whiskers and a single brown tusk hung from his jaws. I grabbed the book and leaped to my feet.

Nellie gasped. "Grandpa!"

He wasn't a rich brown like Nellie; his hands and face were lighter than mine. But his eyes were the same sea gray as hers, and they burned with the same fierce intelligence. He stared at the gaping glass case, the healthy book on the floor, the salt-stained book in my hands. His brows lowered.

"We were going to fix it," said Nellie in a rush. "Aran thinks we should rinse out the salt water, and—"

"Salt water? You took it outside? It's been in the *sea*?" His voice grew louder with every word. He took a menacing step closer. "Give it to me, boy."

Well, what would you do if a walrus came at you? I bared my teeth and growled. The world grew sharp and crisp.

"Stop, Grandpa, you're scaring him," said Nellie.

But I wasn't scared. I was completely alert, my body tensed for action.

"That's my *Songs of the Orkney Islands*," barked the walrus.

He was blocking the stairs so I couldn't escape that way.

Nellie looked at my arms hugging the book, and then at my face. She lifted her chin to the walrus. "He needs it."

"Needs it? A nineteenth-century first edition?"

"Not the book, the selkie song. I couldn't remember all the verses."

I froze, exposed like a fish left gasping on shore. It was bad enough that he'd seen me; now he'd start asking questions.

"All for a song, eh?" His eyes got a considering look. He reached up to his tusk. I gasped as he pulled it from his mouth.

"Desperate times call for desperate measures," he said, sitting at a table by the window. "And this calls for my pipe." He struck a twig into flame. Smoke spiraled up from the tusk; he waved it toward me. "Bring it here."

I weighed the book. Until it was healed, it probably couldn't sing Nellie the rest of the song, and she couldn't sing it to me. And the walrus's anger—you only get that protective of something very valuable.

The sound of my voice startled me. "Do all the books have songs?"

"Songs, and stories, and the lore of the sea."

I stared at the wall. Maybe there were more songs in there about my folk. What did humans know about selkies? About pups like me? This was the only time in my life I'd have a chance to find out.

I took a step closer to the walrus. Then another. I handed over the book.

He examined the cover, shaking his head. "Nellie, I thought I made it clear. You're never to touch these books unless I'm with you."

She gulped.

"I'll send this off to be repaired. You'll work to help pay for it."

Nellie gave a crisp nod of agreement, blinking back

tears. But at her side, her hand flicked toward the door.

"*Go,*" she whispered.

She was trying to help me get away. But I couldn't leave her to face the old man's anger alone. And I couldn't leave this wall of secrets.

"I'll work, too," I said.

The walrus snorted. "I don't know a thing about you."

Nellie said, "He's just some boy I found at —"

"I'm staying at Maggie's," I said, jumping in to get the story right. "I'm her nephew, except, I'm not there, I mean, it's a secret. My father can't know, with the divorce, and . . . and . . ." I sputtered out of air. They were both staring at me. I took a deep breath. "Don't tell anyone else I'm here. Please."

"All right," said the walrus. "I'll think what work this warrants. Come back tomorrow morning."

Nellie glanced at me. "Grandpa, he can't —"

"I'll be here at seven," I said.

CHAPTER THIRTY-FIVE
❧ BLUE ❧

The next morning I was still out on my sleeping ledge when I smelled coffee. There was a light on in the kitchen window. Maggie was never up this early! As quietly as I could I crept to the side of the house, eased my window open, and climbed in. I tiptoed to the bed, then jumped out again so my feet hit the floor with a *thunk*. I opened a dresser drawer and slammed it shut. Then I walked to the kitchen.

Maggie sat slumped over a steaming mug.

"Morning, Aran." She was trying to sound cheerful, but she looked so hollow, a puff of wind could have carried her away. "Listen, I have to go to the mainland today."

She paused and took a sip. "Jane's husband is taking me across to the big island to get the ferry."

I didn't answer. All I could think about was getting to Nellie's. I rushed to pour myself a bowl of cornflakes and gulped it down. I rinsed the bowl at the sink, flicking the curtain aside to check the height of the sun. I glanced at the door.

Maggie shook her head with a crooked smile. "I know, I know, you're off for your daily dose of sea. But you be extra careful, okay? I'll be back before dark."

I ran off without saying good-bye.

Nellie met me at the bluff. This time I watched our path carefully so I'd be able to find my own way home. At sea, finding a route was easy, with currents and wave patterns to guide me. Here I had to memorize markers: a tree with two trunks, a boulder shaped like a whale. And I was on the alert for people. It was bad enough that Nellie's grandfather had seen me. He was absolutely the last human who could know I was here.

We reached the house and Nellie led me inside. The walrus stood staring out the window. He turned and limped over to a chair. No wonder he was so fierce; he had to be, to survive predators with a leg like that.

He picked up the cold tusk from the table and cradled it in his palm. "I need blue," he barked.

I glanced at Nellie to see if she understood. But she looked confused, so I asked, "What kind?"

"Every kind. Robin's-egg blue. Evening blue. Sun-on-the-water blue." He leaned back in his chair and gestured toward the window and the sea beyond. "How can I paint if I can't get close to *that*? My blasted knee is so bad, I can barely walk. I need to rest it for a few days and hope it stops screaming at me with every step. In the meantime, I need to keep working. So bring me blue."

I followed Nellie outside. I was glad it was misty here. Humans went outside less when it was wet, probably because their clothes got clammy.

"Hold on a second," said Nellie, spinning around. "I'll get my backpack."

Blue. How hard could that be? This shouldn't take long. We'd find our blue, and then somehow I'd sneak up to the aerie and figure out how to listen to the books. The trick would be doing it without letting the walrus know. And I couldn't let Nellie know my plans, either. She and her grandfather were close. No, I had to find my way up the stairs when no one was watching—

Nellie touched my elbow and I jumped. Then she was

racing ahead. I ran after her, winding downhill around fir trees and leafy trees, bushes and brush. We leaped off rocks and crunched down on a pebbled shore. It was a beautiful little cove, peaceful and sheltered.

"I'll look here," said Nellie, bending to the base of the cliff behind us. "You check the beach."

I picked up handfuls of stones but tossed most of them away again. When we met to share what we'd found, only two were good enough to keep: a shiny, black pebble flecked with blue and a blue-gray shard.

We shook our heads. It wasn't enough.

A boat puttered into view. I dashed back up the trail, crouching under the leafy trees at the top. Something rustled in the branches high above me. I glanced up in time to catch a flash of pure, bright blue.

Nellie came running up and I pointed. For a moment, nothing. And then, from behind the leaves, another flicker of blue and a burst of song.

"A bluebird," she said.

She jumped up and grabbed the lowest branch, pulling herself up easily. Then she disappeared into the thick, swaying green. A moment later, the bluebird burst from the leaves and flew to a fir, scolding crossly. I waited for Nellie to come down. Instead, the leaves rustled higher up the tree.

She peeked out near the top, small and far away, and called, "Come see!"

On the rocks where I was raised, trees were bent and stunted by the wind. This one was taller than I'd ever climbed before. I grabbed the branch and pulled myself up, the bark rough under my hands, and then I was climbing high into a dark, cool, whispering world. The leaves brushed gently against my skin. The thinner the branches got, the more they swayed, until it was like riding waves. I almost forgot why I was climbing until I reached Nellie.

She pointed to a hole in the trunk. Inside was a snug nest made of grass, fir needles—and feathers, like slivers of summer sky.

We chose two and left the rest for the bird. Nellie scampered down like a squirrel. I followed, branches bouncing under my weight, and landed in a crackle of brush.

Nearby, we found a cluster of dark blue berries and a sprig of flowers, a soft purple-blue. We spread out our whole collection. The mist had deepened to rain. Nellie's dark hair dripped around her face.

She sighed. "It's not enough."

I scuffed at the ground. She was right. This wasn't

enough to make the walrus welcome me back. I could see it now: a dismissive wave of his hand, a gruff snort, and there went my chances of sneaking up to the books. Colors on land were so feeble compared to those under the sea.

I started walking.

"Where are you going?" Nellie fell in behind me.

"Back to the cove."

"But we already looked there."

"We only looked on shore," I said. "No wonder we didn't find anything good."

I jumped down to the pebbles, waded in thigh-deep, and dove.

A silver-blue fish swished past. I let it go. A fish would be hard to carry back alive, and the dead ones lose their shimmer. I swam deeper.

At the bottom, next to a sun-red sea star, lay fragments of mussel shells. I gathered a handful, kicked up, and lobbed them ashore. I dove again. It didn't take long to find a colony of live mussels nearby. I twisted off a few, hoping their insides would be brighter than the fragments. Besides, I was hungry, and mussels sounded good. As I swam off, I saw some oysters, so I grabbed one of those, too.

I splashed back up on shore. Nellie was looking through the shell fragments.

"These three are best," she said, holding them out.

They were good, but not great. I cracked open a mussel and offered the meat to Nellie. When she shook her head, I slurped it down. Then I held out the glistening inner shell so Nellie could see. It swirled with layers of blue, from bold and dark to pale and mysterious. The center glowed like a pool of silver-blue moonlight.

We grinned at each other.

"That's it!" said Nellie, bending to put the treasures in her pack. She headed up the trail.

I was still hungry, and I wasn't going to let the oyster go to waste. I grabbed a sharp rock and pried it open —

There, atop the meat, nestled a pearl, as round and shining as the Moon. It almost looked like it belonged in the night-blue sky of the mussel shell. I slipped it into my pocket. Then I swallowed the oyster and ran after Nellie. Toward the walrus, and the house made of windows, and the aerie full of secrets.

CHAPTER THIRTY-SIX
❧ THE STORY FIRE ❧

As we neared the house, Nellie grabbed my arm.

"Look! Smoke! He's made a fire!"

I didn't understand her excitement, but it didn't matter. I was going back inside.

The walrus sat before an open hearth. The embers flickered in a constantly shifting pattern, like light dancing through water.

"Let's see what you've got," he said.

Nellie pulled our findings from her pack and spread them out on the low table.

He picked up the pebble with blue flecks and held it to the light. He was staring at the stone, and Nellie was staring at him. . . . I slipped the whole mussel shell out of the pack and into my pocket.

He examined the blue-gray shard, the pale flowers, and the feathers. His brows lowered. "Is that all?"

Nellie pulled out the broken mussel shells and set them down so they caught the light from the fire.

The walrus leaned closer. He picked them up one by one, turning them this way and that.

"Is it enough, Grandpa?" asked Nellie.

The set of his mouth said it wasn't.

"There was one more," she said, turning to the pack.

"Here it is." I placed the whole mussel shell on the table. Closed, so the walrus could open it himself.

He set it on his palm. Firelight flickered across the dark surface. Then he lifted the top.

His eyebrows shot up. Nellie gasped.

There, on the pool of silver-blue nacre, sat the perfect round moon of the pearl.

The walrus stared, trying to figure it out.

"They really grow in oysters," I explained. "Not mussels. But the colors of the shell . . ."

"It's like they're trading light," whispered Nellie.

The walrus was looking at me thoughtfully, his head tilted to one side.

"Now is it enough?" said Nellie.

A smile played at the corner of his mouth. "It will do."

I glanced toward the staircase with a sigh. With Nellie and her grandfather right here, I couldn't sneak up to the aerie.

"I guess I should go," I said, taking a step toward the door.

Nellie's head flew up. "But Aran, there's a fire! It mean's Grandpa's in a storytelling mood. You have to stay!"

I eyed the walrus warily, but the more he accepted me, the closer I'd get to his books. So I sat at the edge of the rug, far from the fire and close to the door. Just in case.

The walrus took his tusk from a pocket and cradled it, unlit, in his palm. "Now," he said, "what do you want to hear a story about?"

"Selkies," I said before I could stop myself. Then I bit my lip. I couldn't believe I'd said the word out loud.

But he didn't seem suspicious, or even surprised. "Ah! A tale from my homeland. Let's see, there's 'Westwood Pier,' about the man who followed the selkie. But no, that wouldn't do for children." He stared into the fire. "I know, we'll start with the classic tale of the selkie wife. Go get the cookies, Nellie."

She ran into the kitchen and came back a moment later carrying a plate piled with flat, brown circles. She offered me one, but I shook my head. She and the walrus each took two.

Nellie sat on the rug halfway between the walrus and me. She glanced at him, and I could tell she usually sat right beside him for stories, like I did with Grandmam. I took it as a sign of friendship, so I wouldn't be too far outside the story's circle.

She didn't have to worry. The moment the story started, the walrus's gravelly voice drew me in, deeper and deeper, until I was under the story's spell.

"Once upon a time," said the walrus, "when the world was newer than it is now and the magic fresher, there was a man named Sean O'Casey. One night he stumbled back to his boat, a bit the worse for drink. 'I'll sit for a moment and catch my breath,' said he, leaning back against the rocks above the beach. Soon he was sound asleep.

"The moon rose as round and bright as a silver platter. Sean woke to the sounds of lively music and laughter rising from below. Now, who could be having a party this time of night? He peered over the rocks. The shore was full of dancers, their steps graceful, their skin pale, their hair as dark as night. To his great surprise, not one of them wore a thread of clothing.

"That's when Sean noticed the sealskins piled on the rocks. Black, silver, speckled; each one sleeker than the last. Ah, so the dancers were selkies! In the water, selkies look like seals. But when they come ashore, they slip off their sealskins and step out in the same form as you and me, to dance by the light of the moon.

"Now Sean O'Casey was a lonely man in want of a wife, and these black-haired beauties made his heart beat faster. He waited until a spirited reel carried the crowd away. Then he crept down and searched through the furs until he found the prettiest one of all. A soft, speckled brown it was, and as sleek as can be. He tucked it inside his satchel and crept back to his hiding place.

"The music stopped and the dancers ran laughing back to the rocks. Each one found a fur, slipped it on, and swam away, until only one selkie remained on shore. 'Where can it be?' she cried in anguish, searching around the rocks. 'Oh, where can it be?'

"'You won't find your sealskin there,' said Sean, stepping out from his hiding place. 'It's gone. You're coming home with me.'

"How she wept, then, and pleaded with him to let her

return to the sea. But he only draped his coat over her shoulders and rowed her back to his cottage. A big silver seal followed the boat, staring at them as if his heart were breaking.

"The selkie became Sean's wife, and a good wife she was, bearing him four fine children, keeping his house, and cooking his meals. Things might have stayed that way forever. But one day her young son ran up, calling, 'Mother, look what I found in the loft!' In his hands he held a sealskin, a soft, speckled brown, and as sleek as can be.

"Now, they say when a selkie has her sealskin, she can't resist the ocean's call. Without a word she thrust her babe into the oldest child's arms, slipped on the sealskin, and swam away.

"Sean O'Casey came home that night to find his children standing at the shoreline. He followed their gaze. A speckled brown seal stared back at him from the waves. A big silver seal swam by her side.

"'Come back!' Sean cried. 'Come back to your children and your home! After all these years, don't you love me?'

"Without a word, she dove and disappeared into the great, gray sea."

∾ ∾ ∾

The room grew silent, except for the gentle crackle and spark of the fire.

"And the children?" I asked, still deep in the story.

The walrus leaned forward. "What do you mean?"

"What happened when they got their pelts? Now that their mam is back in the sea, and the Moon . . ."

"Well, now," said the walrus. "The story doesn't say."

He set his pipe down with a loud *thunk*. All at once I was aware of his eyes on me.

It took all my willpower to stand up slowly. "What do you need us to find tomorrow?" I said, trying to keep my voice steady.

The walrus had picked up the pearl and was rolling it around in his palm. "I'll tell you in the morning." His voice came from far away.

Nellie jumped up and started walking with me to the door, but I needed to be alone.

"I'll find my own way back," I said. Before she could protest, I was gone.

I was walking through the forest, but all I saw was that selkie's face when she couldn't find her pelt on the beach. That man said he loved her, but he kept her trapped in his house.

Like my father trapped Mam.

I felt dizzy. It was Mam's story, but twisted and told from the other side. Everything was reversed, like looking in Maggie's mirror and seeing myself the wrong way around.

How strange to see a selkie through human eyes! And those children, staring after their mam as she swam away . . .

Like my mam swam away.

A shiver ran down my spine. I stopped and took a deep breath, pushing the feeling away. There wasn't any need for me to be uneasy! *My* mam had borne me at sea. She raised me with salt and moonlight on my skin, taught me the songs for the rites. And I didn't get cold, did I? Or need fresh water?

I pulled the stone selkie from my pocket and walked on with her clasped in my hand.

No, I wasn't worried. I was *interested*. Stories were places where the two worlds met, swirling around each other like ribbons of foam. The more I heard, the more I wanted to know. Now I was even more determined to get into the aerie. Before Mam came back for me, I'd find out as much from human tales as I could. Then I'd share my discoveries with the clan.

∾ ∾ ∾

I got back to find Maggie sunken in the big chair, gray and exhausted. She hadn't even taken off her coat.

"Where have you been, Ocean Boy?" That was all it took to start her coughing.

"Exploring. I'll make you some coffee."

I went to the kitchen and turned on the heat under the kettle, trying to figure out what to say when she asked me more. But when I returned with the coffee, her eyes were closed. I set the steaming mug gently on the table at her side and started to tiptoe away.

"They want me to go in for tests," she rasped.

I turned. "Go in?"

"To the hospital on the mainland. They want me to stay there awhile. I had to tell them I'd think about it before they'd let me out the door." She reached for the mug. "Bring me the calendar."

I brought it over and her finger traced the rows.

"Not long now until your mom's back. I'll wait until then to decide."

Her sunken cheeks, her tired eyes . . .

"Are you . . . I mean . . ." I looked out the window at the trees in the distance. "Can they heal you there?"

She blew on the steam and took a slow sip. "I don't know. And I don't think they know, either, for all their talk. I don't have much truck with hospitals, after Tommy."

I almost asked what happened to him, but part of me didn't want to know. "Maybe you should go," I said. "I'll be fine on my own."

She shook her head with a half smile. "We made a deal, you and me. I keep my promises. We'll stay here together until your mom comes back."

CHAPTER THIRTY-SEVEN
❧ THE TREE CAVE ❧

The next day I found my own way to Nellie's house. I knocked and she let me in.

"Come look," she said, leading me to the big table by the window.

Our blue feathers and shells lay scattered across the wood. Next to them was a half-filled sheet of thick paper. It wasn't a picture of a thing, just colors and shapes. A sphere swirled with silver-blue light. Beside it, three stripes—just lines, but somehow they carried both the stillness of the shell and the swiftness of the stroke. The space between the pearl and the stripes felt alive. Like whispers were passing back and forth. I drew in my breath.

"Don't stand there gawking," barked the walrus.

Nellie and I jumped and turned around.

"I need rough," he said. "Rough you can see and rough you can only feel. As many kinds as you can bring me. Well, what are you waiting for? Go!"

This time Nellie led me inland, in a direction we hadn't gone before. We ran through a thick fir forest and across a meadow. We skirted a house with peeling red paint; it looked deserted, but Nellie kept us out of sight anyway. She didn't even need me to remind her.

The ground began to climb. Now we were hiking up a steep hill, with rocks and scraggly grass underfoot. We crested the top.

"There!" said Nellie, proudly.

Spindle Island lay spread out below us. There was the harbor, with miniature boats bobbing at the pier. The buildings looked like tiny boxes. The bigger one must be Jane's store. I was surprised how few other houses there were. From the dock, in the dark, the town had seemed much bigger. A single black road wound inland like a snake with a yellow stripe down its back. Here and there, ribbons of dirt road branched off toward solitary houses.

I could have stayed looking for a long time, but Nellie

was pointing down to the bottom of the hill. "See that creek? That's where we're going."

She took off down the hill. I followed, and when she spread her arms and started leaping, I did the same, my arms as wide as wings. The slope got steeper and a breeze pushed me from behind and my feet barely touched the ground. I'd never gone so fast on land!

At the bottom we skidded to a stop, panting, our hands on our knees. Nellie looked up at me, her eyes sparkling, and grinned. I couldn't help it: I grinned back. At that moment a kind of weight lifted from me. I felt I could run forever without getting tired.

We wandered along the creek. I didn't know plants could grow like this, so dense and green. Fir trees towered overhead, and the ground was a sweep and tumble of ferns, their long arms draped over rich, black earth. Everywhere I looked there was brilliant green moss, growing on rocks, coating tree trunks in soft, thick pelts. Swaying branches swallowed up sound, muting our footsteps, hushing even our breath. Where were we going to find *rough* in a place like this?

Nellie was bending down with her pack open. I ran ahead, jumping from rock to mossy rock across the creek. On the far side, the soil was even softer. It gave a little with every step.

"Wait up!" called Nellie, bounding toward me. And then we were racing and chasing each other through the trees.

It was late afternoon when we ran out of the woods and onto a new stretch of shore. The sun lit the madrone trees sideways, painting their bark red.

"Where are we?" said Nellie.

I pointed to the rocks out in the strait, where I'd carried her, and then to the jut of land that led to Maggie's. "So we're halfway between your house and mine," I said.

As I lowered my arm I saw, barely above the high-tide line, what looked like a bright green dome. Nellie followed my gaze, and then we were running over to investigate.

A short tree, only shoulder high, leaned toward the water. Its branches draped down to shelter a broad rock at its base. We pulled a branch aside and crawled in. It was like a cave woven of leaves and sparks of light.

"It feels like magic," I said.

Nellie nodded. "But better, because it's real."

The space was just big enough for us to sit and examine what we'd found. Fern fronds and tufts of yellow-green lichen. Some stones from the hillside. Fragments of bark that looked like they'd fit together if you could only figure out the pattern.

Nellie picked up a fern frond and ran her finger along the jagged edges, then turned it over. On the underside were two rows of tiny bumps.

"Those are the spores," she said. "That's what my mom studies."

"Your mom?" I hadn't pictured her with anyone but the walrus.

Nellie nodded. "She's a biologist. So is my dad. They're working in the rain forest. I wanted to go, but Mom said if I was running loose around all those snakes and germs, she couldn't concentrate. Dad was going to stay behind, but then Grandpa said I could live with him. Mom said there's no school here"—she gave a little smile—"but Grandpa said I'd learn plenty from the plants and the animals. Which was a pretty good argument since they're scientists. And he said I could read his books."

I caught my breath. *Read.* Was that how they gave her their songs? I started to ask, "How—"

"Mom said he didn't even get a decent internet signal, and Grandpa said, Who needs the internet when you've got the sea and sky? That's when Mom said yes. So I get to live with Grandpa for now. Mom and Dad send letters, and Grandpa checks for email when he goes to places with decent reception, and once in a while they call when they can get to a phone."

Nellie leaned back. Her face was hidden in the shadows.

She'd said a lot of words that I didn't understand, but I knew the feeling in her voice. "You miss them," I said.

"Yes," she said softly. "I do."

A breeze rustled the branches, and drops of sun rippled across the rock like light through water. And then the light seemed to thin, and I saw Mam swimming under a layer of ice—her determined eyes, her powerful tail. She must be heading back to me by now. A thrum of excitement ran through me, but then it got muddled up with a longing so deep it hurt.

"I miss my mother, too," I said.

I knew Nellie understood because she didn't say a thing.

When we got back to Nellie's, smoke was rising from the chimney. This time I walked right in without hesitation. We spread everything out and the walrus leaned forward in his chair with a grunt.

"Hmm." He held the bit of yellow lichen up to the window. "That might do it."

"Grandpa?" said Nellie.

He picked up the bark and rubbed it between his thumb and fingers.

"Grandpa, shall I get the cookies?"

He set the bark down and pulled the pipe from his pocket. "Ah, yes, a story. What would you like today?"

"What's the one you didn't tell us yesterday?" said Nellie. "About the man who follows a selkie?"

I looked up eagerly. Of course she wanted the same story I did.

The walrus sniffed his cold pipe with obvious longing. "'Westwood Pier'? I won't be keeping you up with nightmares."

"We don't get nightmares, do we, Aran?"

"Never," I lied.

The walrus leaned back in his chair, looking thoughtful. Then his eyes lit up and he gave a quick nod. "Right, then. Get the cookies, Nellie. I know just the story."

This time I took a cookie. And then another. I decided to ask Maggie if she'd heard of cookies; they were much better than cornflakes.

The walrus cleared his throat. "In the old days," he began, "there was a king who had ruled for fifty years of peace and prosperity. . . ."

A king: Was that like a chief? I leaned forward, eager to catch every word. But the story droned on and on, and there wasn't a selkie in sight. There wasn't even any ocean. My feet started jiggling; I sat cross-legged to keep them still. Finally I slumped over, chin in hand. This story had nothing to do with my folk, or me. It didn't even make my heart beat faster.

What was the tale the walrus wouldn't tell?

CHAPTER THIRTY-EIGHT

❧ THE REST ❧ OF THE SONG

Nellie and I kept working for the walrus. We found shades of black, and things that were mottled, and the colors just under the waves. Then one afternoon we met the walrus hobbling with his stick to the store. His knee was better, he said, and our debt was paid in full.

My head flew up. "Does that mean the book is fixed?"

"Fixed! I've barely sent it off."

I scuffed at the dirt as he clomped away. "I'll never get the rest of the song," I said.

Nellie looked at me thoughtfully with those clear, gray eyes, and then we were dashing into the woods.

But as day followed day, I spent less time longing

for human tales. The second full Moon was coming. The closer it came, the more it filled my thoughts, like a rising tide sweeping over the shore.

Soon I'd see Mam. Soon I'd have my pelt.

Would the rest of the clan be coming, too? It had been so long since I'd felt the brush of whiskers, the touch of a flipper, the softness of fur.

And my pelt—was Mam bringing it with her? Or did the wise ones give her secrets instead, words or actions that would make me turn?

I stared at the Moon for hours. I felt her tug on the tides.

Maggie was watching, too. She pulled out her calendar and drew a line through another box. "Only two weeks until your mom's back," she said.

She left the room. I slid the calendar drawer back open. I touched my finger to each empty box, and then traced the perfect, round circle of the Moon.

Soon it was hard to think of anything else. I could almost hear Mam calling out the ritual greeting—*Come to me! Come!* I could see myself diving deep with a flick of my tail, swooping up behind rockfish and gulping them down. Every night, as I lay outside waiting to fall asleep, I checked my fingers for webbing, in case it came first as some kind of preparation.

"Only one week," said Maggie.

I spent hours in the bathroom with the door closed, staring at myself in the mirror. How would I look in my pelt? I'd probably be just a bit smaller than Finn. Maybe I'd be black like Lyr or dappled like Mam. I hoped I wouldn't be brown like Maura, but even that would be all right. I pictured my eyes looking out from a whiskered face. I rolled my shoulders, imagining the pelt sliding on.

"Only two days now," said Maggie.

The next morning I came into the kitchen to find her setting down the calendar. "Tomorrow," she said with a sigh, staring out the window.

Tomorrow I'd be heading back home. I'd close my nostrils and dive deep, swimming as far and as fast as everyone else in my clan.

I knew the path to Nellie's so well, I didn't need landmarks anymore. I paused at each one all the same—the tree with two trunks, the whale rock—seeing them for the last time.

Would I tell Nellie I was going? *Could* I?

She was pacing in front of her house. The moment she saw me, she grabbed her backpack. "Want to go to the tree cave?" she said, her eyes bright with excitement. "I have a surprise."

I nodded. "Let's take the long way."

We ran across the meadow, up the hill, and down. We leaped from stone to mossy stone across the creek and zigzagged through the trees, bursting out into the bright light of the shore.

I gazed across the waves to the horizon, and my heart swelled. Tomorrow I'd be swimming those waters with Mam.

"Come on!" called Nellie from inside the tree cave.

I lifted a branch and crawled in, sitting cross-legged beside her.

She tugged off her pack. "You know that song from the day we met? And how you wanted to hear the rest? Well, guess what. I found it!" She reached in the pack and pulled out a skinny white book.

"But I thought it lived in the blue book," I said.

"It's in lots of books. I don't know why I didn't think of it before. Grandpa said I could bring this one outside."

I was getting the whole song after all! It felt like a farewell gift.

Nellie opened the book and set it in my hands. Black markings clustered in little groups on the page.

It didn't sing to me.

I handed it back. "You sing it," I said. It was better this way. I'd hear the whole song in her sweet voice and carry the memory away with me.

She pushed her hair behind her ear.

"In Norway land there lived a maid . . ."

Could I tell her? Just that I was leaving, and nothing more?

"'It shall come to pass on a summer's day
When the sun shines hot on every stone
That I will come for my little wee son
And teach him how to swim the foam. . . .'"

The song swept through me, verse after verse. The woman raised their child on land for seven years. Then the selkie came back for the pup and they swam away. That must mean the pup got his pelt after all those years in longlimbs, like I'd be getting mine. I almost said something, but then Nellie was singing,

"And she has wed a gunner good
And a proud, good gunner it was he

And he went out on a May morning
And shot the son and the gray selkie."

The words struck me in the chest, and I jerked back with a gasp. Shot? That was all wrong! They should be fine at the end of the song—the selkie and pup with their clan, the mother with her new mate on land.

"'Alas, alas, this woeful fate,
This weary fate that's been laid on me!'
She sobbed and sighed and bitter cried
And her tender heart did break in three."

Nellie looked up and saw my face. "I know," she said, closing the book. "I don't like that ending, either."

I was breathing hard. The selkies were dead. The mother was dying of sorrow. They should never have gotten together in the first place.

Worst of all, it was Nellie singing those words. We'd climbed trees together. We'd explored the island and found this cave of leaves and light and made it another home. Human and selkie . . .

My teeth clenched. It was good I was leaving. But

then why was there a tug of loss in my chest, pulling like a strong ebb tide?

"I have to go," said Nellie. "I told Grandpa I'd help him pack up one of his paintings. We're getting it ready for the next mail boat." She slipped the book in her pack. "I'm hoping there'll be a letter from my parents. We're trying to figure out when we can all talk on the computer. It's been so long since I've seen them, even on a screen." She sighed. "But they have to get to a city with good wi-fi, and so do we."

She crawled out of the tree cave. I took a long, deep breath before I followed. I wished Nellie could come wait with me tomorrow. I wished she could meet Mam. Could I at least say good-bye?

I ducked through the branches and stood, murmuring, "Nellie, I—"

She was already disappearing into the trees.

CHAPTER THIRTY-NINE

❦ THE SECOND ❦ FULL MOON

All morning Maggie was fussing, glancing at her calendar every few minutes and trying to hide her worry. Her problem was, she hoped Mam was coming. I didn't hope; I knew.

I helped Maggie with things she'd need once I was gone. I brought in firewood, building a stack so high it toppled over and I had to take half of it outside again. I grabbed the broom and swept so hard, I broke a lamp. Maggie finally asked if I wanted to wait outside.

So here I sat with my feet in the waves, waiting.

After a while the door clicked open.

"Aran?" called Maggie.

I climbed to the top of the cliff and waved.

"Don't you go swimming off," she said. "You'll want to be here the second she comes."

As if I'd be going anywhere! But I nodded and climbed back down.

I kept hearing the door open. Maggie must be watching the road. She didn't know Mam would come from the sea.

I tossed stones into the waves as the sun crept slowly across the sky. The heat of midday. The shift of my shadow. The long light of late afternoon. I called to a gull, hoping for news, but it was too high up to hear me. Maybe I'd go higher, too, so I could see farther. I climbed back up and sat at the top of the cliff.

The next time Maggie opened the door, she called, "Do you want some supper?"

I shook my head no.

The sun was sinking in a fiery orange ball. The sky faded to pink, then purple, then gray. Finally the Moon began to rise. I held my breath. Nothing was ever more beautiful than that Moon.

I reached in my pocket and pulled out the stone selkie. I longed to bring her with me, but I wouldn't be able to carry anything in sealform. I stroked the curve of her back one last time. Then I put her in her cave, facing out, so she could watch me swim away.

The higher the Moon climbed, the harder it was to wait. Mam would be here any time now. I'd never be able to wait for her to reach land. The instant I saw her, I'd swim out and we'd roll in the waves—her shining eyes, the brush of her whiskers! We'd streak back here and she'd pull my pelt from a woven pouch. . . .

The door opened again, and then Maggie was walking out toward me. She spread a blanket on the ground and sat down. Side by side, we watched the moonlight spread across the waves like a great silver road.

After a few minutes she held out a closed hand. "Here," she said with a crooked smile. "Don't forget your pirate gold."

She clinked the coins into my palm.

It was a joke, a reminder of the night I arrived. How wild I must have looked, wide-eyed and dripping from the storm! How little I'd known of the human world, seeing a couch, a rug, a bed for the very first time. Thinking the gold was real.

"Worth a fortune," I said.

I smiled, and she started laughing, and then we were both laughing so hard we had to hold our sides. It was only Maggie's light cough that stopped us.

I put the coins back in her hand.

"For you, to help with the costs," I said. The same words as when I gave them to her two moons ago. And then, staring out across the waves, I added, "I wish it was real gold for you."

Her smile turned wistful. "Oh, Ocean Boy, the real gold was you."

The Moon kept rising. The stars came out. Maggie had draped the blanket over her shoulders long ago. Now she started to shiver.

"Aran," she said. "It's too late for a boat. Come back inside."

"She'll be here."

Maggie sighed. "Well, then, you come say good-bye before you take off." She stood and rested her hand on my shoulder, and then she walked back to the house. The door closed behind her.

The Moon was nearing the center of the sky. This was the perfect time for Mam to come. Excitement stretched me as taut as a kelp bubble. I stared out across the waves until my eyes hurt. The Moon was right overhead. . . .

And then she began her descent.

A gust of wind from the north swept over the waves, splintering the silver path into shards. A bat sailed overhead on shadow wings. The waves lapped, and lapped, and lapped against the rocks. I was still staring as the Moon began to sink into the sea.

I tried to hold on to my excitement, but it was turning brittle, the hope leaching away.

Where was Mam?

She said she'd be here by the second full Moon. Mam kept her promises. She'd be here, she *had* to be here. Unless . . .

The words of Nellie's song came pounding through my head. *"And she has wed a gunner good, and a proud, good gunner it was he. And he went out on a May morning —"*

My stomach churned. Guns. Harry said he was keeping his loaded. I pictured a gun pointing at a silver head in the water. And then the pictures were whirling around faster and faster, an eddy pulling me down: metal cages — walls of ice — an orca's gaping jaws —

I jumped to my feet, gasping for breath. *Where was Mam?*

I strained to see out over the waves. The Moon was disappearing — a half circle, a sliver — and then she was gone, cut off by the horizon's sharp blade.

I shuddered. Mam would have come if she could. She must be lying somewhere, hurt or sick or trapped. She was in danger! And here I was, stuck on this stupid island in stupid longlimbs.

My hands clenched into fists. Mam needed me.

A crow's caw raked the dawn. I looked back at the house. Behind the window, Maggie was asleep, slumped in her chair. She must have lugged it over to keep an eye on me. Her hands splayed across a white page in her lap. The calendar. With last night's Moon, and four rows of empty boxes, and the blood-red slash that meant Jack was coming home.

CHAPTER FORTY
❧ SPEAK ❧

I crouched in the bushes outside Nellie's house. But it wasn't Nellie I'd come to see.

For weeks now I'd been wasting my time. Playing. Leaving it up to Mam to come back with my pelt, without me doing anything but hiding. Like all I had to do was stay safe, safe, safe.

Safe wasn't working anymore.

The doorknob turned and Nellie poked her head out, looking for me. I held my breath until she went back in.

A moment later she came out carrying a large, flat box. That must be the painting. The walrus hobbled after her, leaning heavily on two canes. As he lifted a hand to close the door, he tilted sideways.

Nellie watched warily. "Really, I can take it there myself," she said. "Don't you trust me?"

"I'm fine, Nellie," he said, with a sturdy smile. "Let's go." But when she skipped ahead, he winced with pain.

Stomp-drag, stomp-drag—with him on those canes, they'd be gone a long time.

The steps faded away. I crept silently to the door. But the moment the knob turned in my hand, I couldn't hold back. I dashed in, leaped up the stairs two at a time, and threw open the door to the aerie.

I skidded to a stop, staring. My breath caught in my throat.

The books packed the wall from floor to ceiling, row after row, spine after spine. The air was so thick with their magic, it shimmered. There must be hundreds of books, each with its own tune or tale. And one of them, *one of them*, might have what I needed. Even if it was only clues to patch together, it could be enough. It had to be.

It was Nellie's song that gave me the idea. That pup turned late from longlimbs. His mother might have seen how it happened. Humans *could* know. The song skipped over the moment of turning itself. But another might show a pup just as he got his pelt, with words that were chanted, or some kind of rite that made it happen. And that song could be in one of these books.

My jaw set in determination. I wasn't going to cower on this island forever. I'd get my pelt, and I'd swim off and find Mam, and, Moon willing, I'd save her. I stepped up to the shelves.

The books in the glass case were forbidden. That meant they had the most power. I opened the glass door and squatted down, listening for a thin thread of tune, a murmur of voices.

Nothing.

I didn't have time for every book. How would I choose? Most of them were clad in cloth, but a few wore leather. One of those was mottled, light brown and dark, like a pelt. There were ridges on the spine, like vertebrae—the bones of a living creature.

I pulled it down and gripped it tight, praying without words. Then I lifted the cover.

Black marks pressed deep into thick, pebbled paper. They marched in straight rows. So orderly. So disciplined. So silent.

Nellie said you *read* books. What did that mean? Was it a special way you held a book so its voice reached you?

I closed the cover and opened it again. I pressed the book to my ear.

But in the tree cave, Nellie had been looking down at the white book. And I hadn't heard it singing. Was its voice too soft to hear under Nellie's? Or did it whisper its words right into her head? How did she ask it to start?

"Please, speak," I asked politely.

Maybe it worked by touch. I fanned a group of pages. Then I held a page flat and ran a finger along a line. Some marks stood on their own; others clustered together.

"Speak!" I begged, louder.

The marks started spinning in front of my eyes. Was the book trying to keep them hidden? I pressed them down with my finger, but they wouldn't stay still. I didn't have forever. I had to find something fast.

I tossed the book on the floor and grabbed another. But it was silent, too—a conspiracy of books. They perched smugly on their shelves, their mouths clamped shut. I threw the book down and jerked out another, and another. They littered the floor, taunting me. The clues to my turning were right here, but they might as well be at the bottom of the sea.

I grabbed the biggest book on the shelf and shook it hard, trying to force the words loose. *"SPEAK!"*

The door swung open and crashed into the wall.

I whirled around as Nellie burst into the room. Her eyes blazed at the books strewn across the floor, at the pages still shuddering in my hands.

"What are you doing?" she cried. "You're not supposed to be up here! You're wrecking Grandpa's books!"

My face was burning. Anger and despair rose in my throat. I clamped my jaw shut, trying to hold the terrible feelings in.

"You just wait until he gets home!" Nellie's hands clenched into fists. "Why didn't you ask me? Why—"

"They won't talk!"

Nellie stopped, startled.

"The books," I said. "They talk to *you*. They give you songs and secrets, whatever you want to know. I asked them, but they won't tell me one stupid word!"

Nellie was staring at me with a strange, intent expression. She thought I was an idiot. She'd never want to see me again. I'd lost Nellie, and I'd never learn the books' secrets, and I couldn't save Mam—

"It's called reading," she said. "I'll show you how."

CHAPTER FORTY-ONE
❧ PATTERNS ❧

When I came back, Maggie surprised me by grabbing me in a hug. She must have thought I'd left last night when she was sleeping.

"How long—" I said, and then stopped. I was going to ask her about the calendar, about Jack and when she was going to call the child-taking people. But if I didn't say the words, maybe she wouldn't think them.

Too late. "We still have a little time," said Maggie, her eyes glistening. Then she went into the bathroom and washed her face for a very long time.

∾ ∾ ∾

The next morning I met Nellie at the tree cave. She'd brought a book with pictures of an animal called a bear. There were hardly any black markings. I looked at it scornfully. What could a book like this have to say?

Nellie pointed to a mark standing by itself. "That's a small letter *a*." She moved her finger to the center of a dense clump. "And so is that one."

It was the same shape: a beak curving over a round belly, like a well-fed puffin.

There were patterns! My eyes raced across the page, and I pointed to another *a* and another.

Nellie nodded. "There are twenty-six letters. Each one can look two ways, so that makes fifty-two shapes to learn. Then you learn the sounds they make. After that it's just practice."

I worked with Nellie all morning. *A, B, C, D, E.* When she went home for lunch, I traced letters in the sand. I dipped my finger in the surf and drew dripping letters on the rocks.

I went back the next day, and the next. I had to learn to read fast and get back to the aerie and start searching. Every day that passed was another day that Mam could be caged or caught or lying injured somewhere.

When I wasn't learning to read, I had to do something else, or I'd be eaten alive by worry. So I swam. Before, I'd gone swimming to explore. Now I swam to get stronger. I had to be ready to take off as soon as I had my pelt. And if Maggie called the child-taking people, I'd have to swim off in longlimbs. I couldn't let them take me away from the sea.

Every morning I woke before dawn and swam as hard as I could before first light. Out to the rock where I'd pulled Nellie, five times out and back without stopping. Then I climbed the cliff, shook off the wet, and snuck inside to put on a dry pair of shorts. I always held the stone selkie in my palm for a moment before switching her to my new pocket. She was my courage. I needed to be even braver now, for Mam.

When I heard Maggie fill the kettle, I came out rubbing my eyes as if I'd just woken. I ate a bowl of cornflakes and headed out the door, with Maggie calling after me yet again to be sure I didn't let anyone see me. I still hadn't told her about Nellie and the walrus, and now it felt too late. She'd be disappointed in me. She'd worry, and start coughing. It was better not to tell.

Then I worked with Nellie in the tree cave. All the way to *O, P, Q*. Then to *X, Y, Z*. But we still weren't done! I had to learn how to put the letters together. Sometimes a pair of them made a whole new sound. I had to memorize where they acted differently than they should have.

A hard swim back to Maggie's, and then I spent the

afternoon and evening doing my chores, and more and more of hers as her cough got worse. Sometimes it sounded like she couldn't breathe. She had something she called pills, small and round as fish eggs, and she'd take one and go to bed in the daytime. So I cut wood and piled wood. I swept and scrubbed the house before she could. I brought her fish and mussels so she wouldn't have to go to the store as often.

As I worked, I was always watching for letters. I ran my fingers across them—on the calendar, on boxes, on cans of food—putting the sounds together so they flowed into words.

At night I shut the door to the bedroom and pretended to go to sleep. When Maggie turned out the lights and her steps dragged to her room, I snuck out the window. I set the stone selkie beside me on the rocks, and I thought about Mam and prayed to the Moon, until somehow I fell asleep.

I was at the tree cave with Nellie. I read the bear book aloud without stopping. I looked up with a flash of pride. But with my next breath, I slammed the cover shut.

"What?" said Nellie.

"This is stupid," I said. "I don't need to know about bears. I need . . . I need . . ." A wave slapped the rocks below. I thought of Mam, and my chest grew tight. I took a deep breath. "I need songs and stories and the lore of the sea."

Nellie nodded. "I think I know something you'll like."

"Go get it now," I urged.

"Why are you so impatient? I'll bring it tomorrow."

I wanted to tell her there wasn't time, but I forced the words back down.

The next day she brought a book with lots of letters and only a few pictures. I started reading aloud. It was the story of the selkie wife. I read faster, and then I wasn't reading aloud anymore, but in my own head.

Nellie pulled another book from her pack and started reading silently beside me.

I read and read, clawing my way through the words. It was hard work, but I finished the story before Nellie got up to go.

I scuffed at the stones as she ran off. I'd spent the whole morning on a story I'd already heard. Where were the clues to my turning? The books with magic? I thought back to the walrus and the story he wouldn't tell, so powerful it gave nightmares.

I had to get back into the aerie.

An amazing smell greeted me as I opened the door. Maggie was setting a platter on the kitchen table. She lifted her head with a smile.

"Come on in, Ocean Boy. Do you like chocolate cake?"

I'd never smelled anything like it before, so rich and dark and sweet. She cut thick slices and set them on plates. Three fat layers bound by glistening ribbons of filling.

I'd never eaten much of Maggie's food before, but she'd never baked before, either. I took one tentative bite.

That cake spoke to something in me I hadn't known existed. A kind of hidden . . . humanness. Suddenly I was shoveling the cake into my mouth.

Maggie fiddled with her fork. "You've been working so hard around here, I wanted to make you something special."

I nodded my thanks.

"I wish . . ." Her eyes were glittery. "I wish I wasn't sick. I wish I knew what Jack would do one day to the next. I wish . . ."

I stopped with the fork halfway to my mouth.

She sighed. "I wish I could do something for you. In case—"

I didn't like where this was going. "You made me a cake," I said. And I held up my plate for another slice.

CHAPTER FORTY-TWO
❧ THE THEFT ❧

Nellie didn't want to take me back to the aerie.

"I don't think Grandpa's ready to have you near his special books," she said.

"If we do it right, he'll never know." That didn't convince her, so I went on, "It's just, now that I can read, I want to choose my own books. Some of them could . . . call to me."

Telling the truth worked. Nellie got her determined expression.

"You're right. I need to choose my own books, too. Half the time I don't know if a book is for me until I start reading. Let me think."

In the end, we figured it out together. Nellie would tempt the walrus from the house by offering to carry his painting gear to a beautiful spot. She'd get him settled and leave him there until high sun, which she called noon. Then she'd go back to carry his gear home. That would leave us all morning with the house empty, and he wouldn't catch us by surprise.

He leaped at the offer.

The first day, when Nellie came back and led the way inside, she looked guilty. "He told me how thoughtful I was," she said. "It felt rotten."

And then she opened the door to the aerie.

Finally! I strode to the shelves. The last time I was here, I'd shouted at the books to speak. Why, they'd been speaking all along! I ran my finger down a spine. "*Tales from the Hearthside*," it proclaimed, as bold as thunder.

"What are you looking for?" said Nellie.

She was taking a big risk for me, but I still couldn't tell her. "Maybe stories," I said. After all, the story about the selkie wife had been packed with truth.

I chose a book of folktales. Nellie and I stretched out on the floor and read in silence. Every once in a while I glanced up at her. She was flipping pages quickly, chasing her story through the book.

Me, I trudged along. Reading was hard work, and my pages turned slowly. There were ghost ships, and mermaids, and a boy who rode a turtle to a world under the waves. I could smell the brine and hear the roar of the surf. But the sun was rising higher and I still hadn't found a single word about selkies. I drew in a quick, anxious breath.

Nellie misunderstood. "Don't worry," she said. "Grandpa won't come back until I fetch him. But we'd better go now."

We put our books back. Then we stopped by Nellie's room so she could get her backpack.

It wasn't anything like Tommy's room. She had shelf after shelf of books of her own, and a table with paper and little pots of color, and a row of rocks and shells. Next to her bed a small, round table held a lamp and a picture in a frame. I stepped closer. The picture showed Nellie with a man and a woman. The woman had golden hair and Nellie's gray eyes; the man had dark brown skin and Nellie's mouth and black hair. They both had their arms around Nellie.

"Is that part of your clan?" I asked.

"I guess you could say that." She pulled her pack out from under a pile. "It's my mom and dad."

∾ ∾ ∾

An endless week passed the same way. I'd be there when Nellie came back from taking the walrus, and then we'd run upstairs to the aerie. Each day I read faster. But in the aerie's stillness, time was tightening around me like a net.

One morning I found a book about seals in the far north. I read, hoping to find something about the wise ones. Snow and slush and ice; a low, gray sky—it pulled me deeper and deeper until I fell into a waking dream. *I was in my pelt, turning with a flick of my flippers, an effortless swish of my tail. In the distance, Mam lay on an ice floe. Then I saw three black dots creeping toward her—two eyes, a nose—a polar bear! I put on a burst of speed and vaulted onto the ice with a ferocious growl. As the polar bear reared up in surprise, Mam and I hurled ourselves into the water and sped away. . . .*

"What are you reading now?" said Nellie.

I startled back to the aerie and slammed the book shut.

"Stories," I said, disgusted.

Stupid stories. I'd been reading for days. Page after page, book after book. And what had I found? Nothing. Not one single clue. Not even a hint of magic. I wasn't one splash closer to my pelt and swimming off to help Mam.

I stormed back to the wall of books. Words had power.

That day in the cove, they'd gathered Mam's pelt. They had to help me now.

I shoved the book back on the shelf and tugged out the one next to it, a small, thin book with a dingy paper cover. I tossed it on the floor, opened a page at random, and read:

"*Sometimes the child of a selkie and a man is born—*"

I gasped.

"What?" said Nellie.

My heart was pounding so fast I couldn't answer.

Suddenly her head jerked up and she leaped to her feet. Then I heard it, too. Labored steps were approaching the house, *stomp-drag, stomp-drag—*

The walrus had come back on his own!

"Quick!" whispered Nellie. "Down to my room!"

In a flash we were bounding down the stairs. We flew past the front door—the knob was turning!—skittered around the corner, and flung ourselves through Nellie's door. She landed on the bed. I slid and sat on the floor. We stared at each other wide-eyed.

My fingers were throbbing. I looked down: I was still clutching the book.

"*NELLIE?*" shouted the walrus.

She ran from the room.

The book was burning up my hand. I'd been in the aerie. I'd taken a book. If the walrus found out, he'd never let me in the house again. He'd forbid Nellie to see me.

Down the hall, the walrus cried, "There you are!" I heard his cane clatter to the floor, the rustle of a hug.

I flipped the pages, frantically searching for the words I'd just read. *Sometimes the child of a selkie and a man* — what came next?

"I thought something had happened to you." The walrus's voice was muffled, as if his head was bent down to hers. "I was worried sick."

"I'm really sorry, Grandpa. Aran is here and we were playing. I forgot the time."

I was still turning pages.

"Where is this friend of yours, then?" said the walrus.

"In my room." Then, calling, "Aran!"

I stood and closed the book. The next thing I knew, I'd slipped it under the back waistband of my shorts and pulled my T-shirt down over it. I walked out carefully.

The walrus stood by the still-open door, an arm circling Nellie's shoulders.

"Hello, Aran," he said, smiling.

"Hi." I leaned my back against the wall. "Sorry I kept Nellie so long."

"Well, no harm done. My knee was better today. Perhaps I'll start going out on my own again."

"Oh, no, Grandpa!" Nellie gave me an anxious glance. "I like carrying your stuff. And . . . and getting fresh air and everything."

He motioned to the satchel at his feet. "Why don't you start by carrying that to the table, then? And you can get some fresh air fetching the rest of my gear after lunch."

He shuffled toward the living room. When he reached me, he paused. His eyes seemed to see right through me to the book gouging into my back.

"Will you join us for lunch?" he said.

It was all I could do to shake my head.

"Next time, then."

I sidled toward the door. Nellie was bending to pick up the satchel. I slipped past her, muttered a quick good-bye, and pulled the door shut behind me. I managed to walk slowly all the way to the corner of the house. Then I grabbed the book and ran.

CHAPTER FORTY-THREE

A CIRCLE OF LIGHT

I got back to find Maggie coughing worse than ever. She pressed a cloth to her mouth and it came away spotted with blood. She was gasping for air. I got her in the chair, brought her a blanket, and made her some coffee.

"Is there someone who can make you better?" I said. "Does that hospital have healers? Will Jack help you when I'm gone?"

"Never you mind," said Maggie. "And stop fussing over me like an old mother hen."

But I made her a can of soup, and I did her chores, and I watched her until she went to sleep.

Now I was lying on Tommy's bed. The lamp made a

small circle of light in the dark. I opened the book.

I wished I could skim through like Nellie, but I had to work for every word. It was old people telling true stories about selkies and seals. There were gruesome tales about hunting. Humans battered seals bloody on land and speared them at sea. They slashed off the fur to make coats and purses. One man said his purse was magic because it came from a selkie's pelt. There were stories of drowning men saved by seals, and selkies seen dancing beneath the full Moon—

And then there it was. *Sometimes the child* . . .

My heart pounded and the page went spinning. I had to stop and take a deep breath until the words settled into place.

An old woman was talking about a fisherman in her village who'd married a selkie, with dark eyes, white skin, and a voice like music. They had a son.

"*Sometimes the child of a selkie and a man is born in sealskin,*" the old woman said. "*Such a child soon slips into the sea and swims away. Other times the child's like his da, and never changes into a seal at all. But once in a rare while they come late to the changing. This lad grew up looking like every other child in the village. Then one day, on the verge of manhood, he ran to his da crying, 'What's gone wrong with my hands?' Between his fingers* were half-moons of skin, like the webbing between a seal's claws. The fisherman's heart was like to break. That morning he had a wife and a fine son. But come evening, he watched two seals swim away, and they never came home again."

On the verge of manhood—the boy was older than me when his pelt came! I turned the page.

"It was just as well they left. Why, you ask? If you're wishing to know what happens with those born half-selkie, you've only to look at 'The Tale of Westwood Pier.' And then you'll never ask again."

That was the end of her story. There was nothing about how he turned. For a moment I felt disappointed. But then I realized another clue was right in front of me. You've only to look at 'The Tale of Westwood Pier.' I read the rest of the book word for word, but the tale wasn't there.

Westwood Pier.

It started to rain, a steady pattering on the roof. I stared out the window at the dim light of morning. In my mind it became a fire's glowing embers, and there sat the walrus, the unlit pipe in his hand, saying, "'Westwood Pier'? But no, that wouldn't do for children."

I turned off the lamp and slipped the book under my pillow. I knew exactly what I had to do.

CHAPTER FORTY-FOUR
❧ THE TALE OF ❧ WESTWOOD PIER

I shook myself dry at Nellie's door and knocked.

"Come in!" she called.

I ran into the living room. A fire glowed red in the hearth and the walrus was settled in his chair. Nellie smiled at me.

"A story fire!" I said.

The walrus nodded. "If someone will fetch me my pipe."

Nellie dashed off and came back with the pipe, and I got the cookies. I sat down right across from the walrus in spite of the fire.

"I've got a fine South Sea adventure for you today," he said.

"Actually," I said, "we were hoping for 'The Tale of Westwood Pier.'"

Nellie's head shot up.

"Where did you hear about that one?" asked the walrus.

I shrugged. "You mentioned it once."

"Strong stuff, that story. A bit much for children."

"We're not babies!" said Nellie. "There are lots of scary stories in the books we read. What about the girl whose hair was knotted to the rocks by seaweed when the tide came in?"

He leaned back in his chair, looking at me with a raised eyebrow.

"I don't scare easily," I said.

"All right, then, but don't you come running to me complaining of nightmares. You know, I might need a match for this one."

He lit his pipe. The smoke curled around his white whiskers as he gazed into the fire, gathering the story's spark.

"Long ago," said the walrus, "in the village of Westwood, there lived a young man and his beautiful, black-haired bride. They'd been married for almost a year, and yet she was still a mystery to him. He'd never met her family—

'They wouldn't take to one like you!' was all she'd say—and she never once spoke about where she was raised. It didn't matter, because he loved her to distraction. She was his sun and his moon, his salt and his sweet. There was only one thing that bothered him. When the moon was full, he'd wake to find her slipping back under the covers before dawn, her hair damp and her skin smelling of the sea. 'Where have you been?' he'd ask her, and she'd laugh lightly and reply, 'Why, you've been dreaming again! I've been nowhere but right here beside you.'

"For a long time he chose to believe her. But one such morning, he left the house earlier than usual, and there was the path of her wet footprints, glistening in the morning sun. He followed them to the harbor and out to the end of the pier. With each step his heart grew blacker. 'A dream?' he said to himself. 'Another man, more likely.' And he came up with a plan.

"Come the next full moon, he told his wife he was going away for the night on business. But instead he went to the pub to gather his courage, and then he snuck down to the pier and hid beneath an overturned dinghy.

"Darkness settled in. The moon began to rise. The man heard an owl hoot a warning in the distance, and the flutter of bats on their nighttime hunt, and the pounding of his own suspicious heart. Finally he heard footsteps, and his wife's bare feet skipped right past his hiding place.

"He tilted the boat up a few inches and peered out. There she stood at the end of the pier, her long, black hair gleaming in the moonlight, her beauty more unearthly than ever before. She spread her arms wide and sang out in an eerie tune, 'Come to me! Come!'

"The man shivered. A splash came from the dark. It was no boat, no man, but a seal swimming toward her, and as it swam it sang in human tongue, 'Come to us! Come!' Another sleek head rose, and another, until the sea was full of seals swimming toward his wife, singing, 'Come to us! Come!'

"She dove, piercing the water with barely a ripple.

"Who was this woman he'd married, this woman he thought he knew? Sneaking off to swim with seals— no, not seals; they were selkies to sing like that—and she'd greeted them like kin. Now she was splashing and cavorting with the fey beasts. Though she had no sealskin, she looked at home in the water, strong and graceful, and never had he seen such happiness on her face. A thought pierced him like a dagger: What if she swam away with them and never came back? He leaped up, toppling the dinghy, and strode to the end of the pier.

"'Come here!' he shouted. 'Come here and come home with me!'

"The waters stilled. Every face turned toward him with those huge, dark eyes. And his wife's eyes—why, hers were as dark as theirs.

"'Go!' she cried, in a frightened voice. But it only made him more determined. If she wouldn't come, he'd catch her and drag her home. He dove into the bitter cold water. When he rose, the beasts had circled him. He took a stroke toward his wife.

"'No!' she cried. 'Go back, my love, go back!'

"But it was too late. The selkies had already slipped under the waves. Now they attacked from below. Jaws clamped around his feet, tighter than steel traps, and dragged him down into darkness. The man was strong— he thrashed to the surface once, and even once more— but the selkies were remorseless. They couldn't risk him telling the rest of the world what he'd seen. Their tails struck like hammers, their claws slashed flesh, and their teeth bit through bone. The roiling waters turned red.

"When all was done, nothing was left but a pile of bones on the ocean floor.

"His wife walked home alone that night. They say she never smiled again. She'd rise from her bed each full moon,

not to swim with the selkies—no, they never returned—
but to dive down and circle those bleached white bones.
You can still see them there, if you look closely among the
oyster shells off the end of Westwood Pier."

The walrus set his pipe down with a *thunk*. The story was
over. The fire was just a fire again. But the world had
changed.

"Aran?" Nellie's voice came from far away.

I saw the churning water, the pale arms thrashing, the
gleam of dark fur. The air was sharp with screaming and
the metallic scent of blood.

My head flew up. "It's a lie!"

"I warned you it's strong stuff," said the walrus.

"It's a lie! Selkies don't kill humans. Humans are
the killers! They catch selkies and cut off their pelts and
render their fat! They trap them in nets until they drown!
They put them in zoos and—"

My voice rang out so loud, it startled me into silence.
Nellie and the walrus were staring at me slack-jawed. I
was breathing fast. Too fast.

Finally the walrus spoke. "I admit it's an unusual tale."

"It's just a story," said Nellie.

I'd gone too far. "I know that," I said, trying to smile,

though from the look on Nellie's face it must have been a strange sort of grimace. "I mean, it's not what selkies in stories are supposed to be like, and that's, well, it's wrong, and . . ."

The walrus stepped in to save me. "I'm inclined to agree with you. It's almost as if the storyteller had confused a shark attack with a selkie tale. And there are other problematic points. If the wife is a selkie, why does she remain on land? Where is her sealskin, or the classic webbing between the fingers? And even if she's half-selkie, half-human, how could the husband not know? Such a jealous, suspicious man. Many of them are, in these stories." The walrus gave a disapproving sigh. "At any rate, I consider the story an oddity, an outlier. But no less interesting for that." He reached for his cane and hefted himself to his feet. "Who's joining me for a piece of toast?"

I shook my head. "I have to get back to Maggie's."

Nellie knew it was a lie. She followed me to the door and whispered, "What is it, Aran? Tell me."

I couldn't even look at her. I jerked the door open and ran out into the rain.

CHAPTER FORTY-FIVE
❧ THE TORRENT ❧

I ran and the land felt wrong under my feet and the air burned my lungs. I needed to be in the water away from houses and humans and smoke. I needed to be with my kin.

Was the story true?

It had our ritual greeting: *Come to me! Come!* That woman had no webbing, like I had no webbing. Her eyes were like theirs. She was half-selkie, I knew it, and she loved her kin, and she loved that man, and they killed him. Ripped off his flesh like salmon skin and left a pile of bones.

And my clan? At the first hint of humans, they'd

always rushed me into hiding. I'd thought they were just protecting me. But it was more than that. They couldn't risk being discovered. How far would they go to keep their existence a secret?

I shivered and stumbled as I ran. I'd begged for that story, but it wasn't about turning at all. It was a warning. About what happens if a half-selkie never turns.

Somewhere behind me, Nellie called, "Aran!" I glanced over my shoulder. There was a flash of movement back in the trees. "Aran, wait!"

That pile of bones at the foot of the pier. The man died. The selkies never came back. And that woman, the half-selkie, now she had no one.

I ran faster. The forest was a whirlwind of whipping branches and cracking twigs. The low roar of surf came through thinning trees. I'd dive in and never see Nellie again—

Her hand grabbed my shoulder and whipped me around. "You're one of them!" she cried.

My breath scraped the air like stone on stone.

"You're a selkie!" Nellie was smiling, a strange brightness in her eyes, like this was some kind of game. "I should have known. Remember how I thought you were a seal, that first time I saw you? And when I was drowning and you carried me to the rocks—no kid can swim like that! And the way you have to be so secret—"

I had to make her stop. I had to get away. But my feet were stuck to the ground.

"And the way you're so desperate to find stories about selkies, and how you said the one today was a lie, like you *knew*—"

Heat was rising inside me. Nellie's words were like dry wood tossed on a fire, sparking and ready to catch.

"You knew because you're one of them. You're a selkie, aren't you? Change for me! Show me how you do it!" She was so eager, like it was the easiest thing in the world. Like all I had to do was reach behind the closest rock and pull out a pelt—

It all burst into roaring flame. "Go away!" I shouted. Fire burned through my veins, and the world turned a searing, blinding red. "*Go away. GO AWAY!*"

But my voice faded, and Nellie was still there. She took a deep breath. Her eyes were thoughtful, figuring it out.

Now I could see too clearly. The red rage was slipping away. I tried to grab it back, so I wouldn't have to think or feel.

"That woman in the story," said Nellie. "The selkies were her family, weren't they?"

I gulped.

"But she didn't leave with them." Her voice dropped. "Maybe she couldn't. Maybe . . ."

"She didn't have a pelt," I said.

It was like a stick shifting in a logjam. The dam shuddered and burst, and the truth came rushing out in a wild, whirling torrent. "I don't have a pelt, either!" I cried. "I'm the only one in my clan in longlimbs and I can't keep up. I can't go on the long journeys or even the hunts, and Mam kept saying it would come any day, but it never did. And then the clan came back—"

I told her how the man came to our haulout, and I found out about my father, and how I'd counted on Moon Day. About Finn and the fight and the pelt cave, and how Mam insisted on swimming north to the wise ones instead of me. How she should have been back by the second full Moon, and I knew she was in danger. . . .

Nellie listened until it was all out. Every last, terrible word.

We walked from the trees to the top of the bluff. I sat beside her in the rain.

"You need your family," she said, soft but determined.

I nodded.

"And your pelt." She turned and looked into my eyes.

"I'll be your partner. We'll figure it out together."

"No. Not after that story. What if you're with me and . . ." I couldn't finish the sentence. I was seeing the attack again, but this time the arms rising from the water were Nellie's, thin and brown.

"Selkies aren't like that," she said firmly. "You said so yourself. And you know better than some stupid story."

I should refuse. I should swim away and never see her again. But to have her by my side, not to be alone with the searching anymore . . .

"You wouldn't tell?" I said.

She shook her head. "What do you think I am?"

In the old days, I would have said, *human*. But now I put my hand on hers, on the rain-speckled grass, and said, "My friend."

CHAPTER FORTY-SIX
❧ BIRDTALK ❧

I burst from the water and slapped the rock near shore, sending a spray of drops sparkling in the sun.

"Time?" I called, panting.

Back on the beach, Nellie looked up from her watch. "Four minutes, thirty-seven seconds." She wrote the time in her notebook. "Only five seconds faster. Do it again."

"What am I aiming for?"

"Four and a half."

I had cut my time from here to a rock in the strait by half a minute. But Nellie insisted I should be doing it in four minutes flat. She was keeping track of my times in her book. She'd set up what she called a training schedule, so

I'd be strong enough to swim off, with a pelt or without. And maybe, just maybe, the Moon would notice. I thought I'd been pushing myself hard before, but it was nothing compared to how strong I was getting with Nellie on my side.

"Come on, lazybones," she said. "Get going."

I threw my head back in mock agony. And there, peering down from the top of the rocks, was a puffin. She nodded a greeting.

It was the puffin I'd helped at Maggie's!

I wanted Nellie to meet her. I stood and called in birdtalk, "Where does the wind carry you?"

The puffin cocked her head toward Nellie.

"She good," I said. "Friend."

The puffin flew down and settled on my outstretched arm.

Nellie gasped, her pencil clattering onto the pebbles. But she didn't jump or shout or do anything to scare the puffin. That was how she was—she just knew.

The puffin bowed her head and grunted, "Me find flock. Good."

She looked plump and healthy, and her feathers were sleek.

"You alone?" I asked.

"Flock near. Me come find you. Thank you." She nuzzled my ear.

"Oh!" Nellie said softly. "You're talking with it!"

I grinned. "Basic birdtalk. Want to learn some?"

She nodded, wonderstruck. I motioned her over. She set down the watch and notebook and waded in, thigh deep, over to my rock. I explained to the puffin what we were doing, and she perched between us.

"What do you want to learn to say?" I asked Nellie.

"Um, how about your name."

I said my name in birdtalk. Then the puffin grunted it, nodding to show she was glad to know what to call me. Then Nellie tried. But she had no idea which part of the sounds mattered. She sounded like a sick goose. The puffin and I laughed.

"Cut it out!" said Nellie, laughing, too. "Let me try again."

I said, "Aran."

The puffin said, "Aran."

Nellie said, "Eel bottom."

The puffin chortled so hard, she lost her footing and flapped to catch her balance.

"Stop it!" said Nellie, laughing. "Say it again."

"Aran," said the puffin.

Nellie's brows lowered in concentration. "Flat bottom."

"Aran," said the puffin.

"Ar-tom," said Nellie. "Ar-om. Aran!"

"That's it!" I cried.

Nellie clasped her hands overhead.

"Good, good," said the puffin. "More talk."

I pulled the stone selkie from my pocket. No one else had ever seen it before.

Nellie drew in a breath, then reached over and ran a finger along its smooth stone back. "It's beautiful," she said.

"Selkie," I said in birdtalk.

"Selkie," said the puffin, with an encouraging look.

"Sea foot," said Nellie.

But with every word, she learned faster, sorting out the trills from the chirps, discovering the importance of pitch. She had almost mastered, "Where does the wind carry you?" when the puffin hopped to my shoulder, nuzzled my cheek, and said, "Me go. See flock."

I translated for Nellie.

"Please tell her thank you," she said.

We watched the puffin flap away across the water.

Nellie sighed in contentment. "This is the best day ever."

As usual, I felt the boat before I saw it. This time Nellie felt it, too. It crested the horizon, chugging its way toward Spindle Harbor.

"There goes your chance to make a better time," said Nellie.

"Just wait until tomorrow." I waded with her through the water, the pebbles rolling underfoot. "I'm going to break four and a half, easy."

We ran up the trail, then slowed and walked side by side through the trees until our paths split.

"Good-bye," I said in birdtalk.

"What did you say?"

"Eel bottom!"

Our laughter was a ray of light, linking us as we waved good-bye.

I walked the long way back to Maggie's, holding on to the bright afternoon, and the joy of seeing the puffin again, and Nellie's attempts at birdtalk. I rolled the stone selkie in my hand. "Sea foot," I said, laughing. I barely noticed when I stepped out of the trees and started walking across the gravel toward Maggie's door. I was hearing the puffin chortle and seeing the concentration on Nellie's face —

And then a huge hand clamped down on my shoulder.

"Tommy?" said a deep voice, breaking. "Tommy, is that you?"

CHAPTER FORTY-SEVEN
❧ JACK ❧

He spun me around. I stared up into a stubbled face, lined and leathered by the sun. I smelled smoke and sweat, and something sickly sweet on his breath. He pulled me closer, his eyes struggling to focus.

"Tommy?" he said, less certain this time.

My heart was pounding out of my chest. He wasn't supposed to be here yet! I forced myself not to run.

Now he really saw me. His brows lowered. "Who are you?" he demanded. "What are you doing at my house? In Tommy's clothes?" His grip tightened on my shoulder. *"What are you doing with his seal?"*

He shook my shoulder until words came tumbling

out. "I—I—I live here," I stuttered. "My mam's finding a place for us to live, and it's secret with the divorce—"

"Maggie would have told me," he growled.

But I couldn't stop, and now Maggie's story got mixed in with Mam's. "—And my father can't know, and I'm Maggie's nephew, and my mam will—"

"Well, that's a lie. She doesn't have a nephew." He let go of my shoulder and grabbed my wrist. "Give it to me."

My stone selkie, my gift from the Moon—

And then Maggie was at the door. "Aran!" she shouted. "Give it to him!" It was too much for her. She shuddered, struggling to hold back a cough, and then hunched in pain as it ripped through her. Jack and I stared, frozen.

"Go on," Maggie gasped between coughs. "Give him the seal."

I opened my hand. The stone selkie lay on my palm, staring up at me—and then Jack snatched her and she was gone.

Inside, I rubbed my sore wrist while Maggie made Jack a cup of coffee. They sat at the kitchen table. He took a slim bottle from his pocket and poured something into the mug. It was the sickly sweet smell on his breath.

"Welcome home," said Maggie. "I didn't expect you for a few weeks yet."

Jack's head drooped and he stared down at his mug. "Yeah, well, that idiot captain decided he wanted a smaller crew. Too cheap to split the profits. Didn't even give me half of what I should've made." He took a leather holder from his pocket and threw it on the table.

But Maggie's sad eyes were resting on the bottle. "Again, Jack?"

He glowered at her, his hands tightening around the mug. "That's not the point, Maggie." He lifted his head and leaned forward like he was ready to fight. "What's this kid doing here, in my house, in my son's room? He's wearing Tommy's clothes! What the hell haven't you been telling me, Maggie?" Now he was yelling, and Maggie shrank down small. "I go off to work and it's like I don't even exist! Who's the kid, and what's he doing living in my house?" He slapped his hands down on the table, like he was going to push himself up. Then he'd be towering over her.

"I'll go," I said, inching toward the door.

"Oh, no you don't," said Jack. "Not until someone tells me what's going on."

For some reason Maggie didn't tell him about Mam coming in the middle of the night. She spun a story with lots of fake details about how she'd met my mother at the store, and something about common names and a phone number that wasn't working. But the last part was all too true. "She should have been back by now," said Maggie. "She must have run into trouble."

Jack shook his head. "Not our problem. Call Social Services. What do we pay taxes for? He can go into foster care."

My gut wrenched around. I hadn't expected to have to swim off so soon.

Then Jack's big hands cradled his mug. In a softer voice, he said, "You're sick, Maggie. Taking care of a kid's going to make you sicker. And we can't afford another mouth to feed."

I was waiting for her to agree. She was wringing her hands, over and under, over and under. She looked up at him. "I . . . I like having him here, Jack."

The softness fled. His face darkened. He stood, banging his chair into the table. At the counter, he jerked a drawer open and pulled out a ring jangling with metal shards.

"I'm going to have a drink with Harry," he said.

"You shouldn't be driving," said Maggie.

He slammed the drawer and stormed out. The truck sped off in a spray of gravel.

∾ ∾ ∾

Maggie was breathing shallow and fast, with a strange, wheezing sound. I helped her into the big chair by the fire. Her head fell back against the faded fabric. In her lap, her hands lay still and twisted, the dried-out roots of a toppled tree.

When she finally spoke, her voice came from far away. "Oh, Lord, Aran. What were you doing with Tommy's seal?"

It felt like a slap in the face. The stone selkie couldn't be Tommy's. She was my courage. My gift from the Moon.

"Jack won it in a card game in Alaska. Said it was worth something, given how much they were betting. He carried it around like a lucky charm. Things were good back then. He worked hard. Didn't drink much. The captains always took him on."

I didn't want to listen. I turned my head away, but she kept talking.

"He gave it to Tommy on his fifth birthday. You should have seen that boy's eyes light up. He was always playing with it, making it little hidey-holes. He slept with it under his pillow. Jack would come home after months on the boat, and there'd come Tommy, running up with that seal in his hand." She gave a deep sigh. "Lord, he loved that boy."

Her voice grew lower.

"Jack was off on a salmon boat when Tommy got the fever. He was burning up. No matter what I did, the fever wouldn't go down. Then he was writhing and twisting and didn't know me anymore. I was so scared! I carried him out to the pickup and drove to the dock. The boat, the ambulance . . . I was sitting by his bed in the hospital, that cold, white room. Trying to get through to Jack on his boat. Holding Tommy's hand. And then the doctor's face . . ."

Her own face was as white as bone. The only thing left was sorrow; everything else had leached away.

"Back home, after we buried him, Jack searched for that seal for days. Like it could bring Tommy back." She looked at me, shaking her head. "And now it turns up in your hand."

Then she caught herself. She sat up straighter and tried to smile. "Don't you worry, Aran. Jack's all right when he doesn't drink. I'll figure something out. We still have a little time."

Her words were brave, but her eyes said she didn't know what to do.

CHAPTER FORTY-EIGHT
❧ THREE LITTLE COINS ❧

Jack got up late the next morning. He filled the whole house. His steps were loud, and his voice was loud, and he kept banging things down or crashing into them. The louder he got, the quieter Maggie got. She was shrinking away.

He was walking through the living room when he knocked against the round table by Maggie's chair. Everything went skidding off. He picked up the box of Kleenex, the small bowl . . .

"What's this?" he said. In his palm were two of the doubloons. He stood and turned one over. He ran a finger across the raised marks.

Maggie came to the kitchen door, wiping her hands

with a towel. "That's just Aran's pirate gold. Toy gold. He brought them when he came." She walked over and held out her hand. "Here, I'll put them back."

She'd kept them close by her chair since the second full Moon.

He was weighing the coins. "Where'd you say they come from?"

"His mom gave them to him," said Maggie.

Jack held one up to the window. "Maggie, that looks like real gold to me."

She snorted. "And I'm the queen of England."

He picked up the third doubloon from the floor. "Are there more?"

"No, that's it," said Maggie. "Come on, I'll put them back."

But Jack put them in his pocket. They clinked against the stone selkie, and I winced.

"I'm going to find Harry," he said, walking to the kitchen. He came back with the ring of metal shards. "Might take a boat to the big island and have someone take a look at those coins. Just in case." He opened the door. "Don't wait dinner."

As soon as the truck rumbled away, I dashed outside. I had to swim off some tension, or I wouldn't be able to think or sleep or figure out what to do. I was clambering down—and then stopped, staring at the stone selkie's empty cave.

Tommy's seal.

Maggie's story churned around inside me. Was the stone selkie still mine? Had she *ever* been mine? My face was burning hot. Clenching my teeth, I climbed down to the rocks and dove. And then I swam fast and hard for a long, long time, trying to wash the thoughts away.

I was climbing back up the cliff when the truck growled into earshot. It skidded to a stop. I reached the top in time to see Jack striding to the door. "Maggie!" he called, pulling it open. "Maggie, guess what!"

I shook myself dry. Through the window, I saw him standing over Maggie's big chair. He reached into his pocket.

"Look, Maggie, look!" he crowed. "We're rich!"

I walked up to the house and stood quietly by the open door, where I could see better. He was thrusting out a handful of green paper.

"All that for three little coins!" Jack said.

Maggie looked at the wad of green paper in her lap, her eyes widening. "You mean they were *real*?"

"Gen-u-ine, finest quality, treasure-chest gold! So old it's worth a bundle."

She picked up the green paper and started leafing through, staring at the numbers in the corners. Her mouth fell open.

Jack looked taller, his eyes brighter. "Maggie, listen, I got a plan. That's enough right there for a down payment on a fishing boat. Not anything fancy, something used— I'll need to do a lot of work on it—but a boat, Maggie. A boat of my own."

Her hands had stilled in her lap.

"I'll be my own boss," said Jack. "No more getting fired, no more worrying about a paycheck. I'll work hard and make the payments and there'll be enough left over. There'll be money for doctors, Maggie. It'll take awhile, but—"

"No," said Maggie. It was her determined voice, the one that said she wasn't going to budge.

Jack jerked back. The air bristled around him. "*What?*"

Maggie stood up. "That money belongs to Aran."

What was she doing? She needed to stop before he got angry. I took another step into the room. "Maggie . . ." I said.

Maggie kept talking. "His mom gave it to him. If she

doesn't come back, he'll need it. To have a stake. Make something of his life. Maybe go to college."

Didn't she see the tension coiling in Jack's arms? Now I was really getting worried. "I don't need it," I said, but no one seemed to hear me.

Jack's mouth had narrowed to a thin slash. "What about *us*, Maggie?" He was breathing hard. "What about *our* life?"

Maggie shook her head. Her voice was as clear as it was sad. "It's too late for us, Jack."

His hands clenched into huge fists at his sides, tight as rocks. And his eyes—I knew the feeling behind that look. It was red rage, about to spark and set him on fire. If he stopped thinking, if he let loose, what would he do? And Maggie just stood there, unbowed.

The next thing I knew, I was standing between her and Jack.

His chest was heaving up and down. He stared at her, at me—and then he threw back his head and roared, shaking the walls of the room. He raised his fist and my heart stopped—

He turned and slammed his fist right through the wall. Bits of wall exploded everywhere. A picture tumbled down and glass shattered across the floor. Maggie gasped and pulled me close.

Jack yanked his fist back through and stood there panting. We all stared at the jagged, gaping hole. There was nothing but the sound of his rough breath, and Maggie's, and mine.

Without another word, Jack turned and stormed out, slamming the door behind him.

CHAPTER FORTY-NINE

❧ TOO DANGEROUS ❧ TO HANDLE

As soon as he'd driven off, I mumbled an excuse to Maggie and ran out the door. I didn't know what to do. There were too many parts, all crashing together. How could I swim away, now that I'd seen Jack's anger? Maggie usually shrank small around him; that meant he got angry a lot. She wasn't safe alone with him. But I made him even angrier. And then there was the boat. If I could convince Maggie to give him the money, would she be all right? Or would Jack still drink and get angry all over again?

It was too much for me. I needed Nellie's help.

She was pacing in front of her house with a book in

her hands and a strange, intent expression on her face. As soon as she saw me she ran over.

"Nellie, I need to—"

"Aran, I found—" She stopped, staring at the ring of bruises around my wrist.

Before she could start again I said, "Tree cave. Come on."

We ran all the way, and I *needed* to run—up hill and through forest, over stone and stream—my feet striking the ground, the air surging through my lungs. We burst out of the trees and onto the shore. I drew in a deep breath of salty air.

We crawled into the tree cave and sat cross-legged on the smooth rock.

"What happened to your wrist?" said Nellie.

"Jack—" For a moment that was all I could say. Then, "He's back, and he took my stone selkie—"

Nellie gasped.

"And—" I struggled to drag out the words. "He gets really mad. He put his fist through the wall. I—I'm afraid he's going to hurt Maggie."

"What about you?" Nellie reached out and, very gently, traced a finger along my wrist. "Those are bruises. He hurt *you*."

"It's not me I'm worried about. I can handle it."

"Maybe . . ." She swallowed. "Aran, maybe some

things are too dangerous to handle. Like Jack. And like . . ." She paused, clenching the book, and then her words came spilling out.

"Listen, there's a story in here about this old woman. She always wears gloves, but one day she pulls them off and shows her grandson this extra skin between her fingers. That's the webbing, right? So she's a selkie, and—"

"Nellie," I said. "It doesn't matter. We have to help Maggie. If I leave—"

"No, you have to hear this part! Her son told her to hide the webbing, but she says she earned it—that means her pelt, right?—because the Moon set her a test. And then she tells her grandson"—Nellie leafed through the pages—"Here it is. She says, '*Should you ever find yourself facing that test, think long and hard. Don't risk it unless you can't live without it. It might cost you everything. A love, a life—*'"

Nellie slammed the book shut. "See? It's too dangerous, trying to get you to turn."

I shook my head. "Pups turn all the time. Listen, Maggie wants to give—"

"But don't they do it younger? Maybe the older you get, the more dangerous it is. Didn't you hear what the old woman said? It could cost a life. *Your* life, Aran." She looked back down at the book in her lap and said softly,

"You know, being human's not so bad."

I could see her heart beating at the base of her throat.

She sat up tall. "Come live with us!" she urged, her eyes intense and bright. "I know Grandpa will say yes. And Maggie can tell your mother where you are, and we'll be together all the time. Please say yes, Aran. *Please!*"

I thought of story fires and cookies and big windows looking out at the sea.

And then I thought of Jack's fist crashing through the wall.

"I can't," I said. "Not until I know Maggie's safe."

"Come now! Grandpa and I are going to the big island to get online and talk to my parents. I don't like leaving you here. Come with us."

"I told you, I'll be fine. Didn't I come meet you today, same as always?"

She sighed, her shoulders slumping. Then she pulled back a branch and looked out. "The sun's setting. I need to go. Think about what I said, okay?"

We clambered out onto the rocks. She reached for my hand and held it for a moment before she ran off. I kept staring at the spot where she'd disappeared. My head was full of cross currents, all rough chop, and no way through.

CHAPTER FIFTY

❧ A BIT OF ADVICE ❧

I knew I should go right back to Maggie's, but I couldn't face Jack. I swam for a long time, trying to make sense of everything—Maggie, and Mam, and gold, and the boat— but I only got more confused. By the time I got back it was late. The house stood silent, the windows dark. I breathed a sigh of relief.

I hadn't done any chores that day, so now I gathered an armload of firewood and brought it inside. I knelt and, as quietly as I could, stacked it by the woodstove. I stood up—

"Hey, kid," said Jack.

I whirled around. He was leaning back in the other

chair, the one Maggie put me in the first night I came. His legs were spread wide, his shirt unbuttoned and open over his wrinkled T-shirt. His hand rested on the bottle. Now I smelled its sweetness over the wood and ash.

"Have a seat," said Jack, gesturing to Maggie's chair with the bottle. The words were fuzzy at the edges. "Go on, sit. Maggie's asleep with her pain pills. It's too quiet in here."

I backed up and sat at the very end of the chair, alert and wary.

"What?" said Jack. "Can't we have a little talk? I'd offer you a drink—" He looked at the bottle, at me, and then settled it back in his lap. "Nope. Kids don't drink. Shouldn't drink. Bad for you." He nodded sagely.

If I sat still long enough, maybe he'd fall asleep and I could sneak away.

"Tell you what, kid. I'll give you something else. A bit of advice. How's that?" When I didn't answer, he said sharply, "Well?"

"Sure," I said.

He nodded and leaned back in the chair. And then, like it was precious information, he said, "You gotta take care of yourself in this world." He looked at me, waiting.

"Okay," I said.

"No one else is gonna do it for you. You think you got

a job, you can pay your bills, put food on the table. Then it's gone." He took a swig from his bottle. "You think you got a family. Think they love you, got your back. Like I had Tommy . . ."

His voice went raw. "I was at sea. Maggie tried to call. The radio wasn't working. And when it did . . . when it did, he was already dead." He took a long drink. "And Maggie. When I got home, she'd gone stone cold. Her face was white. 'Go work,' she told me. Said we needed the money. But that wasn't the whole story. She wanted to be alone. Shut off her heart. Then her heart started dying for real." He lifted the bottle toward me. "Right?" he barked.

"Right," I whispered. I glanced at the door, longing to be gone.

"I'm not enough for her. Can't make her happy. Can't even keep a roof over her head." He sighed. "I finally get a chance to make a real living, and she won't let me take it."

His free hand was clenching into a fist. I glanced at the hole in the wall.

"You can have it!" I said. "The gold, or the"—what was the word?—"the money. I don't want it. My mam's coming back for me, and if she doesn't I'll go find her. You can have it."

"Coming back." He gave a bitter laugh. "You think

your mom's coming back? You're kidding me, right? How long have you been here?"

I gulped. "Almost three months."

"And she's how late?" The laugh didn't reach his eyes. He took another drink. "She's not coming back. Don't you get it? She doesn't want you anymore. Couldn't handle telling you to your face, so she made up some story and dumped you here."

I clenched the arms of the chair. "No, she's hurt," I said, trying to convince myself. "That's why she's not here. She's hurt or in danger."

He leaned forward, like he was sharing a secret, showing me how the world worked. "If she really loved you, she'd be by your side right now."

I leaped to my feet. "That's a lie!"

He looked lighter now, like the weight of all he'd said had lifted off his chest. But his pain had become my pain. It gnawed at my gut, at my throat. It *couldn't* be true.

Then I remembered Mam dancing with Lyr at Moon Day. She'd looked so alive and free. I hadn't made her that happy for a long time. I was the weight she had to carry on her back. I was why she couldn't go on the long journeys with the clan.

I've found a place for you to stay, she'd said.

And the stone selkie wasn't a selkie; she wasn't even a gift from the Moon. The Moon didn't see me after all. Maybe she'd never seen me. Had Mam ever planned to bring me a pelt, or was it a trick to get me here? Now she could travel as far and as long as she liked. She wasn't stuck alone with me anymore.

"Leave you," muttered Jack, his head falling back against the chair. His eyes closed. "They leave you. Every. Single. One."

I sat on top of the cliff until the tide was ebbing. Then I climbed down, so I could sleep on the rocks with my feet in the waves. Right at the shoreline, because that's what selkies do. The clouds hung low and the sky pressed down, empty and black. The wind sang an eerie tune along the stone walls.

I hated the thoughts Jack had planted in my brain. I tried to shut them out. But the more I pushed them away, the more the waves murmured, "Leave you . . . leave you . . . leave you . . ."

I pressed my hands against my ears.

I'd trusted Mam. I'd counted on her to come back with my pelt. But she'd worked so hard to leave me with humans.

Other times the child's like his da, and never changes into a seal at all . . .

Half human. Half selkie. Not a whole anything. Where did I belong?

CHAPTER FIFTY-ONE
❧ THE KEYS ❧

I woke in the water with a sputter and gasp. A wave had washed me off the rocks. The sky was already light. I hauled out and shook myself dry.

When I reached the top of the cliff, the truck was gone.

Inside, Maggie was leaning over the sink and coughing, the sponge in her hand. "House is a mess," she wheezed.

"Let me," I said.

I led Maggie to her big chair. I made her some coffee. She had a few sips, then her head fell back and she was asleep, the mug still in her hands. I set it on the table. I'd never seen her look so gray. And her legs looked funny— puffy and swollen.

She'd been doing too much. I hadn't been helping enough.

So I got to work. I washed the dishes and dried them and put them away, quietly, so I wouldn't wake her up. I swept the floor in every single room. I emptied the trash into the big bin at the back of the house.

Maggie stirred, and I made her a can of soup. She'd stopped asking me if I wanted some a long time ago. She took a spoonful, and another, then set the bowl back down.

And Jack was still gone. The air in the room felt lighter. We could pretend life was normal again, the way it had been.

I should talk with her about what to do, about where she could go and where I could go. I should make sure she wasn't sending me inland. But I couldn't figure out how to start.

I went gathering, and brought her mussels wrapped in seaweed, and put them in a bowl in the refrigerator. I heated up her soup and brought it back again, and she took another sip. "I'll be up in a minute," she said.

It was already past high sun. Maybe I should tell Maggie about Nellie. We could talk to the walrus. He'd help us figure out what to do.

"Maggie—" I said.

But she heard the tone in my voice and stopped me with

a shake of her head. "I just want to enjoy this quiet with you, Ocean Boy. There'll be plenty of time to talk later."

And then there wasn't.

Because the truck came growling up from the road. It lurched to a stop and Jack stumbled out.

Maggie gripped the arms of her chair.

Jack swept in like a storm. The air crackled in his wake. He reeked of smoke and the stuff he drank. He reached in his pocket and threw something down on the round table beside Maggie. Pieces of metal on a metal cord. He looked at Maggie like he was daring her. His chest rose and fell.

"What's that?" said Maggie, too quiet. It wasn't a question. She already knew.

"That's the keys to my new boat."

"Your boat." Her mouth was a thin, hard line.

"I had to act fast, or she might have been gone."

Her hands tightened. "I told you, that money belongs to Aran."

I wanted to tell her it was fine, that Jack should keep the boat, but my mouth wouldn't open.

Jack shoved his hands in his pockets. He looked out the window. "I figured you didn't really think it through, Maggie."

Slowly, with great effort, she pressed herself to

standing. "You figured wrong," she said. "You're going to take that boat back."

He tugged his hands from his pockets. The stone selkie flew out and skittered across the floor. Then his hands were fists. His shoulders lowered. He stepped closer.

"The hell I am," he said.

Maggie stood tall. "If you keep that boat, it's stealing," she said. "The money is Aran's."

How could I make them stop? Jack's tension filled the whole room, so tight it was about to snap—

They both grabbed for the keys at the same instant. Jack fumbled and Maggie snatched the keys in her fist, pulling them up and away from the table. Jack grabbed her wrist and jerked her close, and she stumbled, trying to catch her balance. The room was full of rage and fire, and I was dry tinder.

"Leave her alone!" I shouted, heat growing in my chest.

Jack didn't hear me. He was beyond hearing. His grip tightened on Maggie's wrist. "Give me the keys!" he said, and Maggie's mouth dropped open in pain.

And then I was beyond hearing, too. I had to make him stop. But he was so much bigger than me. I reached for the first thing at hand—an empty bottle in the seat of Jack's chair—and raised it over my head.

The motion caught Jack's eye. He dropped Maggie's

wrist and whirled around, staring at me, panting. He lowered his head, and my grip tightened around the bottle's hard, cold neck, and I held it high—

"Stop it!" screamed Maggie. "Both of you! Stop it right now! Stop—"

Her breath caught. A shudder ran through her like an earthquake. She struggled to draw in a breath—a terrible, endless gasping sound. Her eyes went wide. She froze, and the keys fell from her hand and clattered to the floor. Then she slumped like there was nothing holding her up anymore—no bones, no breath—and slid to the ground.

She wasn't moving. Her arm was crumpled under her.

"Maggie!" Jack dropped to his knees beside her. "Maggie, come on, Maggie, wake up!" He reached an arm under her shoulders. Her head lolled to the side, the whites of her eyes showing.

The bottle dropped from my hand.

Jack stared up at me. *"Look what you've done!"* he cried.

Then he was gathering Maggie up in his arms. "We'll take Harry's speedboat," he said, as if she could hear him. "Get you to the hospital. Hold on." He staggered to his feet.

Was she breathing? I couldn't see her breathing.

He carried her to the truck. The engine roared to life, and they were gone.

CHAPTER FIFTY-TWO
❧ GONE ❧

The air smelled singed. My breath came in short, sharp gasps. The boat keys lay splayed on the floor by Maggie's chair.

What had I done?

The open door swayed back and forth in the wind. The bottle rolled at my feet. The bottle I'd been about to crash down on Jack's head.

I crumpled over. What had happened to me? What was I turning into?

"No," I whispered.

I should have stayed calm. I should have pulled out the words trapped in my throat. But I'd let that rage blind me. I made Maggie scream.

The human side of me was taking hold. I shivered. I couldn't breathe, I couldn't think. I had to get out.

I was halfway across the room when I remembered my knife. I ran back to Tommy's room, shoved the boxes aside, and pulled it from the gap. My hands trembling, I strapped on the sheath—I had to jerk the cord, it had grown so tight—and then I ran outside into the wind.

I ran through the tossing trees, the late afternoon sky low and dark, my feet pounding a raw path. I ran blind, until I skidded around a rock—the whale rock. Now I knew where I was going. Nellie's.

I burst through the trees and pounded on her door. "Nellie!" I cried. There was no answer. I grabbed the knob; it didn't turn. "Nellie, let me in!"

I ran around the house trying every window. Nellie's slid open. I hoisted myself to the sill and jumped down into her room.

The bed wasn't its usual tumble of pillows; the covers were pulled crisp. She'd shoved the piles of clothes from the floor into the closet. I pulled them out, searching—her backpack was gone. On the bedside table, the picture of her parents was set at a careful angle beside the lamp. What was it she'd said in the tree cave? Something about talking to her parents . . . and going to the big island . . .

I ran into the living room. The fire was dead. The house echoed around me, as empty as an abandoned nest.

They were gone.

A sob wrenched from my throat. I stumbled toward the door.

Nellie said being human wasn't so bad. But that fury had burned through my veins. Just like the men in all the stories. I'd let my human side out, and now look what I'd done. I couldn't let it take hold. I *wasn't* human. I wouldn't be.

Somehow the door was open behind me. There was grass underfoot, then rock . . .

Waves rushed over my ankles. I was standing on the cusp of Nellie's cove.

This was where Nellie and I searched for blue. Where I found the pearl and put it in the mussel shell. The light had shimmered between them like they belonged together.

But it was a lie. You couldn't live in a borrowed shell.

The waves crashed over my legs. My waist. My chest. A whitecap rose higher and higher, foam flying, until it towered over me in a roaring arc.

I dove.

And then I swam, leaving Spindle Island, and my life as a human, behind me forever.

PART THREE
SHORE

CHAPTER FIFTY-THREE
⧸ LOST ⧹

The clouds darkened, the waves raged higher, and still I swam. Spindle Island had disappeared behind me long ago. There was no rock, no resting place. No current to carry me. Day sank and the waters turned black. I dragged up one aching arm and then another, over and over, until I was nothing but a sack of skin, a tumble of bones.

A swell swept me under and spat me out. I rose crying to the Moon for help, but the words stuck in my throat. She didn't see me. She'd never seen me. I was alone.

One arm and then another . . .

∾ ∾ ∾

I woke on an exposed knob of rock, my head pounding, my body crumpled in pain. Hunger gnawed at my gut. I crawled across the rocks and ripped off fistfuls of sea lettuce, cramming them into my mouth, barely stopping to chew.

The rising tide swallowed my rock and I swam.

There were boats. I swam underwater, coming up between swells for quick gulps of air. Another day darkened and fled. One arm and then another.

The tide washed me up on a small, barren island. I crawled above the tideline and fell into a dead sleep. When I woke, the tide was two days higher. I gulped down barnacles and mussels, and slept some more. I dove for crabs and shrimp. Finally I was strong enough to hunt.

I searched in the driftwood and found a long, straight stick. I lashed my knife to the end. The perch in the kelp didn't see me coming. Nothing ever tasted more delicious than that first bite. I sucked every scrap of flesh off the bones.

I took off into open ocean, no land in sight. Somehow, by nightfall, I found a place to haul out. Each night, a different place. The days blurred into each other.

One evening the setting sun broke out from behind

a cloud, filling the sky with red flames. "Nellie, look!" I cried, turning as if she were there by my side. But the rocks beside me were empty.

Tears pricked at my eyes. I blinked them back, furious with myself. I wouldn't think about Nellie. That part of my life was gone. And I wouldn't, I mustn't, give my human side any room to take hold.

Day by day, from skelly to sandbank, from reef to spit, I made my way farther from humankind. Farther from the threat that lurked inside me.

One arm and then another.

One morning I speared my biggest catch yet—a fine black cod—and started lugging it back to my haulout. An eagle circled overhead. Before I could dive, it swooped down in a blur and ripped the fish from my hands, gigantic wings batting my face, bone-crushing talons only a breath away from my hands. It flew off with the fish dangling from its feet. My stomach growled.

I learned to brandish my knife and yell when eagles flew over, so they'd think twice and go scavenge an easier meal somewhere else.

My knife was my salvation: stabbing, slashing, slitting, spearing. Its weight in my hand gave me strength.

Mist gave way to rain, and rain to sleet. One night I

fell asleep on a low island, blind to the clouds gathering on the horizon. In the black of night, a storm surge swept me off the rocks and into the raging sea. I swam in the swells until morning, gasping for air. I finally landed on a higher haulout, and swore I'd never let it happen again.

Now, day after day, I studied the clouds and the currents and the birds. I watched for patterns in the waves. I learned to feel the air's pressure in my head and on my skin. In time I could tell a storm was coming days before the first drop of rain.

Why had I never asked Mam to teach me how to find haulouts? The good ones were few and far between, and if I failed to find one, I had to swim through the night. It was even harder getting enough to eat. Growing up, I'd thought I was a good hunter. Mam had always praised my skills. But I'd only been nabbing easy prey near shore. Now the easy prey wasn't there.

I studied the paths the fish followed, the depth and currents each liked. When I saw gulls diving, I rushed over to hunt alongside them, dodging their beaks and squawks of complaint. When fish leaped in high, frantic arcs, it meant orcas were on the hunt. I waited until the great black fins swam away. Then I swam out and scavenged what was left in their wake.

The Moon waxed and waned and waxed again.

One arm and then another.

I was swimming far from land when the water brought the beat of flippers. At first I thought it was seals, but their motion was too wild and rough. Then they swam into view. Not seals: sea lions.

I kept swimming. They'd ignore me; I wasn't food for them.

A bull broke away and swam over to get a better look. Even though he was young, he must have weighed fifteen times as much as me. He circled once, twice. Then his nose bumped me and I gasped as his entire length grazed my side, rolling me over and over like a log.

I sighed in relief as he swam away. Stupid sea lions and their games!

But when he reached the others, they turned and stared at me with cold, inquisitive eyes. And then the ocean swirled white with froth as they zoomed over to investigate. There were about a dozen of them. I stayed still as they zipped around me. They swam closer and closer, until they were slipping by with just a sliver of space to spare.

As long as they stayed playful, I'd be all right.

Then one of them brushed me with his whiskers. The contact set something loose. The big one barked and now the game changed.

A huge bull surged up from below. This time he didn't swerve away. I gasped as his head pushed up fast and hard under my feet, sending me flying into the air. Instinctively, I yanked in my knees and wrapped my arms around them for protection. The instant I splashed down, another sea lion was tossing me back up again.

I was their toy.

Sea lions are competitive and soon they were seeing who could toss me the farthest. They slammed me from side to side, whacking me with their flippers. Every blow was a bruise. I tucked my chin to shield my neck and wrapped my arms around my head. It wasn't enough. I had to escape before they broke my bones, or worse. I shouted and punched out, but my arms were useless against their bulk. I was lost without sharp teeth and claws—

Claws!

In a single, smooth motion I reached down to my calf and pulled the knife free. When the next sea lion swam up, I struck out. A long, straight gash blossomed along his side. He stopped, stunned—and then I was slashing out in every direction, forcing the beasts back in a widening circle. The big bull gave me an icy stare and dove. He'd be coming at me from below. I felt him rising, fast, and I spun and thrust the knife straight down—felt the blade sink deep—

There was a bark, hard and commanding. In a flash the sea lions were gone.

And with them, my knife.

I was alive, but for how long?

I dragged my battered body to a haulout. Without my knife I had to learn how to hunt all over again.

I picked apart the empty sheath until I had a pile of cedar strips at my side. I thought of the net on the boat, and wove and unwove and wove again, until I'd mastered the diamond pattern. When I was done, I had a net compact enough to strap to my calf, but big enough to scoop up shrimp or small fish for a meal.

I had to be faster, smarter, stronger. My arms grew more muscular. My legs pushed me farther with every kick. Each day was all there was. My hair grew so long, I tied it back with a cedar cord.

The Moon waxed and waned, again and again. And I was still alive.

Mam had thought I couldn't survive on my own. I'd proved her wrong. Here I was, swimming from sunrise to sunset, hunting and finding good haulouts and staying alive. And I was doing it all by myself.

By myself . . .

Now that it didn't take every waking breath to survive, there was room in me to feel.

I sat on a crag at dusk, my belly full, the sky clear — and the loneliness came again, dark and deep. Was this my life now, forever? I couldn't risk going back to humans or my human side. And as for my clan, I'd never make it that far north in longlimbs. I'd stopped looking for webbing between my fingers. The Moon didn't see me. Why should she? I counted my sins over and over again. I cheated to get to Moon Day. I fought with Finn at the rites. I broke a Moon vow.

And so I was alone.

But I needed to hear voices! Something more than a few words in birdtalk now and then with a grumpy grebe. At night I sat with my feet in the surf and sang the old songs.

"The waves lap softly at the shore.
That's where the selkies sleep,
No farther than a splash away
From oceans winding deep.

"A man is fettered to the soil
And fish hold to the wave,
But both the shore and rising swell
The Moon to selkies gave.

"The day is landing like a bird.
She tucks her wings in tight.
Moon keep you cradled in her cusp.
Good night, my love, good night."

I was swimming past an island at dusk when I heard snorting. A herd of seals lay sprawled across the tideline. I swam closer and sat in the shallows, watching. Stupid, dumb creatures, and yet . . .

Their pelts were gray and black and tawny, speckled like pebbles on the shore. They arced up to look at me, heads and tails lifting in a familiar curve. They twitched their whiskers. They scratched their plump bellies with lazy flippers. Seeing that I wasn't a danger, they stretched out long again.

I scooted even closer. Then I slipped up on shore and lay down alongside them, my body stretched out long near their bodies, my feet in the water near their tails. Listening to them breathe.

Pretending.

~ ~ ~

I couldn't stop thinking about my clan. Even though Jack's words still haunted me, and the Moon didn't see me; even though I had no pelt, I longed for them so much it hurt. Where were they now? Had they reached the far north? Where were Lyr and Grandmam, Cormac and Maura and Mist? Where was Mam? *Where?*

I started asking birds for news. When auklets floated by, or gulls strutted along shore, or geese flew high overhead, I'd call, "Where does the wind carry you?" And then quickly, since most birds have such short attention spans, "See selkies?"

Once an oystercatcher squawked about a clan to the west. I swam for half a day. But when I got there, all I found were dolphins poking around in the kelp. Couldn't the stupid bird even tell a dolphin from a selkie?

I almost stopped asking the birds. Each time my hopes were dashed, I ended up lonelier than before.

I needed to find another bird as clever as the puffin on Spindle Island. The birds I spoke with cared only about their own stomachs and mating and nests.

I found their nests. I ate their eggs.

By day, I couldn't stop scanning the waves for my clan: their sleek backs, the curve of their heads. I strained my ears for the sound of their voices. But at night . . .

At night my dreams betrayed me. Instead of the clan, I saw Nellie, bounding across the rocks like a deer, waving and calling out to me in a bright, clear voice. We ran side by side down the hill. We sat in the tree cave, sunlight dappling our arms. And Maggie—in my dreams, she was always walking out of the house to sit beside me atop the cliff, her hand settling on mine.

The Moon waxed and waned.

One arm and then another . . .

CHAPTER FIFTY-FOUR

～ THE COVE ～

I was swimming through sun-flecked water. Fat drops of light drifted down past me, swirling together into long, silver streaks. And then the streaks flicked their tails.

Salmon!

They were big and fat and as long as my arm. What a meal·one would make! They were too big for my net, so I noted the current they were riding and how fast they were swimming. Then I kicked up, looking for land. With luck I'd find a stick right away, sharpen the tip, and come back before the salmon had moved on. I could almost taste the flesh now, pink and sweet.

A curve of land appeared on the horizon. The current

swept me along, and the curve grew and grew until it became an island. I stroked along a wall of rock, looking for a place to haul out. There were gaps in the wall where wind and rain had etched through, leaving windows. On the other side, the calm waters of a cove sparkled in the sun.

I rounded the point and stopped, stunned. That cusp of beach, that flat-topped boulder as big as a throne—this was the island where I first saw a human! And that gap in the rocks, that was where I saw the boat with its blood-red beak.

I slid ashore and ran to the boulder, leaping easily to the top. This was where I'd made the stone spiral with the golden tail. A wave of dizziness washed over me. The past and present were swirling around each other like shining salmon, until I couldn't tell what was light and what was fish.

I jumped off the rock and dashed to the cliff. One rough handhold and then another—it only took me a moment to reach the crevice where I'd hidden from the man. I ducked to squeeze in, but my shoulders were too wide. Had it always been this small?

I sat on a ledge, my legs dangling down. There, that spot in the cove—that was where I'd seen Mam's head rising. Mam, and then every other member of my clan. They had all come back for me.

The salmon had been running that morning. They were running now.

I could almost hear Lyr's voice: *Not you, pup. We're going too far for you today.*

No, I thought, setting my jaw. I jumped down and started searching in the driftwood. It wasn't too far at all.

I found a long, straight stick and sharpened the tip with rocks. I lashed it to my leg and swam out and found the current. The salmon were right where I figured they'd be. I slipped into the silver stream, echoing their movements, and when I'd drifted close enough, I struck. It was easy. The hard part was lugging the fish back to shore.

What a feast I had that night! I stuffed myself to bursting and shared the rest with the gulls.

I stayed on the island another day, and another. The salmon moved on and still I stayed. I told myself it was because the hunting was good, and the cove was sheltered, and the cliff offered a good lookout. But that wasn't really why.

For eleven years, after every long journey, my clan swam back to these waters to find Mam and me. Now a year had passed since they left. In the dark of night, I gazed out across the black waves to the north, trying not to hope.

When it finally happened, it wasn't night after all. It was morning, and the fog lay low across the water, and the call of the gulls came like voices from another world. I was on the rocks, finishing a lazy breakfast of mussels and seaweed, when my skin tensed.

There was a faint disturbance in the air. It grew to a hum, and then a motor's throbbing pulse.

I dashed and crouched at the base of a crag.

A fishing boat chugged out of the fog. It motored past, the stink of its engine filling the air. The fishermen didn't see me, but I saw them: the weatherworn faces staring straight ahead, the cables, the huge spool of net.

When the air was quiet again, I climbed the crag and looked around. The fog was thinning. An auklet flew low, and wind shivered the water, but there was no sign of the boat. My fists relaxed.

Then a movement far out in the waves caught my eye.

There! A head was rising, round and sleek and silvery gray.

A seal, I told myself. I tried to squash down the hope

in my chest, but it kept forcing its way up, an air bubble bound for the surface.

Just a seal.

The head tilted to one side. I knew the expression that went with that tilt, the laughing eyes, the wry twitch of the whiskers. My feet snuck closer to the edge of the crag. I lifted a hand and waved.

She was looking in the other direction.

Another head slipped up and swam to her side. This one was black. One black, one silver . . . My heart caught in my throat. It was them! It had to be!

"Mam!" I cried out. "Lyr! Over here! It's me!"

Now they were spinning around each other. Black and silver twined through the crests. My body remembered those swift spirals, so tight, flipper and tail felt like my own.

The song! I needed to sing the calling song! I drew in a deep breath —

Far in the distance, the boat's motor growled. At any other time, that sound would have sent me scrambling to hide. But my body was pulling toward Mam and Lyr with such force, I could hardly keep my feet on the crag. If I didn't go after them now, I'd lose them forever.

I sliced into the water and raced under the waves,

straining my ears for their undersea voices. Fish fled past me, away from tooth and claw. I was getting close. Close to warm pelts and bright eyes and hearing them say my name. They *had* come back! They'd come back looking for me!

There was a streak of silver right in front of me. She was coming out of a twirl. We burst through the waves at the same moment, my arms opening wide—

The eyes looking back at me were blank and startled. It was a seal. Only a seal.

Disappointment slashed through me, so sharp, it cut something loose. Fear, anger, despair—it all came crashing outward in an unstoppable wave—pounding through my heart, lungs, throat—and it ripped from my mouth in a wild, anguished howl.

The seal startled backward and dove. But I couldn't stop screaming, and now it was both in me and outside me, singeing the air with its harsh smell—

The smell was smoke. The howl was a motor's roar.

"Hang on!" cried a voice. A human voice. "We're coming!"

CHAPTER FIFTY-FIVE
～NETTED～

The scream froze in my throat. A fishing boat pierced through a bank of fog, racing toward me.

My survival instincts took over, stark and clean. I dove straight down. If they couldn't see me, they couldn't catch me. With luck, they'd follow the seals instead.

The water pulsed and pounded with the motor's unearthly roar. A dark shape passed overhead like a gigantic shark. Another moment and I'd be safe.

Something snagged my hand.

I tried to jerk it back, but now the thing was wrapping around the rest of my body. Tentacles pressed into my flesh. Except it wasn't tentacles, it was rope, twisting together in hundreds of little gaping mouths—*a net*. The more I struggled, the tighter it held me. My lungs were bursting—

And then there was nothing. Only silence. Perfect, dark, and still.

Through closed lids I saw light. A beautiful, silvery light. My body hung limp, a deadweight, and yet somehow I was rising through the water toward the Moon.

The water fell away. The light was a red stab of sun.

Rough hands grabbed me, pulled me up, laid me down. The deck shook under my back. The motor pounded through my skin and into my blood until there was nothing but that relentless beat. I couldn't move. I couldn't open my eyes.

Bodies crouched and crowded around me. Voices barked.

"Can't find a pulse—"

"Get on the radio and—"

Fingers tightened on my wrist. A pause, and then a different kind of voice, slow and sad: "It's too late."

The rigging rattled, metal on metal. The wind whipped my skin. I was cold, so cold—me, who'd never been cold in my life. I needed the waves to warm me. Why couldn't I hear the waves?

"Mayday! Mayday! Mayday!" cried a voice behind

me. "This is *Nancy Belle, Nancy Belle, Nancy Belle*. We've picked up a—"

A gentle warmth brushed over my face. Breath. "It's not too late," said a determined voice. Hands pressed down on my chest. Air forced its way into my lungs. A shudder ran through me and my eyes flew open—a blinding light—and then I was coughing and gasping and spitting up water. Hands clutched me from every side.

Men were crouched around me in a tight circle, chests heaving, eyes wide.

A hand curved around my shoulder. "Can you talk?"

But I wouldn't speak. I wasn't one of them. I *wouldn't* be.

A distant voice crackled, "Vessel *Nancy Belle*, this is the Coast Guard station."

Now they were all talking at once. "What happened to—"

"How'd you get way out here? Did your boat—"

"Who are you?"

The railing glinted in the distance, taunting me. I couldn't even hold up my head, let alone break free and dive over.

"That's strange," said a man. "Look at his eyes. One's brown and one's blue. I never saw that before."

"Let me see!" A man with white whiskers leaned over. His eyes stared right into mine. Then he sat back with a brisk nod. "It's him, all right."

"Him?"

"The boy from Spindle Island. The one they were searching for. The one they never found."

CHAPTER FIFTY-SIX
❧ THE WHITE ROOM ❧

I struggled to rise through the darkness. The air smelled strange, like Maggie's cleaning soap, but harsher. A sound pulsed, high and sharp: *beep ... beep ... beep ...*

I dragged my eyes open. A dim room. A dot of red light throbbed in time to the beeping. Where was I?

I struggled to sit up but something bit at my wrist. My heart started racing and the red light quickened. The room swirled back to black.

I wove between unconsciousness and waking—or was it dreams? Faces stared down at me. Bright bursts of pain seared my arms. I couldn't feel the Moon or the tides, and the walls pressed closer, and a smothering weight lay on my chest.

Then I woke and saw the weight was blankets. I was in a white room, in a bed. But it wasn't a bed because there were bars on both sides. Metal bars.

My head pounded, and the beeping got faster again. I was burning up. I reached for the bar and a sharp pain stabbed my wrist. I looked and gasped in horror. Something was biting into my arm. It was attached to a thin, clear tube full of liquid.

The tube led through the bars and up to a bag. There was another sound now, a throbbing—or was it sucking? Was the thing *drinking* from me?

I pulled myself to sitting. That's when I saw the cords dangling from my chest. Each was attached to a small round mouth—a colony, growing on me! I ripped one off with a popping sound. It left a pink circle on my skin. I tore off the rest and stared at them, panting.

I grasped the strap holding the tube onto my wrist and ripped it off in a flash of pain. Drops of blood splattered the sheets. The room was spinning. Somehow I clambered over the metal bars and half fell to the ground. I clutched a bar and pulled myself upright.

The room was strange and terrible, with pillars and

posts and blinking lights. My eyes darted around and found the door. I stumbled over and jerked it open.

Before me stretched an endless hallway lined with doors. A cluster of people stood talking at the other end of the hall. A woman looked up from a table. She saw me and started to stand.

I staggered to an open door. "Who are you?" rasped an old woman, staring at me from a bed-cage. She lifted an arm and tubes trailed after. "Who are you?"

"You shouldn't be up," said a voice. The woman from the table was walking toward me in a swirl of colors and light. "Let's get you back to bed."

No! Panic gave me strength and I stumbled into a run. A man in loose blue clothes loomed before me. I sped up, arms outstretched, and shoved him aside. I ran faster. I was on fire. I needed the sea to cool me. Where was the sea? Windows looked out over treetops so I was upstairs—I needed stairs down.

A voice started chanting from the ceiling, "Code gray. Code gray. Code gray."

I swerved around a corner. At the end of the hall a man was coming out of a door with a little window in it, and behind him was a flight of stairs. I shoved past chairs and rolling carts in a desperate rush—

Strong arms wrapped around me from the back. "Got him," said a voice. "Steady, there." Faces and arms and doors whirled into black.

When I woke, I was back in the bed-cage. Tubes dangled from my arms. I tried to lift my hand but it stopped with a jerk. A strap circled my wrist, tying it to the bars. I drew in a sharp breath.

A woman rose from a chair and walked over.

"How are you feeling?" she said. "Would you like a sip of water?"

She was trying to get me to talk. I wouldn't talk to her. I wouldn't talk to any of them. I stared at the window and acted like I didn't understand. She finally left me alone.

I tried to string thoughts together. The men on the boat must have brought me here. I couldn't feel the pulse of the waves, so I was inland, farther than I'd ever been before. But once in a while a whiff of fresh air brought a hint of salt. The ocean couldn't be too far away.

The men on the boat had said something about my eyes and Spindle Island, and that someone was looking for me. Did Jack tell them what I'd done to Maggie? That I'd—I gulped, blinking back tears—that I'd made her die?

I had to escape. I had to get back to the sea.

Across from the bed was a high, narrow sliver of window, too small to squeeze through. Outside I could see the tip of a fir tree and a taunting strip of sky. Clouds rushed by on a wild, changing wind. A gull soared into view.

Instinctively I called out in birdtalk, "Where does the wind carry you?"

The gull banked and wheeled back in a wide circle.

Did it hear me? My heart started racing. "Me selkie!" I cried in birdtalk. "Trap! Human trap!" With each word I screamed louder, trying to force my voice through walls and glass, until the room was ringing with shrieks and caws and screeches. "ME SELKIE! BRING SELKIES!"

The door flew open and people burst in. They reached at me from every side.

"SELKIES!" I kept shrieking. "FIND! FIND!"

But when I looked up at the window again, the gull was gone.

A tall woman strode in. She took the metal ear that hung around her neck and put it on my chest. She urged me to make the sounds again. The others tried to describe it. One of them squawked, but it wasn't even a word, just a scrape of sound.

A man stuck a sharp silver stick in my arm. Blood flowed into a tube, and I fainted.

When I woke again, the room had stopped spinning.

"You need to eat," they said, showing me plates with mounds of mush. I gagged and turned away.

There was a woman with hair like Nellie's. She noticed more than the others. She took the straps off my wrists. "I don't think we need these anymore," she said. Then she brought a tray piled with lots of kinds of food. There was a bowl of cornflakes, and I gulped it down. She saw me gazing at the window; she walked over and slid it open three fingers wide. That was as far as it would go. She looked back to see my face, nodded, and then left, closing the door behind her.

I breathed in, long and deep. The fresh air brought a hint of pine. A breeze came from the west, carrying the salt of the sea. If I ever got out, I'd follow that scent to the shore.

A man came in and closed the window.

Twice that day I climbed out of the bed-cage and snuck out the door, trying to find my way to the stairs. Both times they led me back to the room and put the tubes back in my arms, talking about blood counts and oxygen levels, looking at each other and shaking their heads. The second time a woman sat in a chair beside me and stayed there the rest of the day.

Night fell. I forced myself to close my eyes and make my breathing slow and steady. Finally the chair scraped back. I felt her standing over me, and then her footsteps walked to the door and she was gone.

I sat up and quietly lowered the bed bars, like the humans had done. My arm was still attached by tubes to a rolling stand. I pulled it beside me over to the window, reached up — I could barely grasp the bottom — and slid the window open. Then I crept back to bed and lay there, trying to smell the sea.

The Moon traced a slow arc across the sky. Somewhere she was shining on the white tips of waves, on the swirling foam of the shoreline. Somewhere, she was shining on my clan.

There was a fluttering at the window, and then —
thump!

I sat up with a gasp. There, on the ledge, perched a round-bellied bird. A puffin. *My* puffin.

"Aran," she grunted.

It was the most beautiful sound I'd ever heard.

The puffin pecked at the window frame. "Trap," she

said. She tried to squeeze through, but the slit was too small. "Bad trap."

I stood at the end of the bed so we were at the same level, as close to her as I could get.

"How . . ." I gulped, blinking back tears. "How find?"

"Gull tell flock. Gulls!" She shook her head to show what she thought of them. "Talk talk talk."

A whisper of hope floated into my chest. The puffin was the smartest bird I'd ever met. If she could spread word far enough, maybe my clan would hear. Maybe they'd come rescue me.

"Find flock. Selkie flock," I said, searching for words she'd know. "Here, me lost. Here, me . . ." A hot tear escaped and ran down my cheek. "Here, me gone."

In birdtalk, the same word means *gone* and *dead*.

The puffin's head jerked back in alarm.

I nodded to show it was true. "Selkie flock. North. Far north." My voice cracked. "Find? Bring?"

The puffin stamped her small, orange foot. "Aran *no* gone," she said firmly, and then she flew off into the night.

The next morning the tall woman brought in a man wearing a blue jacket.

"Hello, Aran," he said in a fake, cheery voice.

How did he know my name? It took all my willpower not to react.

"I'm Mr. Crane from the Department of Social Services. You won't be here much longer, Aran. Dr. Donahoe is coming to get you. And Penelope Donahoe, she's coming, too. You'll be going with them."

My blood was pounding so hard, it drowned out his next words. This was it, then. They were coming to take me away. Social Services—that was what Maggie called foster care. They were going to take me inland and keep me there forever. I'd never find my way back to the sea. I'd lose any chance of seeing my clan again.

I realized they'd stopped talking. The woman murmured, "I told you. No response."

She cocked her head toward the door and they left. But their muffled voices came through from the other side. I eased out of bed and crept closer, listening.

"I'm not sure it's a good idea." All the man's false cheeriness was gone. "No speech. Hysterical screaming. You don't know how the fever or the ordeal might have affected his brain. And you still don't know what's causing those astronomical oxygen levels in his blood. We should reevaluate."

The woman's voice was firm. "We can't keep him here

much longer. And in spite of the blood work, he seems healthy enough."

"But the challenges facing . . ."

Their voices faded.

When was this Donahoe coming to take me away? And where, oh, where was the puffin?

CHAPTER FIFTY-SEVEN

～THE PUFFIN'S PLAN～

Outside the slit of a window, the sky turned gray, then black. The Moon rose huge and bright. Tomorrow she'd be full. She was pulling me like she pulled the tides.

I was still awake, sunk in despair, when dawn broke. There was a flutter of wings. I sat up as the puffin landed on the sill.

"You find—?" I gulped, unable to say the rest.

The puffin nodded. "Find. Fly far, far, far." She tucked her head to her shoulder, shy and proud. "Big Moon, selkies here."

The full Moon—that was tonight! Energy surged through me. My clan was coming! They were coming back for me!

The puffin tossed her beak to the west. "You go, cliff-foot, there."

I pointed to the door. In the simplest words I could find, I told the puffin about the twisting halls, and how the people kept bringing me back, and I'd need time to find the stairs.

We talked and talked. The sun was rising. Footsteps passed outside the door. They'd be bringing in the breakfast tray soon and we still didn't have a plan. If only I could just walk out the door!

My shoulders slumped. "They chase me," I said again.

But this time the puffin lifted her head, an idea sparking in her eyes. "No," she said. "They chase *me*."

She told me what she was going to do. I didn't want her to take such a risk. But she smoothed her feathers with her beak, gathering herself, and then she flapped away.

It felt like a lifetime until she landed back on the sill.

"Me find," she said. "Big hole. Good big. Now?"

But in the daytime, the halls were full of people. To have any chance, we'd need to wait until dark.

"No. Night," I said. I prayed no one would come to take me away before then.

The door began to open and the puffin flew off, bravely carrying all my hopes with her.

~ ~ ~

Now everything depended on timing. There was a whole day to get through. I startled whenever footsteps passed the door. The lower the sun sank in the sky, the tighter my chest grew.

They brought dinner. I forced myself to take a bite and pushed the rest around on the plate. The sun went down. The sky turned deep blue, then black. The stars came out.

I'd already crawled under the covers, eyes shut tight, when two men came in to fix the sheets and tubes. They left, shutting the door behind them.

A moment later there was a rustling at my window. "Now?" asked the puffin.

I sat up. "No. Wait."

We waited until the bustle in the halls quieted and the footsteps stopped. I carefully tugged off the tape and pulled the tube from my arm. Then I crept to the door and opened it a crack, peering out. The hall was empty.

I turned to the puffin. "Now!"

She flew off. I heard her grunt; she must be squeezing through the bigger window she'd found. I watched, my heart pounding, as she came strutting down the hall. I poked my head out the door and waved to show her which room was mine.

The puffin stopped and nodded. She took a few running steps, flapped her wings—and then she was flying! She buzzed up and down the hall, squawking and grunting so loudly, her cries rang off the walls.

A woman poked her head around the corner. Her eyes widened in surprise. "A puffin!" she exclaimed.

The puffin flapped down to a counter and pretended to preen. The woman came sneaking up—and the puffin flew off in a wild zigzag. She careened onto tables, scattering papers and boxes and pens across the floor.

"Help me!" called the woman, laughing. Other people came running and then they stopped, pointing in amazement.

The puffin landed on a cart. A man grabbed a sheet and crept over. The puffin waited until he was close—so close!—and then she took off again. She flew right by my door, glancing at me with what I could have sworn was a smile. Then she turned and went zooming back over their heads and down the hall. A ribbon of people ran after her, arms outstretched, laughing and calling.

The hall was empty.

I stepped out quietly and closed the door behind me. Then I ran in the opposite direction, searching for the stairs.

Halls branched off halls, like colonies of coral, and every hall was lined with doors, but none of them looked right. I turned corner after corner. The sounds of the puffin's call and running feet faded, and then they began to grow louder again. "Catch it!" they were crying, and the puffin was squawking in birdtalk, "Aran! Go! Fast!"— and then there was the door with the little window, and I ripped it open and there were the stairs.

I ran down two steps at a time. At the bottom was another door. I cracked it open—

"Welcome!" boomed a deep voice. "We weren't expecting you yet."

I almost leaped out of my skin.

The voice kept booming, "Yes, yes, come in, Dr. Donahoe. And you must be Penelope." I shrank back against the wall. Footsteps, and then, "Normally we'd wait until morning, but in this situation we can make an exception. The elevator is this way."

I held my breath. I heard a door open and close.

I flung the door open and flew across the spare, echoing room. *Bam!* My outstretched hands struck the metal bar and the glass door flew open into the night. Fresh air hit my face and my feet were pounding down a walkway, and then down the middle of a road.

Buildings crammed tight on both sides, their windows dark. Another road crossed the first and I skidded to a stop, looking for the puffin.

She wasn't there.

She was supposed to come show me the way! I whirled around. She was flying out from behind the building, flapping with all her might. But as I watched, she slowed, fluttering. Did she hear something?

"Come!" I called in birdtalk, as loudly as I dared.

She turned and flew back in the other direction, disappearing around the corner.

Light was blazing from the windows. People were running into the big room and toward the glass doors. I couldn't wait any longer. I'd have to find my own way to the cliff.

CHAPTER FIFTY-EIGHT

‿ IN THIS SKIN ‿

I ran down the black line of pavement, past looming houses and the empty hulls of cars. The houses thinned and night deepened. The hard road gave way to dirt. Then the breeze shifted and there it was: the thick, salty smell of the sea.

I leaped over a fence, running even faster now, over grass and then soft earth, toward a line of trees. There were ferns underfoot, and branches blocking the sky, and the sharp scent of pine. I knew where I was going. I felt it in my bones.

Through the branches came a shimmering light.

I burst out from the trees and stopped, staring. In a

vast, black sky, the Moon was rising, huge and full.

Slowly now, I walked across rough stone to the edge of the cliff. The ocean spread out below me to infinity. Out in the water, three rocks raised their pointed heads. A tiny row of man-made lights showed the sweep of a far shore. The moonlight silvered my skin; it danced on the tips of the waves. But the waves were empty.

Was this the right place?

I stood straight, my shoulders back, my arms stretched long at my sides. I drew in a deep breath and sang, "Come to me! Come!"

The words floated out across the water, each curving wave catching and reflecting the tune.

Where were they?

I lifted my arms out straight before me, palms raised like the Caller at Moon Day, and sang louder, beseeching, "Come to me! Come!"

I could swear the Moon was watching. Her clear, honest light filled me. Full of ache and longing and love, I sang out a third time, "Come to me—"

From out in the waves, a voice sang, "Come!"

A silver head was surging toward the cliff. Mam! Another head popped up behind her, and another, skimming the crests. They sang out together, their voices rising as one: "Come to us! Come!"

I dove from the cliff, piercing the waves.

Never had I swum so fast! I was already past the first rock when—*whoosh!*—Mam zoomed up and braked hard, head back and flippers forward. A glittering splash of silver drops sparkled down as my arms wrapped around her. The warmth of her pelt. The soft brush of her whiskers against my cheek.

"Aran," she whispered. "Aran, my son!"

The rest of the clan zipped around us, laughing and calling my name. I hugged them all, Grandmam first. "I knew you'd be fine," she said, nuzzling my ear.

Lyr exclaimed, "Look how big you are! And how fast you swim! Is this the same Aran we left behind?"

No, I wanted to say, *not the same*. But before I could speak, there was Mist swirling around me, and Maura pretending to nibble my foot, and Cormac, spiraling down and then zipping up into a backflip.

Then I saw someone else, waiting quietly just outside the circle, his fur shining white in the moonlight.

"Finn!" I cried, streaking over. "What—?"

"Our clans are living together now!" he said with a smile.

"But your chief . . ."

"I convinced him to let me come. Because we're all hoping . . ." He stopped and looked at Mam.

The clan had gathered around me in a circle. Anticipation rose from them like steam.

Mam flicked her tail and swam up beside me. "I brought it," she said.

Now I saw the straps holding something close to her body. My mouth fell open; my heart was pounding. She couldn't mean . . .

She nodded, her eyes huge and bright. "Come over here."

I followed her to the jutting rock. She hauled out halfway, her tail still in the water.

"Help me take this off," she said.

The strap and the pouch were made of animal hide, with clasps made of bone.

"Open it," said Mam.

My hands trembled as I lifted the flap and reached inside. I touched fur. Seal fur.

A pelt.

I pulled it out and laid it down on the rock, staring. It was brown and gray, like pebbles jumbled together.

I gasped. "Where — How —"

"The wise ones," said Mam. "They were farther north than we'd ever imagined. The white selkies had ancient tales about where they lived, but not even they had journeyed so far. So far we got iced in. I nearly went mad, not being able to get back to you!"

"That's the truth," sighed Lyr.

"But find them we did," said Grandmam. "And your mam talked them into letting her bring you this pelt."

Mam nudged it forward with her nose. "Spread it out," she said.

My hands moved slowly. So slowly. The fur felt odd and stiff. I spread it out on the rock. The rounded curve of the head. The flippers, hanging lank and empty, black claws clattering against stone.

The Moon was almost directly overhead. Her light picked out every individual hair of the pelt.

And all I had to do was slip it over my shoulders . . .

"Where did it come from?" I said.

There was silence. Then, "A dead selkie," blurted Maura.

My head jerked up.

Mam sighed, as she so often did with Maura. "That's not quite how I'd put it." She turned to me. "Long ago, a selkie died while in longlimbs. So his pelt was left behind. The wise ones said to give it to you beneath a full Moon. They said you'd know what to do."

I lifted the pelt. The gap down the front fell open. I spread it wider, so the shoulders would fit over mine. . . .

"Go on!" urged Mam.

But this wasn't how I'd pictured it at all. I'd imagined my pelt slipping on as smooth and light as a breeze. This pelt felt heavy and stiff. It felt . . . *wrong*.

"Well?" said Mam. "Hurry! I want to see you in it!"

I started to slide my hand into a flipper. And then I stopped. This hand.

With this hand, I fought off sea lions. With these legs, I swam for days at a time. With these ears and eyes and instincts, I sensed the weather. I found the best currents. I foraged and caught all the food I needed. I survived.

In this skin.

I held the pelt in front of me—Mam breathless, expectant—and then I folded it up.

"I can't," I said. "It isn't mine."

"Not yours?" cried Mam, aghast. "Of course it's yours! Didn't I go all the way north to find it for you? Didn't the wise ones—the ones who talk with the Moon, Aran!—didn't they say I could bring it to you?"

She'd risked so much for this pelt. So I could keep up. So I could go on the long journeys. So I could be like everyone else.

I swallowed hard. And then I slipped the pelt back into its pouch.

"It's someone else's skin," I said.

Mam gave a mournful, despairing cry. "But then how will you ever belong? How will you *live*?"

It was the question I'd spent my whole life asking. A lifetime of being different, of feeling I wasn't enough. But now I knew. In my deep heart, in my bones, I knew the answer.

"I guess I'll live as myself," I said.

The pouch slipped off the rock and under the waves.

Overhead, the Moon felt even closer than on Moon Day. The air shimmered, alive with sparks of light. My skin was tingling.

Finn gasped. "Look!"

Everyone startled back in a splash, staring at my hands.

I lifted them before me and spread them wide. My fingers were linked by webbing. With a fingertip, I traced the new line, a curve of soft, almost translucent skin.

And my arms! The silver light shimmered on skin . . . and then on fur, black and sleek and shining.

I sat down quickly with my feet in the water. My legs were together, then tighter, fusing. I kicked in wonder and awe. The water splashed up high in a glistening arc, tossed, not by feet, but by a tail. My arms snugged tight by my sides. My shoulders strengthened around the muscles of my powerful neck.

I didn't just hear the sound when my pelt gathered. I felt it deep inside. There it was—and part of myself slipped into place.

My clan circled around me, their faces radiant with joy.

There was a bright cry of wonder. But it didn't come from the clan.

We all turned and stared back at the shore.

CHAPTER FIFTY-NINE

∾ I COULD SEE ∾ EVERYTHING

She stood at the edge of the cliff. Taller, now, but with the same long legs, that spray of hair, that easy grace: Nellie.

"Aran!" she called.

I felt an instant, instinctive tug. It had been there the first time I saw her, and it was even stronger now.

The puffin was hopping around at her feet. "Me bring!" she grunted proudly. "Friend! Friend!"

"You got your pelt!" cried Nellie.

The clan had grown completely still. The silence was electric, like lightning about to strike.

Maura's eyes narrowed. "A human," she said.

"She saw you turn," muttered Cormac.

"She'll tell," said Grandmam, and the low warning in her voice was the worst of all.

Their bodies were taut with coiled energy, the kind that explodes into fang and claw. That means *attack to defend*.

Like the selkies at Westwood Pier.

The tale flooded back into my mind—the waters roiling white, then red. But this time the arms thrashing to the surface were thin and brown.

"Nellie!" I cried, trying to warn her.

My voice only pulled her closer. She teetered at the edge of the cliff.

"I'm so, so happy for you!" she shouted, straining toward me. "But don't go yet! I have to tell you about Ma—" She leaned too far. Her arms whirled, her hands clutched at air, and then she was falling toward the water far below.

Around the clan, the sharp air, that instant before the surge—

There was no room for thought, for reason. *Slap!* I whacked the water with a flipper, startling the clan just long enough to give me a head start. I pushed off with a powerful thrust of my tail. It was like I'd been in this body forever. All the strength I'd earned living on my own, it was there in the force of my shoulders, my back, my tail.

I reached Nellie as she struck the water. She plummeted down in an eddy of foam and I swam alongside, swerving to stop her descent. There, in the deep, she wrapped her arms around my neck.

A flick of my tail and we shot to the surface. Nellie let go, treading water. I stayed right beside her. The clan had formed a circle around us.

"Listen to me!" I cried.

For a moment, nothing. Then Mam swished her tail. Lyr's shoulders relaxed.

Beside me, Nellie was shivering.

"I'm going to carry Nellie to those rocks," I said. "And then I need to tell you everything that happened while you were gone."

They swam by my side, silent and somber, over to the rocks. Nellie clambered up and sat, hugging her knees for warmth. The puffin flew over and settled at her feet. I hauled out halfway, my shoulders near Nellie, my tail in the waves. Then I started talking. My words rushed out like water that had been stopped up for too long.

I told them about my arrival on Spindle Island, and how Maggie hadn't expected me and I had to convince her to let me stay. I told them about slashing the net, and seeing Nellie for the first time, and the song. How I saved Nellie from drowning, and she taught me to read so I could search for clues and try to save Mam. How she guessed the truth about me and became my partner in searching, and never told a soul.

"I'll never tell," said Nellie. She put her hand to her heart, like I'd shown her so long ago. "I swear to the Moon."

Grandmam watched, nodding.

When I got to the part about Jack coming home, Mam gasped and got so upset, Lyr had to comfort her before I could go on. It was good he was by her side when I told them about Jack's fist crashing through the wall. And then the doubloons and the boat and how I made Maggie die—

"But she's not dead!" cried Nellie.

The world stopped . . . and shifted. "She's alive?" I whispered.

Nellie nodded eagerly. "I knew you thought she was dead or you'd never have left. That's why I ran here so fast, because the puffin said you were swimming away and I had to tell you. She wants to see you, Aran. She *needs* to see you." Nellie sighed, battling with herself. "But now you have your pelt and you're leaving. I'd better figure out how to tell her you're okay."

Maggie. Chocolate cake, and doubloons, and her hand on mine. How she gathered her courage to tell Jack, *I like having him here.*

And Nellie. Nellie with her clear, gray eyes. Nellie who knew me better than anyone in the world. Who'd always had faith in me, and stood by me, and never cared if I was human or selkie.

I scooted all the way out of the water, so I was at her side. The Moon lit my pelt from tail to whiskers.

Nellie looked into my eyes. "One brown and one blue," she said, her voice full of wonder. "Even in that amazing pelt, you're still you."

She'd put into words what I was feeling. Of course she had. Nellie always knew.

That's when I knew, too.

For twelve years I'd lived in longlimbs, resenting it, fighting it. Believing it made me less. Then came Jack with his blinding rage, and that same fire burning in my own veins. Thinking that's what it meant to be human.

Now fear slipped from my shoulders—that terrible weight—and drifted away across the waves.

Human didn't have to be fists and rage. Human could be Maggie making a chocolate cake. The walrus's fire. Nellie running to find me.

What would it be like to live in longlimbs knowing the human part of me was good?

"Mam," I said. "I'm staying."

"But Aran—!" Mam's eyes were black pools of shock and sadness. How could I make her understand?

I took a deep breath. "You risked your life for me. My pelt"—I reached out a flipper to her, my voice catching— "it means everything. But being human—a good human— that means everything, too. I'm *two* everythings, Mam."

Another look came into her eyes and mingled with the sadness. It was more than acceptance; it was pride.

"You're staying," she said softly.

I nodded.

Maura splashed her tail. "Staying? After we came all this way?"

"Hush, Maura," said Grandmam.

But Maura kept on. "After you finally get to be a real selkie? What are you going to do now, take off your pelt the moment you've got it?"

"Yes," I said. "I am."

Mam swallowed hard. "Are you going to be only human now?" From the way she said it, I knew she'd love me no matter what skin I was in.

"No, Mam," I said. "I'll keep my pelt safe, and I'll

swim out and find you and the clan again and again and again. But right now, I need to do this."

"What if your pelt won't bind next time?" said Cormac, in genuine concern. "The Moon doesn't like her gifts to be taken lightly."

That's when Finn swam up. "Don't you see? This is what the Moon knew had to happen. She wants him to be both! Look!"

We followed his gaze. The moonbeams had woven together across the water, blazing a broad silver path from our rock to the shore.

Lyr nodded. "We should go, then."

"Wait," said Mam. She looked at me, a smile playing at the corners of her mouth. She cocked her head toward the waves. "Well?"

I laughed. "Wait here," I said to Nellie.

I rolled off the rocks and into the gleaming water. I arced my back and I flicked my tail and I zoomed down through ripples of moonlight. I swooped from side to side in giant curves, feeling the grace and strength of my new body. My whiskers picked up vibrations in the water I'd never known were there: a shrimp wriggling its legs, a tiny fish slipping into seaweed to hide.

Mam glided to my side. Together we swam deeper,

and deeper, and still I could see everything, from a jellyfish pulsing high above me to a greenling's blue spots fading into the distance. Down to the bottom we swam. Then Mam swerved away, and I sped along the ocean floor. My path was shaped by the slightest curve of my side, the flick of a flipper. The sand lay in rippled waves and I traced every dip and rise. A flat sole saw me coming and burrowed into the sand until only its round eyes poked out.

I swam into a towering, swaying forest of bull kelp. A flash of white swirled down the strands, and another of granite gray—it was Finn and Grandmam, come to play chase. We flew along, darting behind rocks, zipping around so the fronds whipped in our wake. Finn somersaulted in front of me and I flung my tail forward to come to a sudden stop, spinning around to go in the other direction. But the spinning was glorious and I kept spinning and spinning. . . .

I came out of a twirl and slowed down, swimming on my back, gazing up at the underside of the waves. Cormac, Maura, and Mist were at the surface; their tails made soft eddies of foam. Then the seabed was dropping away below me, the water deepened, and I gave an easy roll to follow it down.

And there was Mam slipping to one side of me, with Lyr to the other. As one, we swirled deeper, our tails swishing in unison, the swerve of our shoulders as strong and sure as waves. I had plenty of air; I could have stayed down as long as I liked. But above us, the water was sparkling. It wasn't the silver of moonlight, but a brilliant, glowing green.

We surged upward into swirls of luminescent plankton. Each dot blazed like a miniature green star. I swam through that light—it flickered across my whiskers, my shoulders, my tail—and then with a mighty push, I burst through the waves in a back flip. All around me the others were leaping, too—Mam and Lyr, Cormac and Maura, Grandmam and Finn and Mist—the plankton flying off us in brilliant green arcs across the night sky.

We turned back toward the rocks where Nellie and the puffin were waiting. Mam swam by my side; the others fell behind.

Mam slowed and looked into my eyes. "You're sure?" she asked.

"I'm sure."

I slipped closer, brushing her face with my whiskers. Her flipper reached out and touched mine. We floated there, riding the waves' gentle rise and fall.

And then, a strong flick of my tail and I was speeding to the rocks.

I slid up beside Nellie. The clan bobbed nearby, their faces serious now, because we all knew what came next.

My pelt loosened around me as easily as if I'd done this every day of my life. I lifted it from my shoulders. I stroked the soft nap of the fur. Even now, it felt like part of me. I folded it into a neat packet and tucked it securely under my arm.

"I'll come back a year to this day," said Mam. "And every year after until you're ready to come north. Is this where I'll find you?"

I looked at Nellie. "Let's meet at Spindle Island," I said. "There's a small cove hidden below a house on the eastern shore."

Nellie grinned.

"I'll come, too," said Finn. "We'll have lots of exploring to do!"

I blinked back tears as my clan swam away.

Now that there was room to think, I knew they wouldn't have hurt Nellie. That instinct was in them— I'd felt it, sharp in the air—but they didn't give in to it. Somewhere there might be clans that wouldn't hold back, that would do anything to make sure the folk survive.

Not all selkies were the same, any more than all people. And the rage I'd felt on Spindle Island wasn't a human rage. It was blind fury, pure and simple. Anyone could feel it, selkie or human. I'd have to make the same choices about who I wanted to be, what feelings I'd let rule me, whatever form I was in.

The puffin nudged her head against my arm, waking me from my thoughts. "Me bring," she said proudly.

I stroked the feathers on the back of her neck.

It was Nellie who found words. "You bring. You friend." I could tell she'd been practicing her birdtalk.

The puffin chuckled. "Eel bottom!" she exclaimed, and we all started laughing. The puffin laughed so hard, she had to flap her wings to keep from falling over.

Then it was time for her to go. She flew up to my shoulder and nuzzled my ear. It was a short hop to Nellie's shoulder for another nuzzle and a gentle grunt good-bye. We watched her fly away, a sturdy little bird above a great, wide sea.

A gentle breeze brushed my skin. Nellie sighed with both contentment and loss. I knew, because I felt both, too.

"Now," I said, bracing myself. "Tell me everything."

Nellie took a deep breath. "Grandpa and I went to the

big island to get online and talk to my mom and dad. It got complicated and we had to stay overnight. The next day I kept telling Grandpa to hurry, because I couldn't stop thinking about you. We got back, and everyone was buzzing about how Maggie had had a stroke and Jack rushed her to the hospital. Then Grandpa asked about *you*, and no one knew what he was talking about! He started yelling—you should hear Grandpa when he yells—and Jane drove us out to Maggie's so fast, the car was skidding all over the road.

"We got there and banged on the door and called for you. I was hoping your mom had come to get you after all. But then we went inside. . . ."

There were tears in her eyes.

"We went inside, and the furniture was all shoved around, like there'd been a fight. And your stone selkie was lying on the floor. You'd *never* have left her like that. So I told Grandpa—not that you're a selkie; I'll never tell anyone that! I told him I was afraid you ran away or swam off to sea. And I know you're really strong, Aran, but we were worried you'd gotten hurt somewhere. The sheriff came and searched the whole island, and the Coast Guard put out bulletins and searched the rocks and reefs. They were"—she gulped—"they were searching for your body. But I hoped and hoped and hoped you'd somehow found your clan. And now—look at you!"

I gave a deep sigh. A wave splashed over my feet.

"And Maggie?" I said.

"She's back in her house. She got better enough to go home."

"She shouldn't be alone," I said.

Nellie nodded. "That's why Grandpa got a little car. We check in on her every day, and at night Jack—"

"*Jack?*" I tensed. "She shouldn't—"

"It's better," said Nellie. "He was so scared from her almost dying, he swore that if she lived, he'd never drink again. Maggie says he's keeping his promise. I guess he'd bought a boat—"

"A fishing boat," I said.

"And he took it back, and got a smaller boat instead. Now he takes tourists out fishing and around the islands. He's home almost every night."

"And Maggie's really okay?"

Nellie's face grew more serious. "She'll never be all better again. But she's hanging on. With luck, for a while. And what she wants most in the whole world is to see you again."

I swallowed. I didn't trust Jack, or think he'd be glad

to see me back. But I wasn't going to let that keep me from Maggie.

I looked at the lights on the far shore. Somewhere out there, Maggie was waiting.

"There's just one thing we have to watch out for," I said. "We can't let this Donahoe man hear about me."

Nellie startled. "What?"

"In that place they kept me, they said these people, Dr. Donahoe and Penelope, were coming to take me away. They were already in the building. I heard their footsteps."

Nellie burst out laughing. "That's us!" she said. "Grandpa's whole name is Dr. Robert Donahoe. He used to be a doctor until he gave it up for painting. And Nellie's my nickname. My whole name is Penelope. You know, like the weaver in *The Odyssey*." I shook my head. "It's a great book," she said. "We'll read it together."

Her eyes grew serious. "We came to the hospital as soon as we heard. And then you were gone! Grandpa was shouting, and I didn't know what to do until I saw the puffin. But I'm glad you ran away. From Spindle Island, and then from the hospital. Otherwise you might not have *that*." She gazed in admiration at my pelt. "Black is the best. Oh, Aran, how can you bear to have it and not put it on?"

"I'll spend time in sealform, too," I said, snugging it under my arm. "The cove near your house will be a good place for turning. No one will see me there."

The breeze carried a whiff of pine from shore, brisk and green and full of life. And then something else—a soft, thrumming beat.

A boat was heading our way, a light shining atop the mast like its own little moon. I leaped to my feet.

"Ready?" I said.

Nellie stood beside me, her hand reaching out and holding mine. "Ready."

And then we were jumping and waving and hollering, hailing the boat to come carry us home.

ᵉᵉᵉ AUTHOR'S NOTE ᵉᵉᵉ

Stories are places where worlds meet. That's what Aran says, and that's what I believe. We find each other through stories. Some of the most powerful come from myth and folklore. Even when I was small, their magic took me deep inside myself to a place that felt truer than true.

The first inklings of this book came to me on a trip to Ireland. My family was on a boat to the Skellig Islands. Seals bobbed up to stare at us and dolphins leaped alongside. Then the crags of Little Skellig rose from the waves. A picture flashed into my mind of selkies lounging on those rocks in longlimbs. It was so vivid I can still remember every detail: the pelts piled at their feet, their faces raised to the sun. Soon we landed on Skellig Michael. We climbed stone steps to the top of a pinnacle, and ducked into beehive-shaped huts where monks lived about 1,400 years ago. It felt ancient, elemental, and profound. The next morning I sat down to write, and a few pages about a selkie boy flowed from my pen. I tucked them away.

Later that year, we visited a place we love: Washington's San Juan Islands. We sailed the boat my husband built, landing on lonely beaches and greeting the seals. Orcas breached offshore. Scattered islands, mist and sun, the heartbeat of the waves: this, too, was a perfect place for a selkie boy! I found my earlier scribbles and began to write.

Celtic folklore and music wove their way through these pages. "The Great Silkie of Sule Skerry" is a classic ballad. I've taken lines from several versions and changed a few words. The book Aran steals from the aerie was inspired by *The People of the Sea: A Journey in Search of the Seal Legend*, by David Thomson. My fascination with selkies owes a debt to *The Secret of Roan Inish*, a movie based on Rosalie K. Fry's book *Secret of the Ron Mor Skerry*. "The Tale of the Selkie Wife" is my retelling of a traditional story; "The Tale of Westwood Pier" is my own.

Research is one of the best parts of writing. At a seal haulout, I watched pups ride on their mothers' backs. Visits to the Seattle Aquarium, the Oregon Coast Aquarium, and the Oregon Zoo helped me picture Aran's undersea world. I hope you'll have as much fun exploring seals and ocean life as I did. Online, you can listen to a puffin grunt, watch seals twirling in kelp forests, and see orcas on the hunt. Myth and folklore are rich with tales of the moon, the sea, and beings who can shift shape between animal and human. Seal legends are told around the world, including the Pacific Northwest. You'll find some links to the natural world and the mythical worlds on my website at emilywhitman.com.

Seals, orcas, fish, mollusks, birds: everything depends on a healthy ocean to survive. But the ocean is in danger. Ocean warming, acidification, pollution, overfishing, plastics, and dead zones are serious problems. We share our world with all living things. I hope you'll find out more about the ocean, its wonders and the dangers it faces, and what we can do to make a difference.

The world is full of magic. When my son was young, he'd run along a beach and seals would follow in the surf. He'd be collecting pebbles, unaware of the seal slipping ashore a body length behind him.

Maybe they were selkies.

We've all got ocean inside us. Beautiful, mysterious, and untamed. Like Aran, we are two everythings.

∽ ACKNOWLEDGMENTS ∾

A heartfelt thank you to my editor, Martha Mihalick, who saw what it needed to be true. The Moon must have helped this book, and me, find our way to you. Thank you to Katie Heit and the whole team at Greenwillow Books and HarperCollins—I'm so lucky to be working with you! Vashti Harrison's gorgeous cover perfectly captures the spirit of the book. Thank you to my amazing agents—Nancy Gallt, Marietta Zacker, and Erin Casey.

Thanks to Dyanna Lambourn, marine mammal research biologist with the Washington Department of Fish & Wildlife, for an invaluable visit to a blind overlooking a seal haulout on Gertrude Island. I'm grateful to the Helen Riaboff Whiteley Center for a writing retreat in the heart of Aran's world.

And thank you, thank you to all those who shared insights, knowledge, and support over the years I worked on this story. I'd especially like to thank Kate Whitman, Amy Baskin, and Elisabeth Benfey, wise in the ways of books and life; and Susan Blackaby, Andrew Durkin, Ellen Howard, Barbara Kerley, Annie Lighthart, Sam Lighthart-Faletra, Elena Pettycrew, Elizabeth Rusch, Holly Westlund, and Linda Zuckerman. Thanks to the students in my writing workshops—I'm inspired by our work together. All my love and thanks to my family: Richard, Kate, and Sam Whitman; my mother, Gerda Rovetch; and my sisters, Jennifer Rovetch and Lissa Rovetch. This book is dedicated to my father, Warren Rovetch, in memory. Now, *there* was a storyteller!